The Freak and the Idol

Katy Jones

To Mr Leonard and Josie,
With love from the writer of
The Golden Goose (aged 8 or 9)

KJones

Published by bluechrome publishing 2004

2 4 6 8 10 9 7 5 3 1

First published in Great Britain in 2004 by
bluechrome publishing
An Imprint of KMS Ltd
PO Box 109,
Portishead, Bristol. BS20 7ZJ

www.bluechrome.co.uk

A CIP catalogue record for this book is available from the British Library.

ISBN   1-904781-36-5

Cover design by Katy Jones

www.katyjones.co.uk

This book was edited and prepared for print by
Associated Writing, Editing and Design Services

www.awed-services.com

To

Paul, my spiritual twin,
Mum, Dad, Bert, Em and Ned,
Anna, my feminist ally
and of course Mike,
whose love never fails.

and

With grateful thanks to everyone who said, 'Keep writing',
or 'Keep trying.' It made a difference!

Chapter 1

Opening

Her molten hair ripples down her back, flickers around her face, licks at the white curves of her shoulders. Her eyes are adamantine, sapphire-bright.

Callum makes a conciliatory noise. He touches a fierce, stray strand of her hair, but snatches his hand back in mid-caress as if singed. Her ruthless eyes forbid it.

Her dress is blood red and should, but does not, clash with the violent shade of her hair; some witchy chromatic bargain. The velvet clings to her static body, ending abruptly half way down her taut and slender thighs.

Callum lifts his eyes, but finds himself unable to meet hers.

'What do you want me to say?' he asks.

Her legs are stretched to their full, extraordinary length, crossed at the ankles where thin red straps bind her shoes in place. The heels culminate in cruel spikes.

'Angel,' Callum begins again, and the word is dissonant in the darkened room, 'Can't we just forget this? The point is, nothing *happened*, did it?'

Her sudden movement startles him and his gaze clashes with her stare. Something is seething in her eyes.

'Can't you understand, Callum?' she says, her voice wild. 'Can't you understand that you're mine, you're *mine!*' He can hear a note of threat in her voice. 'I don't expect you to act like you did tonight!'

Now the perfect white of her face is broken by a dark flush on each cheek. She leans forward, her lips shining a gory red. Callum struggles to think clearly. He is writhing within a cage of her creation.

'Just listen,' says Callum, his voice strenuously calm. '*Nothing has happened.* And you have no right to be yelling at me what you do and don't expect…'

She stands abruptly, crushing the broken end of his sentence beneath her vicious heels. Seizing her handbag with red-painted claws, she walks across the room. Callum rises quickly and makes a clumsy attempt to intercept her at the door. Her eyes glow with predatory malevolence.

'I'll show myself out,' she spits.

Chris wanders into the kitchen with a contemplative expression on his face and a pair of tartan slippers on his feet. He sits and pushes two days' worth of breakfast things to the side of the kitchen table in order, presumably, to make room for the elbow he now places upon it.

'It all hinges on the issue of industrialization,' he muses, sounding less than convinced. 'Industrialization and its effect on…religious belief among the working class. Loosely speaking.' He frowns. 'Loosely speaking,' he repeats. 'Of course, one might on the other hand argue…'

A sudden 'Cock-a-doodle-doo!' interrupts Chris' line of reasoning and he jumps.

'Bloody thing.' He reaches across to the top of the fridge, where his house-mate's alarm clock is still crowing raucously. He grabs it by the plastic rooster, and jabs at a button, which seems to have no effect. He jabs another, and the clock announces, in what Chris feels to be unnecessarily upbeat tones, 'It's five-o-clock precisely!'

'It isn't,' says Chris, and returns the clock to its original position. It is a mystery to Chris why Callum's alarm clock apparently now lives in the kitchen; it is a mystery why Callum does not put it forward an hour so that it tells the correct time; and it is a mystery why it has been set to go off at this hour of the evening.

At this moment, Callum himself makes an appearance, possibly, Chris hypothesizes, for some reason connected with the otherwise unaccountable alarm. He doesn't get far into the room, however, before he stops dead and stares at Chris' feet. 'New slippers.'

'Like 'em?'

'No.'

Callum crosses the room and opens a cupboard. 'No coffee,' he announces. He slams the cupboard door. 'Working?'

'Essay.'

'Hmn,' says Callum, and retreats upstairs.

Chris rises abruptly, kicking the table leg and posing considerable threat to the crockery, now balanced precariously near the table's edge. He begins to pace the room – although it is a small room, and Chris is fairly large – so that he can only take three steps in either direction. Even then his progress is considerably inconvenienced by the position of the table.

'Damn,' he says with emphasis. He comes to a halt by the fridge and takes out a bottle of milk. He rinses a mug adorned with Disney characters under the tap, fills it with milk and sticks it in the microwave. As the milk heats, Chris pokes around among a number of empty beer cans, eventually locating a tin of hot chocolate powder. The microwave beeps, and simultaneously the doorbell rings. Chris is temporarily torn between his hot chocolate and the front door, but he reasons with himself that the microwave will switch itself off, whereas the front door will not answer itself…and Callum is almost equally unlikely to.

When Chris opens the front door he finds Shona on the doorstep. Her big, baby-blue eyes momentarily arrest the workings of his mind, but this is usual, and Chris swiftly recovers an appearance of equanimity.

'Callum's upstairs,' he says, and calls, 'Callum!' There is no response, so Chris tries again. 'Callum! He *was* here.'

Chris accidentally catches Shona's eye again, and the effect this time is more than usually severe, because it seems to Chris, although their eyes meet only for a second, that Shona's are almost overflowing with tears.

'Um, he might've gone to buy coffee,' says Chris, semi-audibly. With an effort, he forces his mind to reactivate. 'Come in. I was just making hot chocolate. Want some?'

She nods, mutely. Chris leads the way to the kitchen, feeling rather helpless and wondering, with a degree of desperation, how long Callum is going to be. Surely not long? Surely not longer than it would take to make a couple of mugs of hot chocolate? A thought strikes Chris, and he takes a surreptitious look in the fridge. Only a drain of milk. Oh well.

'Is it low calorie?' Shona asks, suddenly.

A third time Chris makes the mistake of looking directly at her. She looks guilelessly back out of round, limpid eyes. No sign of tears any more. For a single mad moment Chris gazes into pellucid blue and marvels that anyone can seriously have eyelashes that long, that…luxuriant. I really *am* losing it, Chris thinks to himself, and snatches his eyes away from her face. But there is another problem he hasn't yet considered: Shona has perched on a high stool which displays her lovely legs to alarming advantage...when he notices this, Chris' brain lurches dangerously.

'Low calorie?' Chris hears a voice say. After a second it occurs to him that it must have been his own. 'The hot chocolate? I wouldn't have thought so.'

'Never mind.' She smiles a fragile smile. She is fingering the rim of lace which runs around the v-shaped neckline of her clingy little forget-me-not blue top.

Chris ponders whether this means 'never mind about the calories', or 'never mind about the hot chocolate, I'll do without.' By the time he's finished stirring the chocolate powder into the hot milk he still hasn't decided, so he offers it to her, and she accepts it, smiling like a little girl on her birthday. She is looking rather little girly today, in fact. The soft, reddish curls of her hair are drawn into bunches. A couple of rebellious ringlets have escaped, and sometimes fall in front of her eyes. Chris almost expects her to put one of these loose strands in her mouth and suck it, the way his youngest sister used to do when she first started school.

Well, he's made the chocolate and Callum still isn't back. Chris supposes this means he's going to have to try and make conversation. He chooses a seat which means he isn't directly facing her, and tries not to notice that she is swinging her feet back and forth. She nearly always wears a short skirt to the office. Chris wishes she wouldn't.

'How was work, today?' Chris begins, after a long debate with himself about what is the safest and most appropriate topic.

Shona looks at him blankly a moment, then shrugs. 'Okay,' she says. 'Pretty boring, actually.'

Chris waits, but it seems that no other information is going to be forthcoming. He is just trying to assemble another sensible-sounding sentence in his mind when fortunately he hears a key in the door.

'Ah, that'll be Callum,' says Chris, superfluously.

Callum enters the kitchen, bearing a plastic bag which suggests that Chris' surmise about his whereabouts had been correct.

'Well, you look very cosy,' Callum says jovially to Shona, and she does, cradling the warm mug in her hands. She looks up at him sulkily, through mutinous coppery tendrils. There is something more than usually alluring about her pinkly petulant lips.

'No there *isn't*,' says Shona, tetchily.

'Sorry?' Callum looks confused. 'Do you want to come upstairs? Or do you want coffee?'

Shona glowers at him, and her carefully glossed lips catch the light. The childish roundness of her cheeks is strangely pathetic, and her eyes have changed to a moody navy. There is something beseeching in this sudden and capricious sullenness that begs for love, that implores to be kissed.

'Shut *up!*' snaps Shona. 'It isn't *true.*'

'Shona, what are you *talking* about?' asks Callum, concerned. He smooths her hair tenderly out of her eyes.

'Where have you been, anyway?' Shona asks, pettishly.

'Buying coffee. I'm sorry, love, but I thought you'd want some.' Callum takes her hand, gently. 'Come on, let's go upstairs.'

When Callum sticks his head around the living room door Chris is watching *Goldfinger*, with *Industrialization: Concepts and Issues*, open on his lap.

'Want to go to The Lion?' Callum asks.

'Yeah, okay. Has Shona gone?'

'Just left.'

Ten minutes later they are sipping their pints in a secluded corner of the darkish and half-empty pub. The majority of The Lion and Lamb's customers are over sixty, and very nearly all are male. Chris likes to come here of an evening, because it is nearby, and quiet, and off the usual student track, and because the beer is good. He likes it when the landlord greets him by name, and he finds the seemingly slow pace of the lives of the drinkers rather soothing…their intermittent conversations, ruminative silences and lengthy card games. Callum prefers the modern decor and lively atmosphere of the trendier bars in town, but Chris always feels vastly uncomfortable standing drinking bottled beer, nudged and buffeted by strangers and not being able to hear anything except the over-amplified music.

After a few minutes of silence, Chris becomes vaguely aware that perhaps he isn't being particularly companionable.

'So,' he says, 'is Shona okay?'

'Oh, yeah, she's all right,' Callum responds, mildly surprised that Chris is inquiring after his girlfriend. 'You mean earlier? You know what it was, don't you, that was upsetting her?'

'Haven't a clue.'

'It was last night. You should have come. It was a good evening,' Callum remarks, tangentially. 'We went to Justine's in the end.'

Justine's was a bar in town but, in Chris' opinion, one of the less repugnant. You could at least usually get a seat.

'Anyhow,' Callum continues, 'we met Becca and the others there, and the girls had some little presents for her – you know it was Becca's birthday? – and we all had cocktails, and Shona was in a great mood.' He pauses, as the elderly bartender intrudes to place an ash tray on their table. 'And everything was absolutely fine until this girl came in.' Callum picks up a beer mat and places it half on, half off the edge of the table. 'No one we *knew*. Just some girl.' With a brisk upward movement he flicks the beer mat into the air and catches it. 'But she was, well, you know the type…blonde hair, short skirt, big…' Callum grins impishly, 'personality.' He puts the beer mat back in its previous precarious position, and places another one on top of it. 'And I mean we all *noticed*, us guys, and some comments were made…she was a very good-looking girl.' Callum grins to himself as he repeats his flicking and catching movement, this time with both beer mats at once. 'But Shona: well, she's used to being the centre of attention. You know how girls can be.' Callum glances at Chris, to see if, indeed, he *does* know how girls can be. Chris nods cooperatively and Callum, satisfied, carries on. 'They say *guys* are competitive, but I don't think that's anything compared to how girls are with each another. Anyway, Shona got pretty annoyed with me, just for happening to notice this other girl. And she was annoyed all evening.' Callum takes a mouthful of lager. 'I thought we sorted it out after we got back, but obviously not. She was still not happy tonight, as you noticed. But she'll be okay now. We talked it over again.' Callum shakes his head in mock despair. 'Anyhow, I told her to spend tomorrow evening with the girls. That'll make her feel better.'

Chris raises his eyebrows slightly.

'*Certainly* I'll be dissected,' Callum responds, smoothly, to Chris' unspoken comment, 'but what does it matter? The girls will go out shopping, they'll bitch about me a bit, but *it won't make any difference.* They'll all have fun and Shona will buy the latest push-up bra, or a lipstick in this season's shade of – what a surprise – pink, and she'll come back to me the day after tomorrow convinced that now she's irresistible, so all her problems are solved.'

'Retail therapy,' murmurs Chris.

'Yes. I'm a great believer in it,' says Callum. He picks up his glass and swills around the last inch of his lager. Then he grins his affable, slightly lop-sided grin. 'But anyway, enough of my problems. How's your essay going on?'

'Awful.'

'You say that every time, but you always get good marks,' says Callum, with simple faith. 'Come on, drink up and I'll get you another.'

Three girls stand giggling on the doorstep. One is tall, slim, and long-legged with a broad grin and lipstick the colour of red wine. She has a tousle of light brown hair, streaks of which look as if they have been dipped in gold. She is wearing dark-coloured trousers and a green velvet jacket. The second girl is smaller and has longer, sunny-coloured hair, pinned up with little pink clips. Her skirt is pink too, and her jacket is white and made of fake leather. She has a round, childish face and is giggling more helplessly than either of the other two. The third and most beautiful has red hair swept up in a frothy pony tail. She is trying to control her laughter, which is only exacerbating her already awkward position; it is this which is amusing her friends so much. She is attempting to hold a shopping bag between her teeth while she roots through her handbag for her door-keys. Another two bags are supported between her high-heeled boots.

'Let me hold that,' says the tousled one, transferring all three of the bags she is carrying to her left hand, and removing the bag from between her friend's teeth with her right. She has a very lovely voice, the tousled girl. It is deep and warm and throaty.

'Do you think we went just a little bit overboard?' asks the one with the pink clips, beginning to giggle anew. 'I don't know *what* Steve's going to say!' she adds, excitably.

'I know *exactly* what Steve's going to say, Lizzie!' says the redhead, regarding Lizzie briefly with indigo eyes. Their already enviable size is exaggerated by the judicious application of eye-liner and by her elaborately curled and darkened lashes. 'He's going to say you look gorgeous in that little blue dress,' she says, finally getting the door open.

'He's going to be so smitten,' says the tousled one, 'that fortunately he's not going to notice that rather expensive pair of shoes.' A hint of mischief animates her carefully shadowed hazel eyes.

'Or the make-up or the manicure kit,' adds the redhead, flecks of silver in her lipstick glittering slightly as she smiles.

'Or the magazines, or the face-pack or the earrings,' the tousled one finishes off, grinning wickedly.

Lizzie looks slightly dismayed.

'I *did* buy rather a lot, didn't I?'

'No more than me!' says the redhead, frivolously, pony-tail bobbing as the three troop inside. 'Oh! We should have got a video!'

'We should've got ice cream,' the tousled one corrects her.

'Oh, Becca!' says the redhead, reproachfully. 'That's all very well for *you* to say, with *your* figure.'

'Yes, Becca!' Lizzie agrees, 'It's *so* unfair!'

'We can get a video later on,' says Becca, 'and we can get some ice cream too. Live a little!' she adds, in response to the disapproving looks her friends are giving her.

By this point, the three have reached the top of the stairs.

'Oh, what have I done with my keys *now?*' the redhead wails.

'You put them in your pocket!'

The redhead unlocks the door, and the girls virtually fall into the flat, dropping bags and shedding coats as they go.

'These shoes are *killing* me!'

'Eeugh, I look a fright! Why didn't someone tell me?'

'Does anyone have some lip balm I could borrow?'

'Oh, hello Chris,' says the redhead, finding him sitting in her lounge.

'Hello Shona,' he replies, rather weakly, disorientated by this sudden flurry of femininity.

'Hi, Chris!' says Lizzie, and smiles at him prettily. 'Does anyone have a hairbrush I could – oh no, I've got one here.'

'What about getting a gateaux?' Becca inquires in Shona's general direction, 'To go with the ice cream?'

Neither of the others seems to consider this suggestion worthy of a response.

'Look at these split ends! My hair is in *such* bad condition.'

'You should worry! You obviously haven't seen mine!'

'Have you tried any of those hot wax treatments?'

'Cheesecake?' says Becca, hopefully.

'I can't wait to try out that new face-pack I got,' Lizzie announces, ignoring her.

'What was it? Aubergine and orchid?' Becca grimaces. 'Dandelion and burdock?'

'It was *not*,' says Lizzie.

'Has anyone tried the self-heating ones?' Shona puts in, with enthusiasm. 'They're the best. The heat opens your pores up and draws out all the impurities.'

'Leaving your skin soft, clean and radiant,' Becca says, as if she's the voice-over in an advertisement. 'Like a highly polished baby's bum,' she adds whimsically. A pause. 'Recently bathed.'

'What?'

'It was *apricot* and orchid,' Lizzie says, undoing her shoes.

'How about getting a lemon meringue pie for later?' Becca suggests, reverting once more to the topic which seems to be her chief concern.

'If anyone wants a drink...'

'Becca?' says Lizzie. '*Apricot.*'

'Whatever,' says Becca. 'I can't believe what a cool nail varnish I got!' she declares unconnectedly, producing a small green bottle from one of her many bags. 'Here, Chris, isn't that cool?' Almost without warning she tosses it across the room. Chris, startled, only just manages to catch it. He looks at it in bewilderment for a moment.

'*Does* anyone want a drink?' Shona asks. 'Chris? Hot chocolate?'

Chris still appears slightly overwhelmed. Lizzie darts across the room to finish doing her hair in the mirror. A shopping bag Becca has abandoned next to Chris' chair falls over and several items spill out: a bottle of foundation, a tube of hair removal cream, a magazine...Chris glimpses the words, 'What your lipstick says about you,' on the front.

'Um, actually I just had one,' says Chris. He sounds slightly nervous.

'Fruit tea?' Lizzie asks Chris. 'Shona has some nice ones.'

Chris hesitates, confused.

'We could just get a nice big bar of chocolate,' suggests Becca, regardless of the conversation the others are engaged in.

'Chocolate!' Shona and Lizzie exclaim together, with a curious mixture of outrage and longing. In the confusion of protests and argument that follows, Chris manages to escape into another room.

Suddenly, it is hot. Walking around outside is like wading up to your neck in bath-water. And in Shona's room it is hot too, although not so much. The window is open, but the curtains are closed, and a languid movement of air, too slight to be called a breeze, occasionally stirs the curtains. Dark, decadent saxophone music is exuding from a CD player in the corner of the room.

The door of the en suite glides open, and a surge of spice-scented steam escapes from within. After a moment Shona emerges, clad in a silk negligee of dusky rose. Her hair is wrapped in a towel. The lines of her face, uncomplicated by the usual profusion of voluptuous red curls, have a sheer, denuded beauty: the slight inflection of her forehead and nose in profile; the smooth arc of her eyebrows; the softening of the curve of the cheekbone into the subtler curve of the cheek.

She drifts across to the dressing table, an empty wine glass trailing from her hand, and sits amid a ripple of silk. She takes a half-empty wine bottle from its place among the perfume bottles, the bottles of body lotion and make-up remover, and refills her glass with the rich red liquid. Then she unfastens her turban. The towel falls to the floor and wet hair tumbles down about her face, disordered and dark. She loosens the silken sash about her waist, and the negligee slips from her shoulders. The tint of her skin is warmed to amber by the lamp on the table. Fresh from her bath, she is soft and damp and firm like some dewy fruit.

A bottle is selected, the cap is removed, and a heavy chocolatey fragrance pervades the air and mingles with the smell of spice. Some of the contents oozes onto Shona's fingertips, and she smooths it luxuriantly over the already smooth skin of her feet, her legs and her stomach. She spreads it over her arms and shoulders with long, gentle strokes. She rubs it into her hands and applies it lingeringly to her lovely neck. There is something exquisite in the angles of her shoulder blades as she massages the chocolate-scented lotion into her back.

Naked, and with unconscious grace, she crosses the room to where her clothes lie ready among the ruffled bed-clothes…on top of the disarrayed blue velvet throw, amid the sumptuous crimson, blue and purple scatter-cushions with their oriental embroidery. She slips on her knickers, draws a pair of lace-topped hold-ups over her feet, her shapely ankles and slender calves, leaving a brief interval of uncovered flesh at the top of her thighs. Next, she puts on a purple satin top. It is shaped to reveal the curve of the waist and the shoulder straps are embroidered with tiny golden roses. The skirt she has chosen is darker; the colour of deadly nightshade. It is the sort that wraps around and ties at the side, and it reaches to the ankles. Finally, she slips her feet into a pair of elegant black suede ankle boots, with high heels and a zip fastening on the inside.

Shona moves over to the dressing table, her silken skirt undulating softly. She switches off the lamp and pulls back the curtains, and the natural light turns her shoulders and bare arms from apricot flesh to apple. She sits, squeezes mousse from a can and massages it into her hair, which is drying rapidly in the heat, and is graduating through tints of burnt chestnut and fox pelt towards more fervid sunset shades. Next, a perfume is selected and sprayed in a musky vanilla haze onto her throat, her wrists…various mysterious creams and powders are applied from little pots and tubes and a slim silver compact. More powders, a pencil and some mascara accentuate Shona's wide-set eyes and somehow heighten their intoxicating blue. Finally, a succulent plum-coloured lipstick defines the curves of her sensual lips.

When all this is completed, Shona opens a drawer filled almost entirely with small, square boxes. She picks out a red velvet one. Inside are three tiny and intricately moulded golden roses. Two of them are earrings; she holds her hair out of the way to put them in place. The third is attached to a fine chain, which she fastens behind her neck. The delicate chain trickles caressingly over her collarbone and the little rose hangs an inch below the tender hollow at the base of her creamy throat.

At this moment an abrupt buzzing signals that someone has arrived at the flat. Shona goes swiftly into the hallway and, without speaking into the intercom, presses the button to open the downstairs door. She returns to her bedroom for a mouthful of wine, the darker liquid flowing over her dark lips. After another voluptuous mouthful, she abandons her glass in the kitchen and drifts back towards the hallway. Just as she gets there, someone taps at the door. It is Callum, bearing a dozen deep red roses.

'My darling,' he murmurs, impressed, 'You look positively ravishable!' He seizes her with his free arm and crushes the esculent plum of her lips against his own. 'Are you nearly ready?'

She nods. 'Just my hair to do.'

'Better put these in some water.'

She accepts the roses with a dreamy smile. Callum follows her into the bedroom where she finds a vase for them, but she reserves a single rose. She cuts the stem very short and places it on her dressing table while she combs her hair.

Callum has taken a seat on the bed. His gaze wanders around the room, taking in a lacy black bra and knickers draped over the back of a chair and a pile of magazines on the floor, one of them open on an article entitled, *Come-to-bed Eyes in Ten Easy Steps*. He picks up the magazine and turns idly to the contents page: *Revealed: What Men Really Want...Dream Dresses and Floral Frocks...Daring to Put Your Relationship First.*

One of the fashion pages has a portion cut out. Callum takes a look at the pictures that cover almost the whole of the wall next to Shona's bed, but he can't tell which one is new – there must be hundreds. Many of them are taken from magazines, but some are fine art prints, mainly Pre-Raphaelite; some are pictures of models, or actresses dressed up for award ceremonies; and some are adverts for perfume or make-up.

Shona has finished brushing her hair and is twisting a portion of it into a spiral on the back of her head. She holds it in place with one hand while she picks up a grip from the table, but the hair slips and the shining tresses unravel and cascade over her shoulders. She takes the brush again and smooths her hair into a rippled coppery sea. Then she begins to twine the hair once more, and this time successfully manages to pin it up. Now the procedure is repeated, creating another spiral next to the first, while the rest of her hair flows from underneath in burnished ringlets. Finally, Shona pins the gorgeous, velvety rose into place between the two lustrous coils. She turns around, ready to go, and finds Callum watching her.

'Absolutely stunning,' says Callum reverently; and Shona smiles.

It is Saturday. Yesterday was the deadline for the essay that had been plaguing Chris for weeks and, rather to his surprise, he handed it in with a good half hour to spare. Since then he has allowed himself to allot his time rather whimsically, and today's activities have so far involved not much more than a leisurely, loping walk to the corner shop in the breezy morning sunshine. However, in spite of his newly liberated state, a sort of muted anxiety is lolling about in the back of Chris' mind. It is impeding his concentration, as he lies stretched out on the bed, trying to read the newspaper he has bought, sleeves rolled up, head supported on his large, ugly hands. He is just about to give up, just beginning to think about lunch, when he hears Callum stumble out of his room and into the bathroom. The door is locked with a small clunk; there is a second's pause; then a brief expletive outburst and the door opens again. With uncharacteristic speed, Chris darts out of his room and intercepts Callum on the landing, almost tripping over in the process.

'*What?*' says Callum, with distinctly less than his customary charm. He does his best to glare at Chris through his dishevelled fringe, but it is difficult to be intimidating in a bathrobe. 'Left my towel in my room, that's all.'

Chris feels that perhaps he hasn't picked the best moment to begin a discussion, but he plunges in, regardless.

'I wanted to ask you about last night,' he begins, avoiding Callum's eyes, directing his gaze slipperwards.

'What? Last night?' Callum responds, as if it is a concept entirely unfamiliar to him. 'Don't remember. Don't remember anything.'

'You took Shona out for a meal, didn't you?'

'Wait. Yeah, that's right.' Callum screws up his face with the effort of remembering. 'Posh veggie place. Silly name.'

'Yes, but…what happened? Did you split up with her?'

'No!' says Callum, a look of shock appearing briefly on his face, swiftly superseded by one of relief. 'No,' he repeats, with more conviction. He passes both hands rapidly through his hair and fixes Chris with a look of confusion.

'Well, did you have a fight?' Chris prompts.

'No! What is this? We had a great evening,' says Callum,

his memory of the previous evening now in focus. 'Fine. No fights,' he stresses. 'No one dumping anyone else. What are you talking about?'

Chris rumples his brow, seemingly baffled by this. 'Well, I was round there last night,' he says. 'At Shona's flat. After she got back. She didn't *seem* fine.'

'What time was this?'

'About one-thirty. Why?'

Callum leans back against the railings at the top of the stairs and pushes his dark hair out of his eyes once more.

'She made me take her back for twelve,' he says, slowly. 'She wouldn't let me come in. She said she had to be round at Becca's for nine this morning and she wanted an earlyish night. But she was still up at one-thirty, you say? Chris?'

'Maybe she couldn't sleep,' Chris suggests, rather lamely. Callum looks as unconvinced as Chris sounds. 'The thing is, Callum,' Chris continues, 'the reason I was asking, is that she seemed really upset.'

'Upset? How?'

'Well, she looked upset,' says Chris. 'She looked like she'd been crying. She nearly ran into me in the hallway and she didn't say anything, just looked at me as if she was angry…furious. And I don't know what she was doing in her room, but it sounded like she was tearing the place apart.'

'That doesn't make any sense.'

'No.'

'No. She had a great evening. I made sure she did, after that business on Tuesday. I brought her roses and everything.' Callum looks at Chris, as if hoping he has some sort of explanation, but Chris is silent. 'We had a fantastic evening,' Callum insists 'It was perfect. Candlelight, mellow music…And Shona – she was *sparkling*. She looked amazing. So it just doesn't make any sense,' he repeats, 'for her to insist I take her home early because she needs to get some sleep, and then to stay up half the night rearranging her bedroom.'

Chris contemplates his house-mate a moment. He isn't at all sure he's managed to communicate the seriousness of the situation to Callum.

'I'm going round there this afternoon,' Chris says. 'Maybe if Shona's in you should come too and find out what's happened to upset her.'

'Yeah,' says Callum. 'Good idea.' He disappears momentarily into his room and comes out towel in hand. 'You'd better not wear that shirt though, not if I'm going to be seen out with you in public.'

By the time Chris and Callum get to Shona's flat the sun is inexorable and the air is unpleasantly clammy, but Shona's gelid manner is an unwelcome antidote.

'I wasn't expecting you,' she says to Callum, eyes ice-blue.

'No, I thought I'd drop round, see how you are,' he replies, accompanying the words with his amiable grin. His eyes are a clear, ingenuous green.

She is leaning against the door frame, hand on hip. She looks distinctly reluctant to allow them into the flat. Chris finds himself staring at the frayed edge of her denim shorts, which reveal more than enough leg to make him feel distinctly uncomfortable. Embarrassed, he shifts his gaze, trying not to look at the snowy skin left bare by the little black vest top she's wearing.

'Are you going to let us in?' Callum asks, affably.

Shona glares at him as if trying to blight his verdant eyes with her frosty stare, but she moves to one side. She leaves so little room for her guests to get past that Chris almost falls over a collection of stuffed bin liners just inside the door.

'What's in these?' Callum asks.

'Clothes.'

'Whose?'

'Mine.'

'Why?'

'I have too many,' she tells him, with glacial composure.

As if to provide a distraction from the lengthy silence that follows this unlikely declaration, one of the straps of Shona's vest top slips off her shoulder. Chris' brain begins to gyrate. Shona looks, today, as if she has dressed quickly, carelessly, but somehow to Chris this state of déshabillé is no less alluring than her usual consummate elegance. Her hair is looped up casually with a black hair-band, in an arrangement part way between a pony-tail and a bun, and her bra straps are fully visible and conspicuously blue.

'Oh *please,*' says Shona bleakly, 'I'm really not in the mood for this.'

'But Shona,' says Callum, puzzled, after a pause. 'I don't understand what's going on. You've got three bags of clothes here! You can't be going to throw them *all* away!'

'There *were* four. I've already taken one bag to Oxfam.'

'But you won't have any left!'

Shona doesn't reply.

'What's wrong?' Callum asks her. 'You don't seem at all well. Are you ill?'

Shona stares at him a moment. Then she says, 'I have a headache.'

Callum tries to place a sympathetic arm around her, but Shona flinches so violently he doesn't quite manage.

'You should lie down for a while,' Callum says. 'A rest might make you feel better.'

Again Shona says nothing. She doesn't move. Her face and shoulders are the motionless white face and shoulders of a marble statue, but her shorts and the black strap still hanging raunchily off the shoulder breathe heat into her otherwise wintry presence. As if her own provocative dress has brought about a sudden change of temperature, her icy composure melts.

'Can't you for one moment take some sort of interest in *me*? Shut your eyes!' she almost yells. 'You don't understand, you say! If you'd shut your eyes and *listen* for once then maybe you *would!*'

Her face seems to have whitened a shade, throwing her angry hair into bright relief. Her eyes are wide and dark as a troubled sea, and flicker nervously between Callum and Chris, Chris and Callum. She looks like a wild creature, cornered and panicking.

'No!' she wails, a long, agonising sound. She covers her ears with slender, trembling hands. 'Let me have peace!'

'Come on love,' says Callum, gently removing her hands from her ears. 'Come on love, you're ill, you need to lie down.' He pushes open her bedroom door and guides her inside.

Once Callum shuts the door, Shona retreats to the opposite side of the room.

'Don't come anywhere near me!' she cries, frantically. 'If you do, I shall scream!'

Callum is looking around Shona's room, too astonished to respond to this bizarre pronouncement. The room has been desecrated; it is unrecognizable. The wardrobe doors are open and there are very few clothes left hanging within. A drawer pulled off its rails lies empty on the floor. The dressing table, previously crowded with bottles and tubes and tubs, sachets and packets and pots, is bare. A pillowcase has been hung over the mirror. All the pictures have been pulled off the walls, now white and blank but for a few sad blobs of Blu-Tac. The cushions and the throw which used to adorn the bed are gone and there is no duvet, even, just white sheets. Strewn about the carpet are a number of dismembered magazines.

'What *have* you done, you poor, silly girl,' murmurs Callum. Then he notices that the steel waste paper bin, usually kept in the corner, is on top of the chest of drawers. He takes hold of it, intending to put it back in its usual place, but suddenly Shona is beside him. The next instant a match flares.

'What the…?'

Shona drops the match into the bin, and for a second Callum sees a bright, lewd spark in her eyes, the flash of a weird, defiant smile. Then he grabs the bin and dashes into the en suite. The metal bin clatters in the bath, and he puts the tap on; a sudden rush of water and the flames are out. Callum turns the tap off, but it continues to drip idly onto the screwed up, drenched and half-scorched contents of Shona's waste paper basket…tepid drops falling repetitively onto the sodden paper face of a smiling model in a tiara and a ruffley dress.

Callum emerges from the bathroom, wiping damp hands distractedly on his trousers, incredulity evident on his face.

'What was that for?' he asks, the muscles under his eyes twitching as he struggles to comprehend the situation.

'Don't worry,' says Shona, placidly. 'It was only rubbish. Just pictures from old magazines.'

She smiles, serenely. There is a silence, during which Callum runs his hands through his hair several times.

'Shona,' he says at last. 'I *really* don't think you're well. Maybe it's the heat, maybe it's your headache, but take it from me, you're not behaving in a normal way. Think about it a minute. What would Becca or Lizzie say if they saw what you just did?'

A look of slight dismay enters Shona's eyes. She sits down on the edge of the bed; briefly examines her hands, which are trembling again; pushes them under her thighs.

'I strongly advise you to have a rest,' Callum says. He spots her night clothes, lying on the pillow. 'Put these on, you'll be cooler. Then you can have a lie down.'

There is a soft knock at the door. Callum goes over to open it.

'Yes?'

It is Chris. 'There's tea being made, if either of you want a cup,' he says, apologetically. 'Or there's cold drinks.'

'I'll come and help myself,' says Callum. 'I'll fetch you something too, Shona. Get changed, and I'll be back in a minute.'

She is still sitting on her hands...her eyes are large and lovely.

'Okay?'

Shona nods, meekly. Callum shuts the door behind him.

There is a low rumble of thunder as Callum drops ice into two glasses of lemonade. He turns around to find Shona behind him in white cotton shortie pyjamas, bare feet on brown lino.

'Oh, you decided to fetch your own drink, did you? Come into the lounge, then,' he says.

Chris is already in there, spreadeagled in an armchair. He looks up, taking in the white simplicity of Shona's apparel, unadorned but for the little tucks at the top of the cap sleeves and a diffident swirl of embroidery around the neckline, white on white.

'Take your band out and I'll do your hair for you,' says Callum, picking up the hairbrush which is lying on the coffee table.

Obediently, Shona releases her hair. Chris tries to muffle a spasm of envy as Callum begins to smooth the chaotic, deep-coloured waves into submission.

'Right,' says Callum, when Shona's hair is neat and settled modestly behind her shoulders. 'I've been thinking, Shona. I think I should go and get some work from home while you're having a rest. And then later you can come back to mine and stay over. I don't like to leave you by yourself when you're not well. I'm afraid you'll have to entertain yourself, though, because I need to do some problem sheets. And there's a lab report due in on Tuesday, which I should make a start on. Is there anything you can bring with you to do?'

'I have some paperwork I brought home from work.' Her voice is low, subdued. Her eyes are downcast, and Chris finds himself fascinated by the soft curl of the dusky lashes.

'No, I don't want you pushing yourself when you're ill. I meant something relaxing. Bring a magazine or something. Or you can watch TV, of course.'

As Callum finishes speaking, voices and laughter rise from below and waft in through the open window. He springs to his feet and moves swiftly over to the window.

'It's Steve and dizzy Lizzie!' he exclaims. 'Hey, come on up!' he calls down to them. 'I'll let you in!'

In a few minutes, Steve and Lizzie have joined the group in the lounge. Steve is tall and fairly stocky, with a crew cut. Lizzie's hair has lightened a couple of shades and is pinned up prettily. She wobbles a little in her high heeled sandals.

'Ooh! We didn't expect to find you all here!' she cries, gleefully.

'Lizzie wanted to come by because we're going to the cinema later on,' says Steve.

'I don't know what's on!' Lizzie interjects.

'She doesn't know what's on, but she's been nagging me

to take her to see a film for weeks,' Steve says. 'So does anyone want to join us?'

'Shona's not well, I'm afraid,' Callum responds. 'I don't think either of us will be going out this evening.'

'Oh, what a shame, what's the matter?' says Lizzie, tottering over to Shona and perching on the arm of the sofa.

'I've a bit of a headache.'

'What about you, Chris?' Steve asks. 'Fancy it? We're going to ask some of the others as well.'

'Yes, I might come,' says Chris. 'I've got nothing arranged…nothing planned.' There is something about Steve's boisterous manner that always makes Chris feel slightly uneasy.

'What about the Science Faculty Ball, Chris?' Steve says, thrusting his hands into the pockets of his khaki coloured shorts. 'Are you coming?'

'I'm not in the science faculty…' Chris points out.

'Well I know that,' Steve replies. 'But are you coming? A whole bunch of us are.'

'Yeah, you ought to,' Callum puts in. '*We* are.' He places a proprietorial hand on Shona's bare thigh.

'The tickets are for couples, though, aren't they? I don't have anyone to take,' says Chris, feeling very awkward.

'Ask Becca,' Lizzie suggests, brightly. 'She's not got a partner yet!'

'I don't know…I'm not sure that Becca…I don't think –

'Can't say I blame you,' Steve says, brusquely.

'What do you mean?' Lizzie asks her boyfriend rather sharply.

'About Becca? Well…' Steve exchanges a significant look with Callum.

'She's a bit of a…' Callum tails off, glances over at Chris, grins. 'Handful. I mean, she's quite *loud*, isn't she?'

'Mmm,' Chris agrees.

'Becca's lovely,' says Lizzie. 'Isn't she, Shona?'

'She's lovely,' Shona echoes, her voice pallid. There is another distant sound of thunder.

'I only meant that I'm not sure we're very well suited,' Chris explains, tactfully. 'She has quite a dominant personality, she's very outgoing...extrovert...I'm not at all like that.'

Lizzie looks a little mollified by this.

'Why don't you ask Frances to go with you?' Callum facetiously inquires. He smirks. Frances is Shona's reclusive flatmate. Her full name is Frances Freak, a surname all the more unfortunate for being, some would say, remarkably apt.

Chris ignores Callum's comment. 'I tell you what, I'll ask Sasha,' he concedes. 'If she wants to go with me, I'll come.'

The clouds, Chris notices, seem to be darkening inauspiciously.

'Of course, the ball's always a bit of a nightmare for us blokes,' says Callum, settling his feet nonchalantly on the coffee table. 'It means endless trips to the shops. The girls wanting to drag us around looking at ball-dresses.'

'Oh, yeah,' Steve agrees. 'If you let them get away with it. Lizzie knows better than to try that with me, don't you?'

'Nightmare,' Chris murmurs, because Callum is looking at him expectantly.

'And for some reason,' Steve continues, 'girls always seem to buy their frocks a size too small. 'As soon as they've bought one they panic about whether they'll fit into it.'

'Yeah, definitely. Diets are all part of the fun! I reckon you'll be off the cream cakes for the next few weeks, won't you, Shona?' says Callum.

Somewhere nearby, an ice-cream van is playing a tinkling, childish tune. There is a sudden glare of lightning.

'It's so hot in here,' Shona moans.

'Yes, it's horrible,' agrees Lizzie. 'Poor thing, it can't be helping your headache.'

Outside, relentlessly, the rain begins to fall.

'Would anyone like another cup of tea?' asks Frances Freak. She is hunched in a vulture-like posture, in a big, leather armchair on the periphery of the room.

Chapter 2

Falling

A blur of men in grey and navy suits surges from the multi-storey building, and in their wake comes Shona, tripping along with the breeze riffling her long, loose hair, tugging at the hem of her skirt. A smile glimmers in her eyes.

'Well, if there's one thing that can take the glimmer out of a girl's eyes it's this…persecution.'

She runs a hand through her redly billowing hair.

'Can you not just *shut up* for once? Can't I have the evening off, or something?'

She seems to be addressing these nonsensical remarks to the empty air.

'Nonsensical?' She has stopped halfway down the steps that lead to the street from the double doors of the large building. 'I'm talking to *you*, as you very well know. *You!*'

She utters these words so fiercely that one of the besuited men turns around to see who she is talking to. When he sees that there is no one there, he looks away quickly, embarrassed. He takes the remaining steps two at a time.

Shona's cheeks grow suddenly, endearingly pink, and she resumes her progress down the front steps. She has a lovely, lilting walk.

'I shall probably have a lovely, lilting limp by the time I get home,' she murmurs. 'These shoes really rub and I'm getting *huge* blisters.'

She has reached the kerb and is about to cross over when to her surprise, she sees Callum sitting on a bench on the other side of the road, flicking through a magazine. He hasn't seen her yet, but as she hesitates, he looks up.

'Shona!' he stands and waits for her to cross. She does so, slowly. Her hair seems to ignite the grey street.

'Would it help if I shaved it off?' she says under her breath as she evades Callum's embrace.

'What did you say?'

'Nothing.'

She looks up at him with...

'Not *up*. I'm as tall as him in these heels.'

...expectant eyes; eyes so bright they are almost turquoise.

'Since when did I have *turquoise* eyes?'

'Shona? You're not making any sense.' He looks at his girlfriend curiously, but she is examining her nails, unvarnished today, but perfectly manicured. 'Do you feel ill again?'

'No, I don't feel ill. Not in the least. What are you doing here, Callum?'

'I thought I'd surprise you,' he says, after a startled pause.

'Oh. Well. I'm busy, you know.'

'What?' Shona's moods are becoming alarmingly unpredictable. 'Don't you want to go out for a coffee or something?'

'Not really.' She smiles, nonchalantly. Her lipstick is a rich, melting, chocolatey colour. Her teeth glint disconcertingly.

'Are you sure you're okay, Shona? You seem a little...
weird.'

And indeed she does. Her manner towards him is inexplicable, and her smile appears unnatural. There is a lurid light of challenge in her eyes.

She doesn't respond to Callum's comment, but just says, 'Call me later, okay?'

'Well, I guess, whatever,' Callum says, bemused. 'At least let me give you a lift, though.'

'I'll be fine on the bus, thanks.'

She repeats that unnerving smile and is about to walk away when Callum speaks again.

'Oh – Shona. – I almost forgot. I was going to give you these. I found them in the bin in my bathroom. They must have fallen out of your wash-bag.' He is holding out a small, metal contraption.

'Like some elaborate torture-implement.'

'What?'

'Tell you what, Callum, you keep them. Curl your own eyelashes,' she says, and smiles very sweetly.

'Shona...' He looks at her in consternation. 'Shona, what is *wrong* with you? I can't understand...you keep saying such weird things! What was that you said about torture? And then before, something about turquoise eyes?'

Shona sighs delicately. 'As I'm sure you realise, I'm talking to the voice,' she explains, patiently. 'The voice that talks about what I'm doing. What I look like. What *you're* doing, sometimes. Don't tell me you don't hear it,' she adds, 'because I shan't believe you.'

'You're hearing *voices?*'

'Surely you hear it, too. No one ever mentions it, but I can't be the only one.' She pauses, waiting for confirmation.

'I'm sure I can't be the only one.'

Callum is staring at her, alarm in his eyes. 'I can assure you, Shona,' he says, firmly, 'I'm not hearing any voices except yours and my own.'

'You *really* don't hear a voice describing how you're looking at me? The way we're speaking to each other?'

Shona is watching him closely, as if hoping to detect some sign that he is trying to delude her.

'I told you, Shona. The only voices I can hear right now are yours and mine.'

Still she keeps those lovely, overbright eyes fixed on his steady green ones. Her hands writhe purposelessly, neurotically, rubbing her fingers, twisting her rings.

'You think this is some sort of mental health problem, don't you?' she says, at last. She says this very quietly and it doesn't sound like a question.

'I didn't say you're mad, Shona,' Callum replies evenly, 'but certainly it's seriously worrying that you're hearing voices no one else can hear. You have to see a doctor as soon as you can get an appointment.' Shona seems about to make some fierce rejoinder to this advice, but Callum continues. 'And another thing, I don't think going to work today did you any good. You spent yesterday quietly at home with me, and you were fine, perfectly calm. Today you went to work and you've ended up in this state. You do seem very disturbed, Shona, to be honest.' Again, she seems to be about to argue, so Callum explains further. 'Obviously what you've been saying about hearing voices is totally irrational. And considering that I came to meet you especially to take you out, you've been rather selfish and unpleasant, which is not like you at all.'

Callum is disconcerted to find that Shona seems to be looking straight through him.

'Shona? Did you hear what I said?'

'It's not as if my work puts me under a lot of strain,' she says, still looking through him, 'I only do thirty hours and it's hardly the most stressful of jobs.'

'I know you like having this job, Shona. And I know you basically just answer the phone and file information, but any job can be stressful if you're…not well. I really recommend you take some time off, at least until you've seen the doctor.'

'I don't need to see a doctor.' Her eyes are like blue flame. 'All I need is to be left alone.'

'Shona,' says Callum very seriously, 'when you're hallucinating voices and starting fires in your own bedroom you *do* need to see a doctor.'

'You just want to control me.' The words twist from her mouth with a terrible bitterness. She turns and walks away, as fast as she can in her rather impractical pink, patent platforms. Callum thinks it wisest to let her go. Better to call her later on, when she's calmed down.

Chris meanders in at about six-thirty that evening. When Callum hears the front door he swiftly locates the remote and turns the TV off. He follows Chris into the kitchen.

'Hi.'

Chris looks around the untidy kitchen with a sad resignation. 'Hi.'

Callum idly picks up an empty cereal packet; reads through the ingredients; puts it down again. 'Where've you been?' he asks, suddenly.

'The library. The shop.' Chris places his rucksack on a relatively uncluttered corner of the kitchen table.

'We really should tidy up,' says Callum, conversationally.

'Mm.'

'What are you doing this Wednesday evening?'

Chris frowns. 'Hm?' Surely Callum isn't seriously suggesting that they set a date to clean the house? He removes a tin of hot chocolate from his rucksack and places it reverently on the table.

'Are you going to be round at Shona's?'

Chris produces another tin of chocolate. On this tin the writing is greenish and the chocolate is, apparently, mint-flavoured. 'On Wednesday? I don't know.' He extracts a third tin from the depths of his bag: orange-flavoured.

'How much hot chocolate do you need?' asks Callum, who has never really seen the attraction.

'It was three for two. That orange one,' says Chris, placing a finger on top of the relevant tin, 'is really nice.'

'But about Wednesday...'

'Yes?'

'Did I tell you it's my Mum's birthday? And that I said I'd go home to see her?'

'No.'

'Both my brothers are going to be there. I was going to take Shona.' Callum stops. 'Do you want a coffee?'

Chris indicates that he is in the process of making some hot chocolate.

'Oh. Well, stick the kettle on, will you.' Callum clears some unopened mail from a chair and sits down. 'The thing is,' he says meditatively, 'Shona isn't very well.' He waits for a response, but Chris is busy shovelling chocolate powder into a mug of hot milk. 'I met her after work and she wouldn't even let me take her out for a coffee! Just said she wasn't interested and went off home on her own. She was really catty with me. Chris,' he says, abruptly, 'why are you stirring that drink with a fork?'

'There are no clean spoons.' Chris has, however, managed to locate a clean mug for Callum, which he now tips some coffee granules into.

'And also,' Callum continues, 'she was saying some very weird things. She said she hallucinates that voices are speaking to her! I mean, that's not normal, is it!'

Chris presents Callum with a mug of coffee. 'No, it's not normal.'

'Thanks. You don't think it could be PMT or something? All these mood swings? You have sisters. What do you think?'

Chris raises his eyebrows marginally. 'I wouldn't know.'

'Of course I've said she has to go to the doctor's ASAP. In fact, when I ring her later I'll tell her I'm going to make her an appointment. That'll be easiest,' Callum says, thinking aloud. 'But anyway, the thing is, I can't take her to meet my family when she's like this. I sort of wanted them to see her. They never have and we've been going out two years, nearly! My brothers only ever have fat, ugly girlfriends, so they would've been in *awe*!' he grins, briefly. 'But I can hardly introduce her when she's acting like a head-case.'

Chris takes a seat. A blissful smile dawns across his face as he takes a first, careful sip of his chocolate. Callum appears not to notice.

'Actually, though, I wasn't totally sure about it even before all this. You know how it is when you bring girlfriends home. If I left the room for five minutes I'm sure I'd come back to find Mum and Shona planning the wedding.' He pauses for a mouthful of coffee. 'So the thing is,' he concludes, 'I'm leaving here on Wednesday afternoon and coming back on Thursday. And I'd feel better if I knew someone was keeping an eye on Shona on Wednesday evening.'

This suggestion startles Chris into unusual volubility. 'Why don't you get her to ask Becca or Lizzie round? If Shona's ill I don't see how I can just turn up and look after her! I'm not really her friend, am I? I only know her through you.'

Callum is undeterred by this response. 'The problem is,' he explains, 'I know Steve and Lizzie are out on Wednesday night. And as for Becca...I'm kind of afraid she might do something bitchy.'

'What do you mean?'

'Well, Becca's a funny sort of girl and she clearly doesn't like me. And when Shona's feeling unwell...when she's in an odd mood anyway...Becca might just take advantage of that and tell her to dump me. I reckon it's the sort of thing she *would* do.'

Chris isn't sure about this, although Becca does like to take charge...she does tend to have definite opinions and she certainly isn't averse to stating them pretty strongly.

'Look Chris, all I mean is, if you're in the flat anyway can you just be aware that Shona's ill. Just keep an eye on her in case she does something completely crazy. And if you talk to her...she needs to *recognize* that she's ill.'

Chris is stirring the dregs of his chocolate very thoroughly with the fork, which is making unpleasant scraping noises on the bottom of his mug. 'Okay,' he says.

The door whines as Frances Freak scuttles out of her dim room. She stops outside Shona's door, sharp nose tilted upward, poised, listening. Then, quietly, she knocks.

Shona opens the door. She is clad in a short, white satin nightie and her bare limbs are like porcelain. She is a good foot taller than her diminutive flat-mate, who fails to meet her eyes.

'I wanted to say...I think I understand,' says Frances Freak hurriedly. She has a weird, whispery voice. Her lips are thin and colourless.

'What?'

'I mean – on Saturday – the bags of clothes,' Frances says, in an undertone. 'Those things you said. And then that conversation about the Science Faculty Ball.' She fiddles with her ear, which is oddly shaped and prominent. 'Steve and Callum and…even Kit. I think I understand why you were distressed and then…so silent.'

'I had a headache,' Shona answers, rather coldly.

'Yes, but…I think I know what you were feeling.' For the first time, she peers up at Shona, before glancing quickly away again.

Shona looks Frances Freak up and down, taking in the worn jeans a size too big; that ragged, muddy-coloured cardigan she always wears, which reaches almost to her knees; the stooping way she stands; the limp, ashen hair pulled back harshly from a scrawny, unprepossessing face; pallid, papery skin and small, pinched-looking eyes, as if she is perpetually about to sneeze.

'What would *you* know about my problems?' Shona asks, impassively. Frances cringes beneath the heavy azure weight of Shona's gaze. She does not seem to have an answer.

At this moment the strange conversation is interrupted by the phone ringing in the hallway. Frances shrinks back against the wall, allowing Shona to answer it.

'Hello? Oh, hiya, Becs! Are you still coming to the gym tomorrow? Oh! Really? *Really?* Who? Is it the one you've fancied for ages…?'

Shona chatters eagerly into the telephone receiver, which she balances between her chin and shoulder as she picks up the phone and carries it to her room.

'Oh, I bet he is! I bet he's gorgeous…No, it's fantastic news…No, of course I don't mind about cancelling the gym…'

Kneeling down, she places the phone on the floor; her satin nightie is caught in voluptuous folds which reflect the light. The pinkish evening sun caresses her hair as she leans forward to pull the wire into the gap under the door, which she then pushes shut.

In the half-light, Frances Freak stands staring at the blank white door, her face faded, inscrutable. Then, noiselessly, she slinks back into her own darkened room.

Wednesday evening is lovely enough to draw Chris, temporarily, from his usual introspection. The shadows are very dark, the sunlight very bright. Decrepit, time-bleached bluebells form spectral groups among the twisted roots of trees. Flushed foxgloves sway dizzily in the warm breeze, their pale-blotched interiors darkly spotted as if afflicted with some beautiful disease. Near Shona's flat, Chris notices a trail of bindweed, almost ready to burst into white bloom, snaking its way up and around the unsuspecting trunk of an apple tree. It clasps the tree with constrictive tendrils, sprouting ever more of its long, heart-shaped leaves.

By the time he is pressing the intercom button, however, Chris is no longer concerning himself with the plant-life. He is worrying about this evening, as he has been worrying nearly all day. He has only the haziest idea of what he agreed to do and he cannot at all recall why he agreed to do it.

Shona is wearing those white shortie pyjamas again, which doesn't greatly contribute to the stability of Chris' state of mind. Her hair is unbrushed, rather matted, rather wild. She appears to have spent the afternoon where she is now, in the lounge, draped languorously across the sofa. The TV is on, but the sound is turned right down.

'Did you stay off work today?' asks Chris, giving, he feels, a fair impression of being unfazed by Shona, by the situation.

She nods. Disconcertingly, she is not looking at Chris, but through him. Her eyes are unhealthily bright. Dark shadows under them endow her with an unfamiliar, gothic beauty.

'Um, how are you feeling?' Chris asks next, hoping that this is a vague enough inquiry to be acceptable.

For a long moment she doesn't respond at all. Chris is wondering whether or not she has heard him when she says, in a small, wan voice, 'Not so good.'

'Are you still getting headaches?' he asks, hesitantly.

She nods.

'Are you going to the doctor's?'

'On Friday,' she says. It is as if she barely has the energy to speak, but she continues, 'It'll be a relief to find out what's wrong with me.'

Her skin, Chris notices, looks strangely transparent. Luminous, almost. Her cheekbones seem to show more than usual. He has never seen her looking so fragile, has never imagined she could look so vulnerable. Shona's usual fiery allure has caused Chris some pangs, but this brittle loveliness is almost more than he can bear. As he is thinking this he sees her lips move as if she is softly speaking. He thought she did this once before, a few minutes earlier. This time he says, 'Pardon? Did you say something?'

'Sorry,' she says, distantly, and then sighs. It is intolerably tragic, unendurable, that sigh, the look of rapt anguish that has come into her eyes. Chris wrenches his mind round, makes his mouth say something – anything – mundane.

'Did you and Callum go out anywhere last night?'

The words sound harsh to Chris, grossly insensitive. The pain of it wells up inside him, blurring his vision, skewing his mind. Dimly, he is aware of Shona shaking her head.

'He brought flowers,' she says. Then adds, 'We talked.'

She seems to shiver slightly. She twists her legs one

around another and moves her feet restlessly. Chris finds he is fascinated, astonished, by the delicacy of her ankles. He looks again at her face, and a vision springs to mind of Shona in a big white bed, half-conscious, feverish, delirious, moaning softly. She is wearing a long, white, old-fashioned nightie. Her hot skin glows dewily, and Chris is holding her burning hand, wiping her pearly brow with a cool cloth, stroking her hair.

Again, Chris jerks his brain back into control. Shona is looking around the room listlessly. Then, with an effort, she gets to her feet.

'I need to rest,' she murmurs vaguely, and drifts towards her room. Chris follows her into the hallway and watches her disappear into the bare, white space. As she closes the door he glimpses Callum's flowers on the dressing table: huge, pure white lilies and a host of white roses bursting from a haze of gypsophila.

Chris is dashing across the quad outside the Arts Building, struggling with a tower of overdue library books, when a voice calls out, 'Hey! Chris!' He turns, almost tripping over a clump of grass, and sees Callum coming towards him.

'Hi! I just got back! I figured I'd better try and make it to lab. Which is in...' Callum consults his watch, 'ten minutes, and on the other side of campus! What are you doing?'

'Trying to take these books back before my American History lecture,' answers Chris, noting that Callum's Scottish accent has been rejuvenated by his short trip home. It becomes almost imperceptible when he hasn't seen his parents for a while.

'How's Shona?'

'Well...she seemed very ill. Very tired...drained.'

'But she didn't do anything outlandish?'

Chris shakes his head, still rather confused about what kind of strange behaviour Callum is expecting.

'Did she rest?'

'Yes. She went to bed really early.'

'Well, that's good. And she's going to the doctor's tomorrow morning.' He pauses, and Chris begins to feel that maybe there is some hope of getting to his lecture on time; but then Callum launches into an account of his visit to his parents. 'I had quite a good time in Edinburgh,' he says. 'It was okay. I got my mum a plant and a card on the way up, which she was really pleased with. And I brought a photo of Shona with me, so my brothers could see what she's like. They drooled.'

Chris nods and grins appropriately, but inwardly he is trying to control an urge to look at his watch. He's certainly not going to have time to take the books back till after his lecture and he'll probably have to walk in late as it is, which he hates to do.

'And guess what? One of my brothers has a new girlfriend. The older one, Daniel. She came out to the pub with us, for my mum's birthday meal.'

'And was she fat and ugly?' Chris asks, recalling their previous conversation.

'Not fat,' says Callum, 'but she has spots. And, to be blunt, no tits.'

By this stage the desire to look at his watch has become overpowering, and Chris does so.

'Look Callum,' he says, 'I really have to rush now. I'll see you later, okay?'

'Yeah, I have to go, too. Okay then, catch you later!'

Callum strides off across the quad, hands in his pockets, while Chris makes his unsteady way back towards the Arts Building. If the pile of books are going to topple over he hopes they do it here, now, on the steps outside, not as he walks through the doors of the packed lecture hall.

'I have an appointment to see Dr Schwarz at ten-thirty.'
The receptionist scans down a list of names. 'Shona Bell?'
'Yes.'
'Right, if you'd like to go through to the waiting room – first door on the right.'

Shona saunters up the hallway, looking most endearing in a lilac sundress with a pattern of tiny pink flowers. Its rippled hem floats a few inches above her knees. She seems healthier this morning than she has for several days. The shadows under her eyes have nearly gone and if she is a little wobbly on her feet, it is her pink platforms which are to blame.

When Shona reaches the waiting room she finds it empty except for one large, old, toad-like woman. She is reading a large-print book and has a pleated skirt and fat ankles. Her lipstick is seeping into the creases around her lips. Shona sits down opposite her and reaches forward to take a magazine. This is the unfortunate moment the toad-woman chooses to look up, with the result that she gets a better than average view down Shona's cleavage. She eyes Shona's legs and the low V-neck of her dress with open disapproval. Shona evades the toad-woman's stare, crossing her legs one over the other and directing her attention to the magazine. Perhaps she is making a mental note not to wear blue eye-shadow up to her eyebrows when she's seventy; but it does not show in her carefully neutral expression.

Shona hasn't got past the contents page of the magazine before a third patient enters. She looks about thirty and is wearing a black, tent-like dress and strappy black sandals. Her toenails, fingernails and lipstick are a matching shade of puce. She hovers in the doorway for a second before taking the seat nearest to it, folding her hands on her obviously pregnant stomach. The toad-woman's eyes flicker towards the folded hands and an expression of joy springs onto her bloated face. It looks quite alien there.

'When's it due then, dear?' the toad-woman inquires.

The pregnant one looks smug. 'July,' she says.

'Is it your first?' the toad-woman wants to know. 'Ah. So it's all new to you. How are you feeling?'

'Oh, not too bad. I had a lot of problems with sickness to start with. Now it's just that the extra weight is causing me a bit of back pain.'

'Don't I know it! I had five, myself,' the toad-woman confides. 'You're quite large for seven months, aren't you dear? I don't think I ever got to that size.'

At this moment Shona ill-advisedly flicks over a magazine page. The other two turn to look at her. The pregnant one's eyes sweep enviously over Shona's slender body. The toad-woman raises over-plucked eyebrows, her small eyes accusatory.

'I'm usually ever so tiny,' the pregnant one says, defensively.

'So was I, dear,' the toad-woman declares. 'Quite the envy of my sisters.' She is still looking at Shona as she says this and she speaks a little louder than necessary. 'And then I had my five children…I had a very difficult labour the first time. Well, by ordinary standards I had a terrible time with all the first three.' For a long, horrible moment it seems that the toad-woman is about to expand on this, but she seems to think better of it. 'After that I must have got the hang of it. But you never quite get your figure back, you know, and that upset me at the time. What you need to remember is that it's the same for everyone. It happens to us all,' she adds, with extra emphasis.

'I've bought a book with some exercises to do after the birth,' the younger woman responds, not quite managing to hide her irritation. 'It's written by a doctor. Apparently the weight falls off in no time.'

'It's wonderful what the medical profession can do these days. But take it from me, dear, your figure's never the same after you've had children, whatever they tell you.' The toad-woman chuckles unpleasantly.

A middle-aged man, presumably also a patient, has appeared in the doorway. 'Mrs Sanderson? Dr Schwarz is ready for you,' he says, before striding off down the corridor towards reception. The toad-woman gets laboriously to her feet.

'Well, it was nice talking to you,' she tells the pregnant woman. 'My very best wishes.'

As she waddles out she throws Shona a final, hostile look.

'That's what you get for being pregnant,' the woman in the black tent tells Shona, when toad-woman has gone. She examines a chip in her puce nail varnish. 'Complete strangers wanting to reminisce about their own pregnancies and calling you "dear."' Again her gaze sweeps over Shona's fresh, pretty face, her slim figure, her long bare legs. 'You have all this to look forward to,' she says, not entirely kindly, 'in a few years time.'

Shona briefly treats the other woman to her lovely smile and reverts to the magazine. In profile, reading tranquilly, she is very beautiful...even more so than usual. The high white forehead, the lowered lashes, the slight upward tilt of the nose. A curl of auburn hair has escaped from her ponytail and nestles against her neck. She is wearing amethyst earrings...uncut amethysts trapped in a golden mesh.

'I quite enjoy the ante-natal classes really,' the pregnant

woman continues, 'but I didn't expect morning sickness to be anything like as bad as it was. And all these check-ups and urine tests…that takes some getting used to.'

Shona looks up to establish whether the other woman seems concerned that she isn't really listening. She doesn't, so Shona goes back to reading through a questionnaire entitled *Would He Cheat On You?*. She turns the page over. Her lilac-painted fingernails rest briefly on an image of a naked woman sprawling amid folds of pink velvet, advertising the perfume *Softly, Softly*. Shona's fingers seem to tremble slightly. She riffles through the pages, which fall open on an article called, *Take Control of Your Life: Your Beauty Problems Solved*.

'Apart from this back-ache I really do feel healthier than usual,' the pregnant woman is saying. 'I suppose it's because I'm taking special care to eat properly. The dietician has really been very helpful…'

Shona seems to sway slightly in her chair. Then, without warning and without looking at the woman in the tent, she stands up, drops the magazine onto the table where it came from and walks unsteadily out.

The toad-woman is emerging from the doctor's room. As Shona swiftly passes the reception desk, the toad-woman's voice can be heard echoing around the waiting room. She is repeating, with rapidly increasing indignation, 'Shona Bell! Shona Bell!'. Shona rushes towards the exit, dodging around three incoming patients and a nurse. She turns the final corner, pushes a door she is supposed to pull and bursts into white sunlight on the front step of the clinic. She grabs the railings for support as the double doors swing shut behind her.

Shona is standing at the window with her back to the living room and her whole body is shaking. Her hair, tied with a pink scrunchie, is drawn back off her shoulders, revealing her delicate neck and gently curving shoulders. Her shoulder blades look sharp, as if they might burst through the tender white skin; as if they are the buds of an angel's wings. She stands at the window, poised, trembling, as if she is about to open it and take flight into the vivid summer sky.

In the kitchen, the telephone begins to ring.

Slowly, unwillingly, Shona turns around. Her eyes are huge: frightened and unfocused. As she reluctantly makes her way into the kitchen, she wraps her thin arms around her shivering body. She stands before the phone and stares at it as it sits there on the kitchen side, ringing insistently. Then, grudgingly, she picks up the receiver.

'Hello?' She speaks very quietly.

'Hello Shona, it's me. I wanted to ring earlier, but I've had labs since twelve. What did the doctor say?' It is Callum, sounding his usual, jovial self.

'I didn't go.' Her voice sounds brittle.

'What?'

'I didn't see the doctor.'

It is a few seconds before Callum responds. 'Why not, Shona? We've talked about this so much. We need to find out what's wrong with you. The doctor will be able to help get you back to normal. I don't understand –'

'Callum,' Shona interrupts, with an effort. She is gripping the receiver very hard. 'I don't need to see a doctor.'

'You mean you don't *want* to see the doctor. It's only to be expected that you'd feel nervous talking to him about... something of this kind.' There is a fractional pause. 'I should have gone with you,' Callum realizes. 'Next time I will. I'll make another appointment straight away and this time I'll be with you – I can even come into the doctor's room with you and help explain what the problem is.'

'I'm not going to see the doctor,' says Shona in a very low voice, almost as if she is speaking to herself. She is shaking even more violently now.

'Shona,' says Callum, stupefied, 'you're being totally irrational. Of course you need to see the doctor. We've talked it through and we decided you needed to go. I tell you what: I'm going to come round right now so that we can have a proper discussion about this.'

'You can't,' she says, quickly. 'I'm about to go out.'

'Why? Where are you going?'

'I'm going to meet Becca for a coffee.' She has picked up a biro which is kept next to the phone. There is a button on the top, which she presses frantically, making the nib spring in and out, in and out.

Callum is silent for quite a while. At last he says, 'Right. Whatever. I'll call you later, then.'

After she hangs up, Shona stands looking blankly at the kitchen wall. Her trembling gradually subsides, but she continues to press the little button on top of the biro, in and out, in and out.

Shona meets Becca outside an elegant coffee shop called *Casa Nostra*. Becca looks slim and sophisticated in a dark green trouser suit. Her hair is the colour, and her voice the texture, of honey.

'Nice to see you!' Becca exclaims. 'And nice to be back at our favourite haunt. I've had an awful day at work, but let's not talk about it. You look pretty,' she adds, superfluously.

'Can't you see these awful shadows under my eyes?' asks Shona. 'If you can't it's only 'cause I plastered on the concealer. And this dress,' she says, tugging at the fabric, 'is about three years old.'

'Are you wearing a strapless bra with it?' Becca inquires.

'I have one, but it always ends up round my waist. Not that I need to worry about bras too much,' she adds. 'I'm not quite as lucky as you in the bust department. By the way, I *love* your shoes!'

'Do you? Callum thinks they're silly.'

'I think Callum's silly. They're cool. Shall we go inside?'

The interior of Casa Nostra is painted the colour of terra cotta. There are lots of green plants about the place and the floor is a bright patchwork of different coloured pieces of tile. On the walls there are paintings of Italian towns, Italian mountains and Italian lakes.

'What're you having to drink?' Becca asks. 'Cappucino?'

'Espresso.'

'That's very restrained. Are you doing the cake thing?'

'No…I don't fancy a cake.'

'Me neither.'

'Pardon? That's not like you, Becs!'

'No…' she smiles, a little self-consciously. 'Josh works out a lot. I don't think he'd be too impressed by a flabby girl-friend.'

'You couldn't put on weight if you tried!'

'Well…' says Becca, eyeing the cake cabinet warily. 'You can't be too careful.'

Shona lays claim to their favourite table in the corner while Becca gets the drinks. The espressos come in small, striped, blue and yellow cups with matching saucers.

'I've got loads to tell you,' says Becca, as she places the cups on the table. 'I don't think I've even told you how we got together, have I?' She sits down, shedding her jacket. Her blouse underneath is a periwinkle colour. The sleeves end just below her elbows, revealing lean, tanned forearms.

'So you're officially going out now?' In the shadow, Shona's eyes have a rich cornflower tint and her hair is a burning shade of chestnut.

'Well…' Becca adds sugar to her coffee. 'I *think* so. We're meeting up again this evening, so it should be clearer after that. He did kiss me on Tuesday, but it wasn't, you know, a *real* kiss. I might just grab him and snog him tonight, if he doesn't make the first move. What do you think?'

'I'm surprised you haven't done it already. You're not usually so coy!'

'No, I think it's 'cause I really like him. You must let me tell you the whole story!'

'Go ahead, I'm dying to hear!'

'Right then,' says Becca, leaning back in her chair and fixing Shona with a steady hazel gaze. 'You already know I used to see him around the place, usually at the coffee machine. And we used to talk a bit, and he always called me Becca-from-Personnel. And he was Josh-from-Marketing.'

'Yes,' Shona joins in, her long, white fingers interlaced around her little cup. 'And it's a really unreliable coffee machine, you said, so sometimes you spent quite a while chatting, waiting for it to work.'

'That's right. That coffee machine is our building's equivalent of Dateline,' says Becca, with a half-smile. 'So…it all happened on Monday, when the coffee machine was being even more temperamental than usual. When I arrived, Josh was just giving the machine a good kick, which you have to do, sometimes – it does actually seem to help. But this nasty little man from Sales was there with him, going, "Um, I don't think you should be doing that…I think you're going to break it."' As she says this, Becca's rich, husky voice becomes narrower, more nasal, in imitation of the man from Sales. 'Josh was being jokey with him, saying, "It's already broken. It won't give me any coffee. How can things get worse?" Then I arrived, and Josh is like, "Ah! It's Becca-from-Personnel! You'll help me kick this useless machine in, won't you? Simon here has refused." I told him I didn't think mindless violence was the answer and he said, "Well then, there's only one alternative. We'll have to get coffee elsewhere."

Becca pauses in her narrative to take a sip of her espresso. Her eyes are glowing like amber as she recalls these events. Although both girls are tall, slim and attractive, they look very different sitting there. Shona's hair is long and coppery, Becca's short and golden; Becca's skin tawny and luminous, Shona's soft as white rose petals.

'And?' says Shona, impatiently. 'What happened?'

'Well, the man from Sales started saying, "What do you mean? There's only one drinks machine in the building!" and I said, "Yes, but there's a little café on the corner that'll probably do us a coffee." He looked so shocked when I said that; it was really funny! I mean, obviously we're not supposed to leave the premises except at lunch time, but as Josh said, "We can't be expected to work without coffee! It's an abuse of our human rights!" So, the man from Sales went off all scandalised, and Josh and I went, rather surreptitiously, to this café on the corner. It was hilarious,' says Becca, shaking a butter-coloured whisp of hair out of her eyes and grinning across the table at Shona. 'It was the most horrible place I've ever been in and the coffee tasted like mud. Josh said, "Much as it'd be bad manners to criticise your taste in cafés..." he'd such a nice smile, Shona, you wouldn't believe – "... much as it'd be bad manners to criticise your taste in cafés, next time I think we'll go for something a bit more classy, if it's all the same to you. How about the River Bar, tomorrow night?" I was so excited!' Becca's lambent eyes catch Shona's again, which echo back their enthusiasm. 'But I was really casual, I just said, "Yes, that'd be cool," and we agreed times and everything, and that was it!'

'Fantastic! What happened on Tuesday night?'

'I had *such* a good evening! We just had a few drinks in the River Bar – it's really nice in there – and we talked non-stop. Josh is so funny and he has this dead sexy, totally uninhibited laugh. And he has really broad tastes in music and food…he seems to be a very open-minded person. And he's quite sporty and, like I said before, he has a great body and nice hair.' Becca takes another sip of coffee, but something occurs to her part way through and she almost chokes in her eagerness to continue. 'Did I tell you about his hair? It's very fair, lighter than mine, and it's about shoulder length. He ties it back when he's at the office, but when we went out on Tuesday he had it loose and it looked so cool! I just wanted to run my hands through it!'

'He sounds amazing. When am I going to get to meet him? Are you going to invite him to the Science Faculty Ball?'

'I don't know,' Becca responds. 'It seems a bit funny to invite him to a studenty thing. And I don't know if it's a bit soon to inflict my friends on him,' she adds, coolly. 'Not meaning you, of course…although you're too pretty by half. It's just the thought of Lizzie being all fluttery and giggly and Steve trying to look tall and going, "So, you do weights, do you, Josh? Ever done kick-boxing, Josh?"' Becca pauses, a small smile on her sardonic, perfectly-painted mouth. 'And Callum giving vent to his own unique blend of charm and insensitivity…Sorry, Shona, but you know what I mean.'

There are tiny green flecks caught in the amber of Becca's eyes. She looks at her companion intently for a moment. Shona raises her cup to raspberry-coloured lips.

'Oh, Shona, I meant to ask you,' Becca cries, suddenly changing topic. 'What do you think of this?' Becca produces a little bottle from the small suede hand-bag she has with her.

'That's a nice colour,' says Shona, 'like toffee.'

'I got it in my lunch hour.' Becca examines it contemplatively for a moment. 'I've wanted some that colour for ages and I was meaning to wear it tonight, but...well, what do you think? Some men are funny about nail varnish, aren't they? Andy always was. It's quite a *subtle* colour, but...I'm just not sure.'

Shona considers this. 'Well, yes,' she says. 'I do know of a few men who say nail varnish, *any* nail varnish, is a real turn-off. So I guess the *safest* thing to do is not to wear it. But that's not what you'd tell me, if I asked you that sort of question.'

Becca looks quizzical. 'What would I say?'

'You'd say, "Shona, wear what you like. If he can't cope with that then he's not worth the hassle."'

'Mm...' says Becca, wryly. 'Well, I have to admit, I see my point.' She glances at her watch and screws up her face in irritation. 'Oh damn,' she says, 'I probably ought to go.'

Shona is fingering her coffee spoon. 'Becca...'

'What?'

'I kind of wanted to talk to you about some stuff.'

'Did you?' Becca checks her watch again. 'Important stuff? Can you phone me over the weekend, because I really have to get going.' She pushes her coffee cup into the centre of the table and scrapes her chair back; it sounds harsh on the tile floor. 'I wasn't thinking, but I have to get something to eat and have a shower...and I haven't at all decided what to wear this evening. Which, knowing me, could take some time.'

Shona looks rather traumatised. She bites her lip.

'You'll get lipstick on your teeth,' says Becca. 'Is it okay if we postpone our conversation? Can you cope?'

With an effort, Shona smiles. 'Yes, of course,' she says. 'I'll ring you tomorrow.'

'Cool,' says Becca, picking up her bag and jacket. 'What do *you* think I should wear? Should I wear those satiny trousers and the silver top, or should I dress down? I was wondering about that new fawn blouse…'

Shona is sitting in a narrow alleyway on a low brick wall, in the shadow of a dingy, disused building. Broken glass and a few cigarette butts are scattered about and a plastic bag drifts along the pavement. Shona's dress is crumpled and her pink shoes are dusty. There is a small pool of something black and slimy next to her left foot. Her head is bowed and her red hair trickles like blood over her goose-pimpled shoulders.

She has been sitting like this since Becca dashed off to get ready for her date.

In the distance, the cathedral bell strikes seven. Slowly, Shona raises her head. Her large eyes are smudged with mascara.

There is a small hand-bag next to Shona on the wall. She takes her phone out of it and locates Lizzie's mobile number. The phone rings three times before it is answered.

'Hi, Shona, how are you doing?' Lizzie's voice is painfully, bright. Dazzling.

'I was wondering if we could meet up this evening?'

'Sure!' says Lizzie, then suddenly she squeals. 'Sorry, that's just Steve fooling around,' she explains. 'Yeah, we can meet up. Steve and me are eating out this evening, but we could double-date. That'd be fun.'

Shona is silent for a few seconds.

'Are you still there?' Lizzie asks. 'Cut that out, Steve!' She giggles.

'Will you be busy all evening?'

'We'll probably go to a bar or something afterwards. You could meet us there, if you want. We could go to Justine's and get those banana cocktails!'

There is another short silence, before Shona says heavily, 'It doesn't matter. I don't want to disrupt your plans.'

'Are you sure?' Lizzie asks, anxiously. 'I'd really like to meet up for banana cocktails!'

'Let's do it another time.'

Saturday morning is warm and soporific. Drowsy bees waver from flower to flower. Cats doze slit-eyed on garden walls. A sun-crazed blackbird is basking in the middle of someone's lawn, wings outstretched. As Shona rounds the corner at the end of her road a shower of late blossom floats slowly to the ground, flickering marshmallow colours across her path. She is strolling towards town, dressed in dreamy pastels. A soft pink T-shirt hugs her upper body and her little shorts look snug. Her hair is clasped up absent-mindedly and her bare legs glow.

Shona's indolent stride takes her onto George Street where a new block of student flats is being built, set slightly back from the road. Three of the builders are taking a cigarette break. They loll about on the scaffolding, stretched out on the wooden platform, tanned skin glazed with sweat. An infinite chain of traffic makes lethargic progress along the road.

The sky seems to be reflected in the soft blue of Shona's wide-set eyes. As she approaches, her shining hair draws the idle gaze of the men on the scaffolding. Her easy, long-legged walk is soothing...the comfortable flow of her limbs. Three pairs of eyes drift over Shona's alluring form and settle there, appreciatively.

Shona pauses just next to the scaffolding. She tips her

lovely face back and screams.

The traffic passes tediously on. Up on the scaffolding, the three men look at one another, bewildered.

'Are you all right, love?' one of them asks, leaning over the scaffolding, but Shona is still screaming. The screams come one after another, bright gashes in the lazy day.

'What's wrong with her?'

Shona collapses to her knees on the hot, harsh paving. Deep sobs break from her lips. Frantically, she drags her nails across her face, thrusts her hands through her hair. Then she throws her head back again, exposing her soft white throat.

'Let me out of your heads!' she screams up at the cloudless sky, the words only just comprehensible. Her hair-clip clatters on the ground and dark red ringlets cascade over her shoulders. 'Get out of my head! Let me out of my head!' She seems to choke on her own searing cry. Then, for a moment she is quiet. Her whole frame is shaking violently. Her lips are red as strawberries and her creamy skin glistens with tears.

'It's not pretty,' she wails desolately, staring confusedly into the empty air. 'What do I have to *do*?' The question rises into a shriek and with sudden energy Shona jerks herself to her feet and bolts in the direction of her flat.

Chapter 3

Retreating

Upstairs, someone has left a radio on. Indeterminate words, accompanied by a strong beat and an energetic guitar, emanate from above. Becca and Lizzie are downstairs in the small but comfortable lounge. The worn carpet is an extraordinary shade of green; there are feng shui candles on the mantelpiece. Photos and fine art prints conceal as much of the over-busy wallpaper as possible.

Becca is stretched out on the couch, which is covered in a tiger-print throw – Becca's choice – and decorated with pink fluffy cushions – Lizzie's choice.

'He's *so* gorgeous,' Becca purrs. 'Such fabulous physique.' Her golden eyes glow, watching Lizzie, busy at the table.

'There. That's quite pretty, isn't it?' Lizzie contemplates the work of art she has now almost completed on two matching dinner plates. She has just added red onion to two mounds of shredded salad leaves and chopped peppers.

'And *wonderful* hair,' Becca continues. 'Ever so shiny...*ever* so soft.'

'Oh!' Lizzie pauses, mid-way through dressing the salad. 'You have to find out what he uses on it. Mine's in *awful* condition. I tried this new conditioner, but I think it's made it worse. Do you think it looks worse?' She pulls a strand of hair over her shoulder, frowns at it briefly, then twirls it round a finger. 'Of course, it's never been very soft hair. It's never been like *Rowina's*,' she adds, pouting prettily.

'What *are* you talking about?' asks Becca, rather piqued that the conversation has been diverted from her favourite subject. She yawns, luxuriantly.

'My little sister. You've met Row, haven't you? I've always wanted her hair. It's really fine and soft and really curly and just a bit lighter than mine.' Lizzie holds the strand of hair up to illustrate this point. 'Just a bit lighter than my *natural* colour,' she corrects herself.

'Yes, I remember Row having pretty hair,' says Becca, examining a chip in her nail varnish. 'She's a very pretty girl.'

'Oh…you should see her these days. She wears so much make-up!' Lizzie wrinkles up her cute little freckle-sprinkled nose. 'It's horrible. Like a mask.'

'*How* old is she?' Becca's long legs are black-clad in velvet bootlegs. Her short chenille jumper is a murky shade of green and reveals a tantalizing glimpse of her brown midriff.

'Thirteen,' says Lizzie. 'She must have been about nine or ten when you met her, I think? She was very sweet at that stage. She had this gorgeous blue velour dress she used to wear *all* the time. Do you remember? Now she just wears – eeugh, horrible things. Grubby T-shirts and ripped jeans and sweaters that look like sacks. I don't think she owns anything that's not black.'

'I remember she used to love swimming. Does she still do that?'

'No. She used to go three or four times a week, until

about a year ago. She was in all those galas. But apparently now she even tries to bunk off swimming at school.' Lizzie scatters a few croutons on top of the salads and stands back to admire the effect.

'Really?' Becca says, surprised.

'Yes. She keeps on forging sick-notes to get out of it! Mum says it's because she doesn't like people seeing her in a swimsuit. She said that's what Row told her, but, well, that doesn't make sense, does it? If she's worried about what people think of her appearance then why has she stopped trying to look nice?'

'Teenagers do wear some pretty grim clothes, though, don't they? I did, for a couple of years. And maybe she just hasn't got the hang of make-up yet.' Becca stretches her arms, stands up and stalks over to the table. She eyes the food, hopefully.

'Oh no, I don't think that's it,' says Lizzie, crumpling her brow. 'Row's very artistic. And a few months back, when I told her she was naturally pretty and only needed a bit of make-up – and I said it in a nice way, I was really careful not to offend her – she said she didn't care how she looked! She actually said that!' Lizzie glances into the mirror which hangs over the mantelpiece and exchanges a quizzical glance with her own reflection. 'Oh, and she's dead set against having a boyfriend, that's the other thing. She's really funny about that. If anyone so much as mentions it.'

'I expect it's just a phase. She'll grow out of it,' says Becca. She has picked up a fork and is poking about in one of the salads.

'I guess. Hang on a sec while I get the potatoes.'

Lizzie pops into the kitchen. She returns with two sizeable jacket potatoes which she carefully places onto the respective dinner plates.

'Is that it now? Can we start?' Becca asks, not very patiently. When Lizzie nods, Becca sits down and begins to wedge cream cheese into her potato. Lizzie makes another trip to the kitchen for the mayonnaise before joining her friend at the table.

'What are you wearing to the ball, Liz?' Becca asks, unexpectedly.

'Ooh, that's a point...I'll have to go shopping. I've not really got anything I could wear to a ball...Not anything that *fits*, anyway,' she adds, ruefully. 'What about you?'

'I wondered about getting something long and black and slinky.'

'Oh, that'd really suit you! It sounds a bit like what Sasha's wearing – I asked her the other day.'

'Sasha?' Becca exclaims, aghast.

'Yes. Didn't you know? She's going with Chris. Callum's friend Chris.'

'In that case I'll have to have a rethink,' says Becca, reverting to her lunch.

Lizzie fiddles with an earring. Her hands are small and pretty. 'Why? It won't be the *same*. You always get lots of long black dresses at a ball – but in different styles.'

'Yes, but I don't want to invite comparison with Sasha. I'm not going to try and compete with *her*.'

Lizzie stares at Becca with round, blue baby-eyes. 'You're as pretty as Sasha! And just as slim!' she exclaims.

'But she has a *cleavage*.'

'Becs!'

'And *much* nicer hair. She's so *feminine* compared to me.'

'Oh Becs,' says Lizzie, almost sternly. '*Now* you're beginning to sound like Shona.'

Becca looks uncomprehending for an instant.

'You know what I mean,' Lizzie says. 'Shona in "my

thighs are so huge, my lips are too fat, I'm so jealous of your tan" mode.' She reaches for a bowl of grated cheese and begins to decorate her potato with it.

'Oh. Yeah,' says Becca. '"Look at this huge spot," when there's nothing there. "I wish my hair was like yours," when she must know we'd all kill for hers.'

'Mm.' Lizzie nods in agreement as she prepares her first mouthful. 'When you go shopping with her, though, that's the worst. She's in the changing room for hours and hours and you can't find anything, but she looks *amazing* in everything. And she stands there going, "Oh! This looks awful...I can't find *anything* that looks decent..."'

Delicately, but with obvious satisfaction, Becca licks cream cheese from a long forefinger.

'Did you know Shona's chucked out loads of her clothes and make-up and stuff?' Lizzie asks. 'I don't know why.'

'Probably just an excuse to buy more.'

'Probably.'

In the hall, the phone begins to ring. Lizzie trots out of the room to answer it and while she is gone Becca devours what little remains of her meal.

'Just my Mum. I told her to ring back,' says Lizzie, when she returns. 'I thought it was going to be Shona. I rang her this morning, but no one picked up, which is funny, because I thought Frances was *always* in at weekends.'

'Maybe the library extended its opening hours,' Becca suggests, sardonically. She leans back contentedly in her chair and watches Lizzie from under half-closed eyelids. 'I just can't imagine being such a total recluse.'

'I know. Why doesn't she make some friends? Get some nice clothes?' Lizzie casts a rather smug downward glance at her own clothes – a mini-skirt in bubble-gum pink and a low-cut T-shirt with a cherry motif. The fabric is stretched provocatively across her ample breasts, distorting the cherries just slightly.

'Why doesn't she wash her hair occasionally?' Becca adds, her mellow voice fringed with scorn. The light from the window burnishes her tanned skin.

Lizzie is still eating daintily, taking time to prepare each colourful mouthful. 'Mind you, that Chris seems to be round there an awful lot,' she says.

'Yeah, it's pretty weird, isn't it? I get the impression he's known her a while. What d'you reckon's going on there, then?'

'Maybe he fancies her,' says Lizzie, and giggles at the ridiculous thought. Her small cupid's bow mouth is the colour of strawberry ice-cream.

'What a fine couple they'd make.' Becca grins in an almost predatory manner. 'Chris seems nice, but he's kind of gawky.'

'Oh, I think he's lovely. But Frances…Frances is…'

'Definitely scraping the bottom of the barrel. Even if you are a bit gawky.' Becca passes a lazy hand through her hair. The short tresses shine as they fall back into place. 'Maybe he's being philanthropic. Maybe he's trying to, sort of, rehabilitate her.' She gazes ruminatively into the air for a moment, amusement toying with the corners of her mouth. Then comprehension dawns. 'Ah – unless it's Shona.'

'Of course!'

'How *obvious*. Why didn't we think of that before?' Becca produces a small pot of lip-gloss and reapplies rapidly. 'So, he's joined the long queue of Shona's zealous worshippers! Poor old Chris. Still, serves him right for not showing more originality.'

'If it was me I'd find a better excuse for being around Shona,' says Lizzie. 'Frances kind of scares me.'

'Yeah, *I* think she's creepy. Sometimes I'm sitting in Shona's lounge and I think it's just the two of us, and then suddenly she's *there*, all hunched and dowdy in that awful cardigan that looks like it's never been washed. And she's probably been there, listening, for the past five minutes, only we didn't see her sneaking in.'

'Have you seen the way she watches people, sometimes?'

'With those mean little eyes. Like she's trying to read your mind. Eeugh.'

Lizzie shudders in response. 'It's a real shame it didn't work out so Shona could share with us.' She has eaten all but her potato skin and a token salad leaf. She places her knife and fork neatly together and pushes the plate away, slightly.

Becca stretches her arms above her head and arches her back, as if trying to rouse herself. Her chenille jumper lifts a little, revealing a couple more inches of toned stomach. She slowly extends her long legs and stands up. 'Well, cheers for that,' she says, helping herself to a final fingertip of cream cheese and smiling with feline pleasure.

Lizzie is gazing at the dirty crockery, an expression of mild dismay on her face. Becca follows her eyes and clatters Lizzie's plate hastily on top of her own. 'Leave the washing up, I'll do it later.'

'Thanks,' says Lizzie, dimpling as she smiles.

'I suppose I'd better go and do something useful now,' Becca says, reluctantly. 'Like some shopping, so I don't have to scrounge your food any more. Not that you give me much of an incentive, Liz, when you make such nice lunches. Next time you'd better make it bread and water.'

Callum is watching the football when Chris comes in with a bacon butty. Callum glances up.

'You might've made me one!'

Chris ignores this. He takes a seat, pulls a newspaper towards him and skim-reads the front page as he eats. 'I think I might get a rabbit,' he remarks, casually, in between bites.

'To eat?'

'No!' cries Chris, with more animation than Callum thought him capable of. 'As a pet!'

Callum studies Chris briefly and incredulously, but finds no hint of humour in his bony, brownish face. After a moment's consideration, he judges it best to ignore this latest oddity.

'What are you doing today?' Callum asks at last.

'Baking cookies,' Chris replies, without looking up.

Callum's green eyes brighten. 'Are you doing those peanut butter ones?'

'Could do. I was thinking chocolate chip. But I'll make a batch of the peanut ones too, if you like.'

'Yes, do.' Callum emphasizes his words with a few enthusiastic nods. There is a short silence. Chris has smeared ketchup on the edge of his paper and is trying to remove it with the heel of his hand. Callum follows his movements, apparently slightly troubled.

'How's the Freak?' he asks, suddenly.

'Busy. Why?'

'Are you going to see her today? Could you? As a favour?'

'No,' Chris replies, puzzled. He picks up his bacon butty again. 'She's going to be in university all weekend, working. Why?'

'I need to see Shona.'

There is a short silence as Chris tries to make sense of this. He fails.

'What's wrong with the usual method? Why would you need my help?'

'Because Shona...' Callum sighs, heavily. 'Shona's still not very well.' He looks at Chris as if he hopes this is sufficient explanation, but Chris' expression makes it clear that it isn't. 'She's not answering the phone or the door,' Callum finally admits.

'Maybe she's out.'

'She's *not* out. I went round there and saw her at the window.'

Chris considers this, chewing slowly. He imagines a pale, fragile-minded Shona alone in her flat, her thin limbs huddled into an armchair, oblivious to the incessant ringing of the telephone.

'She was kind of okay on Thursday,' Callum says. 'Not *herself* entirely, but not bad. But on Friday she got too scared to go to the doctor's. I spoke to her on the phone then, but I've not been able to get hold of her since.' He watches Chris keenly, awaiting a response.

Having finished his butty, Chris gnaws thoughtfully on an already bitten nail. 'Well, I can't really help you, because Frances is too busy to see me this weekend.' He adds, hesitantly, 'Even if that wasn't the case I'm not sure it would be a good idea for me to interfere.'

'You don't understand,' says Callum, disturbed. 'That girl has serious problems. I'm really worried about her. I don't know *what* she might do.'

Chris takes a closer look at the picture-Shona in his head. She has huge, frightened, cornflower eyes. Her lovely face is white and wasted, the cheeks slightly hollow.

'Maybe you ought to talk about this to her friends or even her family.'

'I don't know.' Callum passes a weary hand over his eyes. 'Maybe I'm over-reacting. I mean – maybe she's just annoyed with me for some reason. Girls do that: they get annoyed with you and expect you to guess why.'

'Maybe,' says Chris. His mind floods with delicious pity as he visualizes a deteriorating Shona confined to her bed, her vivid hair floating over a snowy pillow. She drifts in and out of consciousness, now opening radiant, unseeing eyes, now sinking back into an uneasy dream.

'And I've got work to do, you know. A lot of work. I don't have time to play silly games with Shona, if that's what she wants.'

It occurs to Chris that in spite of the suave manner he generally adopts with women, there is something insensitive, almost philistine, about Callum. 'No,' he says.

Callum is flicking through the TV channels listlessly. He lingers over a couple of olive-skinned brunettes in bikinis, but returns to the football. 'Maybe I should send her some chocolates.'

Chris raises his eyes, rather bemused, but Callum isn't looking and doesn't notice.

'I reckon it's pointless worrying about this,' Callum continues, thinking aloud. 'The chances are it'll sort itself out, whatever the problem is. I'll leave her alone today, since she seems to want that, and I'm pretty sure that by tomorrow she'll at least be willing to tell me what I've done wrong.' Callum seems pleased to have finally reached a conclusion. He relaxes back into his chair.

Chris is making a last, doomed attempt to clean the ketchup from the edge of the newspaper. Dissatisfied with the result, he carefully tears around the stain, rolls the fragment of newspaper into a tiny ball and aims it at the waste-paper basket.

'Missed!' proclaims Callum, jocularly. Then, with sudden energy, he leaps to his feet and casts the remote control onto the sofa next to Chris. 'If anyone wants me I'll be round at

Steve's,' he says, adding, 'Don't forget about the peanut butter cookies!'

With a comical salute, Callum leaves the room. A few moments after, Chris hears the front door slam.

'That poor, beautiful girl,' he murmurs, as he goes back to his newspaper.

On a Monday night, the Astro Bar is at its quietest. It's easy to get served, dancers are scarce and the music is fairly unobtrusive. This evening Callum, Steve, Lizzie and Becca are sharing a table near the dance floor. The ceiling above them is swathed in dark blue velvet and scattered with little twinkling silver lights.

Steve is in the middle of an anecdote.

'And then, what d'you know, Lizzie stalls the car. Right there, in the middle of the zebra crossing. And there's all these people trying to get across the road, and Lizzie's revving the engine like anything, and then this fat old bag who's been following us for miles, she gets out of her car – would you believe it? – she leaves her car in the road and she comes over and starts yelling at Lizzie!' A bout of laughter overtakes Steve momentarily, but he takes a swig of lager and continues. 'The best bit, though, the best bit was that instead of driving off, Lizzie wound down the window and started yelling back! I tell you, I thought they were going to start laying into each other with their handbags!' Steve lets out a great guffaw. 'So that's why!' he finishes, triumphantly. 'That's why I don't let Lizzie drive any more!'

Callum is still chuckling to himself, when he notices a couple of familiar figures crossing the room. 'It's Sasha and Ellen!'

'Oh yes!' says Lizzie. Her pastel pink lipstick shines in the artificial starlight. 'I sort of invited them.'

Sasha and Ellen make rather a striking pair. Sasha is the taller of the two. Her colouring is sultry and Hispanic, her long hair straight and almost black. She is wearing a long, dark, well-tailored coat. Ellen is smaller but more conspicuous in scarlet flares. A black beret is perched impudently on her brown bobbed hair.

'Hello ladies, can I get you some drinks?' Callum asks, smoothly.

'Please.' Ellen removes her jacket with a flourish. 'Mine's a bacardi and diet coke. Sasha's is probably a G and T, but you'd better confirm.'

'Sasha, I haven't seen you for *days!*' Becca exclaims, over the top of Ellen.

'Mm, well, you've been out a lot,' says Sasha, slightly raising a well-defined eyebrow.

'With this Josh fellow!' says Ellen. 'Sasha's been giving me all the gossip. He sounds like quite a catch.'

The girls start chattering amongst themselves. Callum gives up hope of getting a more definite indication of Sasha's choice of drink and strolls purposefully over to the bar.

Steve isn't exactly pleased to be left alone with the women, but he amuses himself by considering the relative merits of Sasha and Ellen. He's always thought Sasha is a fine woman, very fine, and certainly he wouldn't say no, but she's too tall and Steve prefers a girl with a bit of…He notices Lizzie giggling beside him. Yeah, Sasha would never giggle. And she wouldn't toss her hair about in that flirtatious way Lizzie has. Whereas Ellen…she has a bit more…life about her, a bit more bounce. Cute smile, nice curves, not sure about the hat but you can't have everything.

Becca is talking now and Steve watches her. She's loud and bitchy and arrogant, but all the same he likes the way she laughs. She has a very sexy mouth.

'…couldn't stop laughing about it. Anyway, now he's gone to meet up with this old friend of his, so I thought I'd come out with you lot,' Becca concludes.

'Sounds like a really nice bloke,' says Ellen. 'You want to hang onto that one.'

'I keep telling Becs we're all dying to meet him,' puts in Lizzie, fingering a blonde curl, and Ellen agrees with enthusiasm.

'What did you say his job is?' Sasha asks, slipping her coat from her shoulders. Steve eyes her cleavage with a connoisseur's interest. She does have a very good body, there's no denying that.

'Well he works in Marketing. What it basically involves…'

Steve turns his attention towards the bar. He could do with another drink, really. Then he sees that Callum is already on his way back, Sasha's drink glowing like some strange elixir in the UV light from the dance floor. Ah well, he'll leave it a bit and get a beer when Callum gets his next one in.

'Thanks, Callum,' says Ellen, taking her drink and passing Sasha's. 'Nice shirt, by the way. Is it green or blue? I can't tell in this funny light.'

'A sort of teal, I think,' says Lizzie.

'Your taste is flawless, as usual, Callum,' says Becca, her voice rich and syrupy, but tinged with what could be irony. She meets Callum's eyes from under dark lashes. 'Poor Lizzie's been trying to get Steve to dress like you as long as she's known you, but to no avail.'

'Is it silk?' Sasha asks.

'I'm going to the bar,' Steve says, gruffly. 'Want anything, Callum?' He barely waits for Callum's affirmative before he goes.

'Poor old Steve,' says Becca, laughter in her eyes. 'He'll

be coming to you for tips later on, Callum.' It occurs to Callum that Becca's eyes are more than usually seductive this evening. They look bigger and darker than usual and a dusting of golden glitter glimmers around their corners. He treats her to his charming, careless grin.

'Where's Shona this evening?' Ellen asks.

'She's not very well,' Callum answers, sounding a little doleful.

'Still?' says Becca.

'Afraid so,' says Callum. 'She's stayed in to get some rest.'

'It's nothing serious, is it?' Sasha asks, the silver lights reflecting on the smooth surface of her dusky hair.

'No, don't you worry.' Callum smiles into Sasha's black eyes. 'She's just feeling a wee bit under the weather. She's fine, really, it's just a shame she couldn't join us this evening.' He smiles at her again, bravely.

'You must be desolate,' says Becca.

Steve has just returned with a couple of pints. He places them on the table and retakes his seat.

'Oh, guess what, everybody,' says Ellen suddenly, her lively eyes dancing. 'I'm shopping for my bridesmaid's dress next weekend!'

'Oh wow! I'd *love* to be a bridesmaid!' says Lizzie, with a mixture of excitement and envy. 'I haven't been since I was seven.'

'What's this? Who's getting married?' Steve asks.

Becca rolls her eyes. 'Ellen's sister! Louise!'

'Oh yeah. Phil and Louise,' says Steve.

'Do you know Phil?' Sasha asks.

'Yeah, I know him. You know him, don't you, Callum? Reckon we'll get asked on his stag night?'

'Might do.'

'Should do. I went on this great stag night just before

Christmas. I know some cracking places to go. Although maybe we shouldn't talk about it in front of the ladies.' Steve winks rather lecherously at Ellen.

'Do you know what your dress will be like?' Lizzie asks Ellen, eagerly.

'I think Louise is thinking of something lavender,' Ellen says, with a slight grimace. 'Which I'm not sure will suit me. I'm a bit worried, actually, because the other bridesmaid is Louise's friend Sarah. I don't know how we'll ever find a style and a colour to suit both of us, because Sarah's tall and slim and blonde, and I'm,' Ellen glances down at herself and pulls a face. 'Not.'

'You'll get something lovely,' says Sasha, reassuringly. 'Does Louise have her dress already?'

'Yes, she does,' says Ellen, dreamily. 'It's absolutely gorgeous. Really romantic.'

'Oh, that's what I'd want,' says Lizzie, eyes full of longing. 'Something out of a fairy-tale.'

'Well, it could be you next,' says Ellen, with her quick smile.

Lizzie giggles. 'Or it might be Becca!'

Becca looks rather embarrassed for a moment, but quickly recovers. 'If I get married,' she says, evenly enough, 'I think I'd like quite a simple wedding dress. Something quite sophisticated. Maybe not white; maybe another colour.'

'All sounds like a lot of hassle to me,' Steve says to Callum. 'And for what? A lifetime of some woman nagging you because you haven't put your dirty socks in the washing basket.' He snorts.

'Seems funny when its someone you know,' Callum agrees. 'I can't imagine Phil as a married man. I reckon she must've really put the pressure on.'

'Louise's dress is a size eight,' Ellen is saying. 'She's on a diet already.'

'But she's so slim!' Sasha says. 'She doesn't have any weight to lose!'

'She has, like, the *perfect* figure,' says Becca.

'*Size eight!*' cries Lizzie, in torment.

'My mate who got married before Christmas never comes out any more,' says Steve. He grins. 'I don't know if that's 'cause he's too busy shagging her, or 'cause she won't let him out!'

'That's what happens,' Callum replies. 'You give up your freedom. And what do you get out of it, really? You might think you're marrying a really hot girl, but you don't know what other really hot girls might be out there. And you don't know what *she's* going to be like in a few years time.'

'That's right. Women don't keep themselves nice if they don't have to. I've seen it happen. My cousin Nina, for one. She was a stunner, but you wouldn't think it to see her now. She got married and in only a couple of years she'd totally let herself go.'

Ellen is still telling her rapt female audience about Louise's wedding.

'They've been choosing the pattern of the dinner service and what brand of kitchenware they're going to go for. And Louise has all these fabric swatches so they can decide on the colour of the three piece suite.'

'How exciting!' says Lizzie, eyes wide.

'Okay, now I'm seriously considering getting married,' Becca confides. 'I definitely wouldn't mind all my friends and family buying me expensive presents.'

'Oh, me too!' says Lizzie.

Callum and Steve exchange glances

'Better watch yourself!' says Callum.

Steve bangs on the table with his empty glass to get everyone's attention.

'Now look here, girls, don't you think we're getting a teensy bit carried away?' He looks around the table and Lizzie and Ellen start giggling like a pair of naughty schoolgirls. Steve grins appreciatively. 'How about another round of drinks?'

Lizzie pushes open the front door and fumbles for the light switch. Her cheeks are a little pink from walking. She is wearing her new sparkly lilac trousers and a little white blouse that knots at the front. Her hair is tied up in a high pony-tail that bobs when she moves.

'Hi! Is anyone in?' Lizzie calls, as she bounces along the hallway and nearly trips on the phone line, which has been stretched across her path. She follows the wire into the living room, where she finds Becca, sitting wild-eyed on the sofa. The phone is next to her, balanced precariously on the sofa's arm.

Becca doesn't move when Lizzie comes in. She is wearing jeans and a baggy old jumper striped with pink and purple, which was originally fairly large, and has expanded with the passing years. There are several empty crisp packets on the floor. The TV is on, but Becca doesn't seem to be watching it.

Lizzie casts a practised eye over the scene.

'What's happened, Becs?'

With an effort, Becca shifts her gaze from the bare spot of wall where it is fixed, and attempts to focus on Lizzie.

'Becs?' Lizzie repeats, her sky blue eyes a little anxious now.

Becca is staring at Lizzie blankly.

'He was supposed to phone,' she says at last.

'Josh?'

'Yes. Josh.' Becca's gaze wanders helplessly around the room.

On the TV, a woman with an American accent is saying, 'So *he* says he needs his space. But *you* think he should be spending more time with the kids.'

Lizzie sits down next to Becca and takes her hand. 'What time was he meant to phone, Becs?'

'Before eight.' Becca turns smudgy eyes on Lizzie and regards her miserably. 'And now it's after eight-thirty.'

'Oh Becs, half an hour's nothing,' Lizzie responds, the corners of her mouth dimpling. 'You know what men are like. They say eight, but they think it's fine to phone at nine or even ten.'

'No,' says Becca, shaking her head in an agitated manner. 'Josh is always on time. And anyway, we're meant to be going out. We're meant to be going to a pub to see his friend's band. They were going to start playing at eight.'

'Oh,' says Lizzie, concerned. She sighs. 'I *wish* men weren't so inconsiderate. Steve's always turning up late, or not bothering to phone when he's changed his plans.' She pats Becca's hand, comfortingly.

'But I didn't think Josh was *like* that!' Becca bursts out, hysterically. Her hair is sticking up in random tufts.

Lizzie puts an arm around her friend's shoulders.

'Come on Becs,' she says, gently. 'Men work differently to women. It's very inconvenient, but it's something we just have to accept.'

Becca looks stricken. Lizzie gives her shoulders a reassuring squeeze.

'And what do *you* want to say to *Tiffany* this evening?' the American woman on the TV is saying.

'That she's gotta back off, 'cause she's bugging the hell out of me,' a man's voice replies. 'She's gotta stop telling me what to do.'

There is a sound of someone's brisk step on the stairs. Then Sasha comes in.

'Hello. I thought I was the only one in the house.' Sasha pauses en route to the kitchen. 'Has something happened?' Quietly, Lizzie explains the situation.

'I see.' Sasha is dressed simply but effectively in black trousers and a soft grey jumper. Her understated clothes only accentuate her smouldering good looks.

'I don't know if I should phone him,' Becca begins, hesitantly.

'You shouldn't,' Lizzie and Sasha answer in unison.

'You know it'd be silly,' Lizzie adds. 'First rule of relationships: if he says he'll call you then whatever you do, don't call him first.'

Sasha seats herself opposite the others and crosses one leg elegantly over the other. She pushes back her ebony hair.

'Becca, it's quite easy to understand what's going on here, if you think about it,' she begins. 'It's just like in *The Gaping Chasm: Can the Sexes Talk?* You've got to the stage where Josh can tell you care about him. He's starting to sense that you *need* him and he feels trapped.'

'Yeah, that's a really scary thing for men,' Lizzie agrees, blonde ponytail jigging. 'They just don't like commitment.'

'You're at a really sensitive point in your relationship and you have to give him time to adjust,' Sasha continues, seriously. 'The very worst thing you could do is phone him. He'll take it as confirmation that you want to own and control him.'

'And he'll run a mile,' Lizzie finishes.

'Oh!' Becca cries out in frustration. 'I know you're right.' She runs her hands frantically through her hair. 'Why does it have to *be* like this? Why can't men...just be normal?'

'Do you want a drink of something, maybe?' Sasha asks. 'I was going to get myself some hot water. I could make you a herbal tea, if you like. Camomile is very soothing.'

Becca scowls. 'Do you have any ice cream left?' she asks, defiantly.

Lizzie and Sasha exchange glances.

'Are you sure?' Sasha asks.

'That full fat double chocolate stuff, you mean?' says Lizzie, eyes wide. 'Do you think you should?'

'Just bring the tub,' says Becca, recklessly. 'I'll get you some more, Sasha.'

'No, don't worry,' Sasha replies, cringing slightly at the thought. 'I only bought it because I had people coming round. I can't eat much of that myself.'

Sasha disappears into the kitchen. Lizzie notices that Becca's hand, apparently without the consent of her conscious mind, is creeping towards the phone.

'Becca…' Lizzie says, warningly. She reaches across her friend and gently but firmly pulls her hand back. 'You don't want to do that, do you now?'

Sasha has just returned with the ice cream. She addresses Becca calmly and soothingly.

'Let's put that back in the hall, shall we, Becca? If he *does* ring you'll be able to hear it perfectly well from in here.' As she speaks, she picks up the phone and removes it. Becca seems about to protest, but Lizzie quickly shoves the ice cream tub into her hands.

'And here's a spoon. Go on, I suppose it can't do much harm.'

Her attention diverted from the phone, Becca rips the lid off the tub and tucks in without inhibition. She eats fast but mechanically, not appearing to derive any particular pleasure from the taste.

'And what do our studio audience think?' the voice from the TV drawls into the ensuing silence. 'Is Dan wrong to say he wants some freedom? Should Tiffany lose some weight if she wants him to stay home at night?'

Becca has only been eating for a few minutes when Caroline, the fourth member of the household, returns from an evening out with her current boyfriend.

'Good grief, what's going on here?' she asks, when she comes in to find Sasha and Lizzie watching, grim-faced, as Becca crams spoonful after spoonful of ice cream into her mouth.

'Josh has stood me up,' Becca says concisely, with her mouth full.

'Bastard!' is Caroline's verdict. She has a slight lisp which, combined with her natural facial expression, gives a rather misleading impression of innocence. Her hair is short and dark, and she has light green eyes set in a small, elfin face. 'Of course,' she adds as an afterthought, 'it's only normal for a man.'

'He's just asserting his independence,' says Sasha. 'It's that point in the relationship, isn't it, Caroline? They've been together a week and he's starting to panic.'

'Probably it's that, yes,' Caroline agrees. 'I guess you still want to hold onto him? Well then, you'll just have to wait it out. Don't chase him. That'd be fatal. And when he *does* call you, don't be clingy.'

'Yes. Men need to do the chasing. There's a lot about that in *Accepting the Neanderthal in Men*,' says Sasha. 'How was your evening, by the way?' she asks Caroline. 'How's Pete?'

'Simon. Pete was last week.'

Lizzie frowns. 'I thought Simon was *before* Pete. Or was that Sam?'

'That was Si.. Si with the Harley Davidson. Sam's the musician who works at the chippy. He was *last* month. Simon, *current* Simon, is the one who likes girls with long, blonde hair.' Caroline glances upwards at her dark fringe and shrugs. 'Oh well.'

'He likes *you*, though?' Sasha asks.

'Yeah, he likes me.'

'Although you're back pretty early tonight, aren't you?'

'Actually I just came back to pick up my toothbrush,' says Caroline with a cheeky smile, and vanishes up the stairs.

Sasha turns back to Becca, who has finished the ice cream and is slumped dismally back on the sofa. 'Tomorrow, Becca, is going to be important,' Sasha tells her. 'Don't demand to know why he didn't phone, act like you barely noticed. He'll be expecting you to be upset and annoyed, and when you're just casual about it he'll start worrying that you don't like him as much as he thought.'

'But Sasha,' says Becca, dully. 'I'm not even going to see him tomorrow. I've got a course all day, on the other side of the city. And I haven't even had a chance to tell him about it.'

'All the better,' Sasha replies, with the glimmering of a smile. 'Let him wonder what's happened to you. He'll be desperate to see you by Thursday.'

Becca barely responds to this. Her eyes are distant and lifeless.

'You really don't look well,' Sasha says. 'You should try that camomile tea. And help yourself to my vitamin pills.' With these words, Sasha rises gracefully to her feet. 'I'm going back upstairs now,' she announces. 'I want to catch Caroline before she goes out again. Don't worry too much, Becca. It'll be okay. I'll see you later,' she says, and glides out of the room.

Lizzie looks at Becca and clucks in an indulgent, maternal

manner. 'What are we going to do with you?' she asks. 'Shall we put a video on? Would that cheer you up?' She smiles, a small, coaxing smile. 'I'll get your duvet from upstairs and you can snuggle up. Then you'll be nice and cosy. And you have to let me make you something warm to drink, sweetie. That'll help you feel better. I might even have some of that low calorie hot chocolate left...'

Chapter 4

Emerging

Callum is sitting at his desk, poring over a problem paper. There are already several discarded attempts at answers in the wastepaper bin. Very deliberately, he writes something on a fresh sheet of paper with the slim, black fountain pen he always uses. He glances back at the question and adds something else to what he has written. At the same time and almost without looking up, he presses a button on the mobile phone which is at his elbow. He continues writing as the phone dials automatically and begins to ring. Then the ringing is interrupted and Callum, startled, slams the phone to his ear. He braces himself for the Freak's breathy voice.

'Hello?'

But it isn't the Freak. It is Shona. Shona, whose smooth, familiar tones he hasn't heard for five long days.

'Shona!'

'Hello, Callum,' she responds, with silky composure.

Callum hadn't planned beyond this point. He has been ringing every few minutes for the last hour and had stopped expecting an answer. He tries to think what to say.

'Shona!' he manages, again. 'Shona, I've been trying to get hold of you since Friday!'

There is a conspicuous silence at the other end of the line.

'So...what have you been doing?' Callum asks, anxiously.

'Nothing in particular,' says Shona, letting the words linger. 'Going to work.'

'Oh, so you've been back at the office, have you? I...actually, I hoped to catch you afterwards. I waited outside for you yesterday.'

'Ah. That wouldn't have worked,' she answers, unperturbed. 'I've changed my hours slightly, you see.'

Callum listens to her disembodied voice. It sounds sleek and velvety. He wonders if perhaps she is wearing her black velvet dress...the one with the clingy bodice and the long sleeves. He thinks of her hair, glowing like embers against the dark material, the short flared skirt lying rumpled across her smooth thighs.

'I'm in my pyjamas, Callum,' says Shona, dryly. 'The ones you don't like.'

Callum's eyes widen. 'Uh? Pardon?'

'Never mind.'

'Anyhow...are you feeling any better?' he inquires, hesitantly.

'Yes and no.' It sounds as if she is smiling, which for some reason Callum finds very disconcerting.

'Shall I come round?' he asks, trying to sound nonchalant. 'We could go out, if you wanted to put some clothes on...Or stay in. Whatever you like.'

'No,' says Shona. 'No, don't come round.' There is something strong, dark and lithe beneath the words.

'Are you busy?' Callum asks. 'Do you have someone

there?'

'Meet me after work tomorrow, if you want to,' says Shona, ignoring his questions. 'At six.'

'At six? Okay then. Right. That's fine, then. I'll look forward to it. I'll take you somewhere special – '

'Goodbye, Callum,' says Shona coolly, and hangs up.

Callum is rather surprised by Shona's appearance. For one thing, she's wearing jeans, trainers and a black fleece, which is not the sort of thing she'd usually wear to work...or at all. And for another thing, she emanates health. Her step is energetic and her eyes sparkle like a fast-flowing stream on a hot day.

'Shona, you look so much better!'

'Wonderful, isn't it. I can't do a thing wrong! If I'm ill and haggish and I haven't washed for days then somehow I'm Ophelia. And when I get better I'm...what am I? The woman in the Vitayoghurt ad?'

Understandably, Callum is confused. 'What do you mean?' he asks, warily.

'It's simple enough, Callum. I'm merely remarking that wherever I go and whatever I do, the spotlight follows me. I can take off all my make-up, I can buy my clothes from jumble sales, I can rake my face with my nails till it bleeds, but I can't escape the eyes and I can't plug my ears. Even when I'm dead I'm sure I'll be great material for somebody's necrophilic fantasies.' She smiles brazenly, maniacally. 'Tasty!'

'Right,' says Callum, grinning amenably. 'Whatever you say. Now, if you've quite finished, maybe you'll tell me where you'd like to go this evening.'

'Let's go back to yours.'

'Mine?'

'Yes, you're familiar with the place, aren't you? It's where you wake up in the mornings. Usually.'

'But what would we do?'

'Talk? Revolutionary concept, I know.' She meets Callum's eyes and the clear spring sunlight illuminates her fresh, flawless face. 'Except for this rather fetching zit in the corner of my nose. I don't think even Lizzie could deny the existence of that one. No, Callum, I can see this is all too much for you – we'll postpone the talking part. Let's get a video out. Let's buy some garlic bread.'

'Garlic bread? I thought you were on a diet!'

'No, I'm not.'

This is the first fully comprehensible thing Shona has said so far, but Callum struggles to absorb it. He hasn't ever known Shona not to be on a diet. It is as if some basic part of her has been amputated – an arm or a leg.

'Yes, it's going to *cripple* me, not being on a diet.'

Callum is still grinning in that boyish, lop-sided way he has, but the amusement in his eyes is laced with concern. Shona looks so refreshed, so *glowing,* but her mind seems unbalanced and erratic.

'Goodness me, was that almost an admission that there's more to me than how I look? Did someone suggest I had a *mind?*

Callum watches Shona talking into the empty air. It's obvious he needs to get her to a doctor, but if he mentions it she might panic, poor thing. She's going to need very careful handling.

Walking down the road together, Chris and Frances Freak make a comical pair. Chris is tall even by ordinary standards, but next to his undersized companion he looks like a giant. He has to try and curtail his long, easy stride so that she isn't left behind. Frances scampers along at his side, her skinny limbs lost in her huge drab cardigan. In spite of her youth, she looks somehow decrepit. Her skin seems withered and the flesh on her face only meagrely covers her bones.

The odd duo reach Chris and Callum's house. Chris opens the door and they go into the lounge.

'Hot chocolate?' Chris asks.

'Kit, what's this?' Frances demands, her thin voice chafing. She is gaping at a poster, tacked up on the wall.

'That's Callum's,' Chris replies. 'Obviously.'

'But...why have you let him put it up?' She cannot disguise her irritation.

'Well,' Chris considers. 'This is his lounge as well as mine. I don't think I have any right to stop him putting up pictures if he wants to. Besides which, it doesn't bother me. I don't even notice it any more.'

'It doesn't *bother* you?' Frances sounds furious. She turns an accusatory face towards him. There are purplish stains under her eyes.

'It's not exactly hard core porn, is it? She's wearing a bikini.'

'I wonder,' says Frances, her irksome voice turning acid, 'what Shona makes of it?'

'Shona doesn't complain about it. There's plenty more in his room, you know. She doesn't complain about those, either.'

Frances stares at him resentfully, her skin sickly pale, her greyish hair wilting. 'How can you not care, after what your sister went through? And your mum?'

'This isn't anything to do with my family,' says Chris, stung. He gives her a look which implores her to be reasonable, but she avoids his eyes. 'And it isn't anything to do with you. You just don't have any business telling Callum what to do in his own home...any right.' Resolutely, Chris turns away from the poster. 'Can we please drop this? Can't you just tell me whether you want a drink? You can have one of my home-made cookies with it,' he adds, coaxingly.

'But you have to agree that it's degrading!' Frances persists, in a whine. 'Are you seriously trying to tell me you wouldn't be embarassed by that poster, if your family came to visit?'

Chris sighs heavily, wearied by her nagging.

'Frances, you can indulge in any amount of feminist raving in the privacy of your own thesis. But not here. Not in someone else's house.' He pauses, before adding, quietly, 'And I'd rather you didn't use my family as fodder for your theories.'

'But Kit,' she says, fretfully. 'I thought -'

'I don't want to hear. I just want to go and make the hot chocolate.'

For a single, blissful moment she is silent. Then she says, 'It's all scrambled in my head…' Her voice dwindles. 'I'm going home.'

Without saying anything further or meeting Chris' eyes, the Freak dashes out of the house. Chris stands at the window and watches her diminish as she hurries away up the road.

When Becca returns from work on Thursday, Lizzie is ready to pounce.

'Hey, Becs! How did it go with Josh?' she calls, from the kitchen.

Becca goes into the lounge and removes the navy jacket she is wearing. Underneath, her blouse is blue silk, the fluid material fondling her warm skin. She glances only fleetingly at Lizzie, who has come through from the kitchen and is leaning against the door frame, her hair in bunches. She is holding a glass and drinking what appears to be milkshake through a stripy straw.

'Someone stole his mobile on Tuesday,' Becca says. Her voice sounds huskier than usual. 'He had my number programmed into it.'

Comprehension dawns on Lizzie's freckled face. 'Oh! So he didn't have your number? So he *couldn't* phone you!'

Becca nods, slowly.

'That's *good*, isn't it?' Lizzie asks. 'You don't seem very happy!'

'No, it's not good,' Becca replies. She is standing with her silk-clad arms wrapped around her slim body as if she is cold, her head hanging forward. 'He couldn't understand why I didn't phone. He didn't have my address or anything, so he couldn't contact me, but he was sure I would phone him to find out what was going on, once it got late enough for me to worry.' Her hair has fallen over her eyes, veiling them with gold. The back of her neck forms a graceful curve, but looks exposed and vulnerable. 'I tried to explain why I didn't phone him…and he said he thought I would've been more straight with him. "You of all people," he said.'

'Oh dear.' Lizzie purses her soft, pink lips around the straw and sucks, thoughtfully. 'So he was quite annoyed, was he?'

'Not annoyed. Disappointed, I think. Upset.'

'Oh!' Concern fills Lizzie's round, childlike eyes.

'He didn't go and hear his friend's band, because he was waiting for me to phone,' says Becca. She looks up at Lizzie and her hazel eyes are dark. 'And yesterday, when he couldn't find me at work, he was really worried. He found out I was on a course and he couldn't believe I hadn't let him know. He tried to get my phone number from work, but they're not allowed to give out employees' personal information.'

Lizzie wrinkles her pert little nose in sympathy. 'Poor Josh!' She takes a small slurp of milkshake. 'He still wants to go out with you though, doesn't he?'

'I don't know,' says Becca, her voice mellifluous and sad. 'I don't know.'

Lizzie is on her second banana cocktail already. She is trying to look sophisticated in a long blue-grey dress, but she keeps swinging her legs under the table. Callum is watching Shona over the top of his vodka martini. Her glossy hair is twisted up in a French pleat, leaving her shapely neck bare. She is quiet, but keeps meeting Callum's eyes in what he feels is a challenging manner. He rather likes this, and once he tries winking at her, but gets no response. Steve is swigging lager with enthusiasm.

'Freedom!' announces Steve loudly, for the fifth time since they arrived in Justine's. 'No more lectures! No more bloody boring labs!' He clinks his glass violently against Callum's which, by some miracle, remains unchipped.

'You do still have to sit your exams,' Lizzie points out, with a cute little smile. 'And they *are* your finals!'

'Exams?' says Callum. He waves a dismissive hand. 'No problem.'

'No problem!' Steve repeats, cheerfully.

'I reckon we've got a nice easy few weeks ahead of us,' says Callum. 'A bit of gentle revision, the odd exam, but basically we can just doss around, like you girls do most of the time, actually.' He meets Shona's inscrutable gaze with a grin.

'What do you mean, Callum? I have a job.'

'Yeah, but you only do a thirty hour week. You've forgotten what hard work is. Anyway, what do you do when you're at work?' he asks, teasingly. 'Take lunch breaks and coffee breaks, file your nails, answer the phone…and that's about it.'

'Lizzie's the same,' says Steve. 'She does sod all, compared to what we're used to. We have to work evenings and weekends. And what's her job? Just stacking books on shelves.'

'Actually, Steve, there's more to being a librarian than stacking books,' says Shona, looking at him from under long lashes. 'Why do you think you need a degree? And as for you, Callum, why do you love to imagine I'm some sort of featherbrained secretary whose main duty is making the coffee?' she smiles slowly, her lips a dark ruby. '*You* couldn't do my job, so I wish you'd stop belittling it.'

'No, I couldn't do your job,' says Callum, waggishly. 'I've no experience with nail files.'

'You've no experience with HTML or QuarkXPress,' Shona responds. 'And you're incapable of treating other people with respect or sensitivity, which really wouldn't help.'

Callum doesn't know quite how to respond to this rather cruel remark. Shona leans her chin on elegant, laced fingers, her elbows on the table, and watches him as he sips his drink. Her neckline is high, regrettably, though her arms are naked. Her dress is long and black and covered with silver glitter. There is a slit up to her thigh on one side, but Callum has carelessly sat in the wrong place to reap the benefits. Shona's shining lips curve in a small, sagacious smile. She diverts this smile, turning it towards Lizzie.

'Is there any news about Josh?' Shona asks.

'Oh! Yes! It's all sorted. They talked it all through over lunch. I really think he would have called her last night and saved her all this trauma, but of course he *still* didn't have her number, the silly boy.'

'What's this?' Steve wants to know.

'Becca had a sort of misunderstanding with Josh, but it's all sorted out now,' Lizzie explains, twisting the silver ring which adorns one of her small, white hands.

'That's good,' says Steve. 'She needs a boyfriend, that girl, to keep her in check.'

'Yeah, good luck to him, I say,' says Callum, exchanging a grin with Steve.

'You two can stop smirking at one another,' says Shona, coolly. 'Though I know it must be very difficult for you to tolerate a woman who isn't completely meek and deferential.'

'Talking of women who aren't completely meek and deferential...' says Callum, raising an eyebrow at her.

'Thank you,' Shona replies. The light glitters in her diamante earrings and in her deep indigo eyes. 'Right then, what's the plan for the rest of the evening? Lizzie, what do you want to do?'

Shona is sitting in a boxy little office in front of a computer, going through some emails. Her skirt is black and satiny, and it ends just above her knees. Her blouse is burgundy, a colour that bears an interesting relation to her hair. A more ordinary woman couldn't have carried it off, but when Shona combines such colours, the half-clash between the two intense shades is beautiful and intriguing.

Shona's lovely blue eyes scan across the screen as she reads through the last email of the morning. Her manicured nails tap against the keys as she touch-types a reply. When she is midway through, the phone begins to ring and she reaches out and picks up the receiver with a practised movement. Her eyes do not leave the screen.

'Good morning, this is Jigsaw, Shona speaking,' she says, bright and efficient. 'Mmm...I'm afraid she's not in at the moment. Can I take a message?' Shona pulls a large diary towards her and turns over the pages. 'She'll be in the office tomorrow, between nine and ten. Or I could give you her mobile number. No? Okay. Goodbye, then.'

As soon as Shona puts the phone down, it begins to ring again. 'Jigsaw, Shona speaking. Oh, good morning, Mr Matthews. Yes, that's right. Yes, Thursday. Your appointment's in the book, so she knows to expect you. No, that's fine. Don't worry about it at all. See you on Thursday, then, Mr Matthews. Goodbye.'

After hanging up, Shona rapidly finishes off the email she was working on and sends it. Then she begins going through the day's post. This doesn't usually take long and today there are only a couple of letters. Before Shona has had time to finish dealing with them, however, the door opens and a middle-aged woman comes in. She is tall and thin and wearing a tie-dyed skirt with little bells around the hem. Her blouse is voluminous and made of bright orange velvet. She doesn't quite have Shona's flair with colours.

'Surprise!' she cries, shrilly, as she comes through the door.

'Hello, Elspeth,' says Shona, politely.

'Hello, flower. My dear, I've just come up in the lift.' She rolls her eyes for no discernable reason. 'And it was full of men in grey suits. Scarcely even so much as a coloured shirt among them. It can't be *positive*, can it, to be so *straitened*. One feels they should,' she makes a flamboyant gesture, '*embrace colour!*'

Shona nods, diplomatically.

'Now, this isn't one of my scheduled office times, is it?' Elspeth goes on. 'There was some particular reason why I've come in, though it eludes me. It's conceivable, of course – goodness, what's that?' A nasal, pedestrian version of *Jesu Joy of Man's Desiring* fills the air. It seems to be emanating from her bag.

Elspeth takes the huge raffia-work handbag from her shoulder and proceeds to unload its contents onto Shona's desk.

'It's my mobile phone!' cries Elspeth, apparently astonished. She fumbles frantically in the depths of the oversized bag. 'I must have set it to the wrong ring-tone again – hello?' she says, unnecessarily loudly, clamping the phone to her ear. 'Claudia! Yes, I lost the phone in my bag. Oh yes, I know it's been cancelled, Richard called me.' Elspeth's large earrings jangle against the phone. She is decked in uncoordinated jewellery. Her earrings are gold, her necklace is made of big wooden beads and she has a dozen or so bangles in a variety of colours. 'Oh, well, of course...goodness me!...I imagine they *will* be...Well, that's wonderful...No, I won't keep you dear...Till Friday, then...Wonderful!' Elspeth removes the phone from her ear and examines it confusedly for a moment. 'I suppose that's disconnected,' she says, to no one in particular, and buries it once more in her bag.

'Now what was it I came in for?' Elspeth asks, helplessly. She looks vaguely around the office, as if hoping the answer will present itself in visible form.

'While I think of it, Elspeth,' says Shona, tucking a stray curl briskly behind her ear, 'Gerald phoned. He didn't say what it was about.'

'Oh, you've just reminded me what I was going to do, flower,' says Elspeth, beaming in Shona's direction. 'I was just going to pick up a file or two. The advocacy group in Bidley and the other one, the one that Keith set up.'

'Shertham,' says Shona.

'That's exactly the one. You're a treasure.' Elspeth drifts over towards the filing cabinet.

'I don't think its any use looking in there, though,' Shona

tells her. 'I don't think they've been put away.'

'Not a problem, I'll find them,' says Elspeth airily, and begins to whirl around the office, shuffling piles of folders. She nearly trips over a crate of books. A kirby grip tinkles to the floor as her frizzy hair flies out of control.

'Actually, I think I know where they are,' says Shona, rising from her chair. Elspeth perches inelegantly on the edge of the desk and concentrates on putting her hairstyle back together.

'Oh, Shona,' she says, jabbing a hair grip into her mound of mutinous hair as Shona searches for the files. 'Did you know about the new vegan café on Halsey Street? Well, you *must* pay it a visit, because it's wonderful, absolutely wonderful. Not just the food, but the whole...*ambience.*'

Shona has now located the two files, so she hands them to Elspeth.

'Thanks ever so, you really are a treasure. Now I *must* dash, or I'll miss my bus. Oh! One more thing. Where are you *re* the newsletter? Have you filled it, or would you have room for at least a mention of the Bullseye group?'

Shona looks uncomprehending. 'Bullseye?'

'Haven't you come across Bullseye? It's an arts initiative, *very* positive. Almost entirely user-led. The focus is mental health survivors, but they're very keen to network with all sorts of groups. The current project is reminiscence-based, David was saying. My feeling is that Bullseye's going to *grow*. It could become very important in the Bidley area. They've not really had anything like that before, have they? I'll bring the literature in tomorrow and you can have a read.'

'Okay, that sounds good,' says Shona. 'To be honest, this quarter's newsletter is looking a bit thin, so I'm glad you've come up with that.'

'Wonderful. See you anon!'

Elspeth disappears in a flurry of orange velvet and cro-
cheted shawl. Shona goes back to sorting out the day's post.
One of the letters she puts unopened into a pigeon hole
marked 'Claire'. After rereading the other she attempts to
make a phone call, but no one picks up. She replaces the receiver and looks at her watch.

'Nearly lunchtime,' she says, aloud. 'And for your information, I happen to like Elspeth's clothes. And she isn't
scatty or gushing, as you seem to want to imply. She's full of
life and energy and ideas…and I admire her very much.'

The sky is pale, the colour of blackbirds' eggs. Chris is gazing
at it from his bedroom window, his expression solemn. In
actual fact, he is bored; bored of revision. He has been revising all weekend…and now it is Monday, with nothing to look
forward to all week but yet more revision.

Until Saturday, that is. He'd almost forgotten, but Saturday is the Science Faculty Ball. The thought of it fills Chris
with a vague apprehension. He's really not sure why he's paid
all this money to go. Of course, he likes Sasha and she'll be
perfectly good company for the evening but, well…he can
imagine the conversation during the meal getting very tedi-
ous, since it'll probably be dominated by Steve and Becca and
Lizzie. And he can imagine not wanting to dance much, just
sitting around with Sasha feeling inadequate, while she gets
bored and wonders why she agreed to be his partner.

It occurs to Chris that he might not even have his dinner
suit with him. It might be at his mum's. He goes over to
check in the wardrobe. That's okay, it's in there – and the
dress shirt. The tie might be a problem, though. He can't remember having seen it for a very long time. Still, now isn't
really the time to turn his room upside down looking for it.

Reluctantly, Chris returns to his work, sitting down at a

small table where he has been making notes under the heading, *The Political Impact of Religion in the Sixteenth Century.* He skims through what he has written.

'Hm...there needs to be something about theological influences from abroad...Luther and...the one who had to do with Geneva. What on earth's his name? Good grief! I should know this stuff...'

Chris reaches a file of lecture notes down from the shelf above the bed and flicks through it.

'Ah, *Calvin*, of course. Think I need to do a bit more reading around that.'

Chris writes *Luther and Calvin — doctrine* on his pad. He gazes at the words, pen poised, waiting for further inspiration. It isn't forthcoming. He takes a chocolate chip cookie from a plate at his elbow and nibbles half-heartedly on it.

Maybe, actually, he could make some more cookies. Maybe this afternoon. Chris brightens slightly at the thought. He puts his pen down and wanders over to the bookcase. *The Ultimate Crossword Collection...A Compact Guide to Houseplants...*Hmm. His recipe book isn't in the normal place. *Great Expectations...1066 and All That...*ah, here it is, *Complete Bakery.* Chris turns over the pages, looking at the pictures and scanning through the lists of ingredients. He fancies trying something different this time...cherry crackers? Sounds a bit odd. Honey and lemon cookies...maybe. Mmm. Mocha macaroons. That'd be different. But he'd have to go out and buy almonds.

'However,' Chris says, sternly. 'I could only justify baking cookies this afternoon if I'd actually got some work done this morning. Which I haven't, yet.'

Marvelling at his own self-discipline, Chris resumes his revision. He sits, head in hands, waiting for the thoughts to come.

'Obviously, foreign policy is a major issue…' Chris tells himself, eventually. Very neatly, he writes, *Relationships with France, Spain, Scotland.* *Rome*, he adds, after a moment's thought.

'Yes, but what about Protestant countries?' Chris asks, aloud.

He considers this for a few seconds, then puts, *etc.*

Of course, it might be easier to concentrate if there weren't so many other things to worry about. For instance, it's sort of worrying that it's nearly the end of term and still Chris has no idea where he's going to live next year. He has very little idea what he's going to do, either, but for some reason that concerns him less. Callum will be heading off to London, to take up his job with Chiritelle, the cosmetics company. He's going to be on a graduate programme to become a systems manager or procedural consultant, or something that means equally little to Chris. Which means Chris won't be able to stay in this house unless he can find someone else to share with.

Chris reflects that if he can get a decently paid job, he could maybe get a flat on his own…But could he keep a rabbit in a flat? Probably not. And he badly wants a rabbit. A rabbit would be warm and soft and docile. A rabbit…would be company. Chris sees himself, suddenly, sitting in an armchair reading a book in a small, cosy room, with a log fire blazing in the hearth and a rabbit on his lap. He frowns. Perhaps it would be more normal if it wasn't a rabbit on his lap, but a cat instead. But he doesn't like cats, or not much. He likes rabbits.

Chris dismisses the whole rabbit issue from his mind and tries to think what else is worrying him. Hm…Frances is a bit worrying. He never would've thought she'd freak out like that about Callum's poster. Freak out. Chris smiles despite himself, but only for a moment...only till he remembers what it was like, standing there while Frances went on and on, Chris wondering helplessly whether Callum was in and could hear what she was saying...which he maybe could, though he hasn't mentioned it. Of course, Chris knows Frances has these views...but she doesn't usually impose them on other people. He still can't see why she would think it fair to expect Callum, who she barely even knows, to abide by her rules...and in his own house, too. But, reasonable or not, he doesn't like to feel that she's annoyed with him. Maybe he should phone her later on.

Chris' gaze takes a meandering course around the room, searching for a new distraction.

'Perhaps that cactus needs watering.'

He goes back to the window and examines the diminutive cactus which is sitting on the sill. It is in a little painted pot and was given to him for his birthday by his youngest sister Emma. But no, it doesn't need watering – the soil is still wet.

'If you're not careful,' Chris tells himself, 'you'll kill that poor cactus with overwatering. You're forever using it as an excuse for putting off work.'

Stung by remorse, Chris sits down again and tries to think about sixteenth-century politics. Perhaps he would have succeeded, had it not suddenly occurred to him to wonder what Shona would be wearing at the ball. He pictures her, Cinderella-like, in an elaborate blue ball gown, her shoulders bare, a tiara set amid her dark red locks. She gazes about her in wonderment as she descends a sweeping staircase, at the plush red carpet beneath her feet, the marble pillars, the chandeliers. Or, better still...Shona in a plain white dress – very simple, but made of silk. Chris conjures up the image, seeing the sheen of the silk, almost feeling it under his fingers. Her deeply-coloured hair is as soft and shiny as the silk, her skin pure porcelain white. Her eyes are haunted by dim shadows...and there are wildflowers twisted in her hair.

Unwillingly, Chris returns to the real world. He focuses on the photos and art postcards he has hanging over his desk. He has been staring straight through a photo of his mum and his two sisters in their garden. It makes him think, with a slight pang, how long it is since he last saw them. His mum is in the big floppy sunhat she always wears to do the gardening. She has an arm around each of her two daughters. The photo was taken before Rachael had her hair cut and she looks different, much younger, but her smile is the same. And Emma...her expression is almost identical to Rachael's. The same little crease at the corners of her mouth, the same faint self-consciousness in her eyes. Below this photo, Chris has stuck a postcard of Miranda from *The Tempest*. He read the play for his A levels. He remembers how pleased he was when he first saw Waterhouse's painting in an art book – he had always imagined Miranda looking more or less like that. Next to that, in a wooden frame, is Pissarro's picture of the Boulevard Montmartre at night, yellow lights reflecting in the wet street. He bought that a year ago, just after he got back from Paris, where he'd spent a weekend sightseeing. He found it in the little shop in the art gallery in town. Chris resolves to go back to the art gallery and have another look around, possibly buy some more postcards. Soon. Maybe this week. If only he didn't have so much revision to do.

It is Frances who lets Callum in. She opens the door slowly, lassitude in her dismal eyes. Her gaze slides sluggishly over his face. Then she squashes herself flat against the wall to let him past.

Shona has heard him come in, and is standing in the

doorway of her severe white bedroom. She has an unfamiliar pair of long black leather boots on, with three inch spikes for heels. The rest of her clothes are black, too – a black satin skirt with a black blouse. Her hair burns all the brighter against this dark setting.

'How did you know I have Tuesday afternoons off now?' she demands.

Callum meets her cruel, beautiful eyes with a rascally grin. 'I worked it out.'

'What did you come round for?'

'I came to see *you*, Angel,' Callum responds, fondly. He runs an affectionate finger over her cheek and down the side of her neck. When he reaches her collarbone she moves suddenly away.

'Oh, I see,' she says, her voice hard. 'Have you been drinking?'

'Just a swift lunchtime pint or two.' His hand moves towards her satin-clad thigh, but she takes a step back. 'Not interested?'

'No.' She has turned her back on him and is looking out of the window, her black silhouette stark and shapely.

'You're *not* interested, are you, recently? You're turning frigid.'

'I think you know why.'

'I haven't a clue. Why?'

Shona turns round and fixes him with a long, ruthless stare, as if she is trying to gore him with her eyes. Undaunted, Callum returns her gaze, his grin affable. After a while this seems to have an effect. A suggestive smile begins to play around her voluptuous mouth.

'Maybe I fancy trying something different,' she says in a voice which is suddenly coaxing…alluring.

'You do?'

'Mm.'

'Like what?'

'Well, first you'll need to undress.'

Callum regards her suspiciously, not sure what to make of this sudden change of mood.

'If you want to get into these,' Shona says, opening a drawer and producing a pair of black silk knickers, 'you'll need to undress.'

She spins round and pulls the curtains across the windows. Callum passes a hand confusedly through his dark, wavy hair, but when she turns back he makes sure he is fumbling with his shoelaces. Out of the corner of his eye, he watches as she opens a drawer in her dressing table and takes out one or two small items.

'Aren't *you* going to undress?' Callum asks.

'Just be patient,' Shona says. The silk knickers are still dangling from her finger as she walks across the room and opens the doors of her wardrobe. After a few moments she selects a white negligee edged with lace, which reassures Callum somewhat.

Before long, Callum is perched naked and self-conscious on the edge of Shona's bed. Shona, who is still fully clad, tosses him the black silk knickers.

'Okay, put them on.'

'What?'

'Just do it.'

Callum stares at his girlfriend, amazed. There is a punitive light in her eyes, which evokes a violent churning feeling in his stomach. He cannot tell whether it is excitement or panic.

'Since when do you want me to wear your underwear?' he asks, stupefied. He looks down at the scrap of black silk he has in his hand. 'No, I won't,' he says.

Shona sighs, impatiently. 'Callum, we'll do this my way,

or not at all,' she says, inexorable.

She looks very tall from where Callum is sitting. Tall and rather formidable, Callum reflects. But also – and this is the inconvenient part – so gorgeous it is anguish not to be touching her. Her boots cling to her slender shins. Her legs, clad in black stockings, look very long. She has placed her hands on the curve of her hips, where Callum's would very much like to be. Somehow, though, he isn't sure he'll be able to get that close. Even from this distance he feels that her merciless gaze is scorching him. If he were to touch her fiery hair he almost believes he would be reduced to ashes. He has never seen her like this before – she has never looked so…dangerous. For a moment Callum considers his options. Then, quickly, he puts the knickers on.

'Well, you could do with a shave,' Shona says when he has done so, eyeing his legs, 'and your bikini line wants a good waxing. But I suppose you'll do.'

Callum looks down at himself. He is bulging out of her skimpy underwear in a somewhat unseemly fashion. 'Have you completely flipped?' he asks. 'Are you trying to tell me this turns you on?'

'Is it so difficult to believe?' she asks, hitting him with a smile that could raise welts. 'You're quite partial to me in those knickers, I seem to remember. You ought to put this on, too,' she says, holding up the negligee.

'Ought I?'

'Yes.'

'It's transparent!'

'All the better.'

Wondering what on earth has got into Shona, Callum puts the negligee on. It feels very light and insubstantial. And, for some reason, ticklish.

'Now, one last thing,' says Shona, in a businesslike tone.

She opens her hand to reveal a lipstick and a tiny plastic case of eye shadow.

'I hope you're not planning to put that stuff on me!' Callum says, alarmed.

'Oh, Callum,' says Shona, cajolingly. 'It's only for fun. Please? You did want to try something different...'

This latest absurdity doesn't appeal to Callum at all, but it seems to him that having gone this far he might as well completely abandon himself to her whim. He hopes it will turn out to have been worthwhile.

'We're going to need some more light,' says Shona, whipping back the curtains the instant he agrees. She sits down next to him on the bed. 'This skin isn't in very good condition,' she comments. 'You need to moisturise on a twice-daily basis.'

Callum stares at her in disbelief. He feels himself losing any sense of involvement in the situation. It is as if he is looking on while some surreal drama is played out before him.

'His lips,' says Shona, applying lipstick liberally, 'are a dark, seductive red...'

'What's up with you?' says Callum, hollowly.

'Don't talk or you'll get lipstick all round your mouth,' Shona replies. 'His already long, dark lashes don't need the help of mascara...which is fortunate, because I'd probably poke your eyes out.'

She opens the little compact of eye shadow and loads a small, sponge-tipped stick with silver powder.

'Don't cringe like that,' she says, as she tries to apply it to his face. 'And don't screw up your eyelids! It's not going to hurt!'

Callum attempts to relax, but it isn't easy while Shona is subjecting him to these indignities. Has she seriously developed some sort of makeup fetish, he wonders? A liking for men in silk panties? Although he isn't opposed to the idea of fetishism in principle, this particular penchant of Shona's seems perverse to an unpleasant degree.

'His deep green eyes are dusted with silver,' she is saying. 'Complementing their hue and defining their...their attractive shape.'

She sits back to contemplate her handiwork. Callum isn't reassured by her expression, which shows satisfaction and amusement in equal quantities.

'You look lovely,' she announces. 'Go and have a look at yourself in the bathroom mirror.'

Obediently, Callum goes into Shona's en suite bathroom and stands in front of the full length mirror, staring at his transformed self. He had expected to look ridiculous, but he wasn't prepared for this. He wasn't prepared for the way his too-skinny legs would look, sticking out from under the short negligee, or the way his chest hair would bristle up through the delicate white lace. He hadn't expected his face to look so strange, and yet eerily familiar. He stares at his mouth, which looks large and moist...and at his eyelids, which are twinkling alarmingly. Several expletives spring to mind, but he is too astounded to utter them.

'Try taking yourself seriously now!' Shona says. Or that is what he thought she said. He makes it out of the bathroom just in time to see the bedroom door close.

'Shona!' Callum opens the door a crack. Having established that there is no one but Shona out there, he opens it further and sticks his unusually colourful face through the aperture. 'Where are you going?'

'I'm just having a quick coffee and then I'm going out.'

'What? Aren't we going to...?'

'No,' says Shona, unelaborately. With distinctly sadistic

pleasure, she adds, 'By the way, your clothes are on the front lawn.'

As he struggles to process this last piece of information, the dim remembrance of a sound comes back to Callum...a sound he heard but didn't consciously register while he was looking at himself in the bathroom mirror...a sound like an opening window. The bitch!

'If you hurry you'll get to them before I do,' Shona says, conversationally. In spite of her casual tone, she lacerates him with her eyes as she continues, 'Otherwise I might stick them in a dustbin somewhere not at all obvious.'

She turns quickly and the blaze of her hair singes his eyeballs. He cannot think what to say and he can barely focus on her tantalising curves, as with excruciating slowness her beautiful body disappears down the hallway.

The girls have a long-standing tradition of meeting up for lunch on a Wednesday. It is a way of breaking up the working week. Each Wednesday lunchtime is like an island in the great ocean separating one weekend from the next.

'Where's Becca?' Shona asks. She is wearing a short leather coat and a trim black suit. She has a dusky pink top underneath and her hair is drawn back into a sleek plait.

'She has another lunch date with Josh,' says Sasha, who has dressed with her usual understated style. She has her long, dark coat on, with a white angora scarf at the neck. Her trousers are soft grey and well-cut.

'And Lizzie?' Shona queries.

'She's with Steve.'

'Just the two of us, then,' Shona says, her smile sparkling like snow. 'Have you got your lunch already?' Sasha holds up a large baguette brimming with cheese and salad, wrapped in a paper bag.

'Oh, that looks nice,' says Shona. 'Where was it from? The bakery? I've just got a boring supermarket sandwich. Actually, not that boring. Smoked salmon. Shall we eat, then?'

The two girls walk briskly across the square together, Sasha's coat swirling around her ankles. Shona's shapely legs are clad in matt black stockings.

'Tights, actually,' says Shona, under her breath, and Sasha gives her a funny look.

The two girls sit down on the bench outside the cathedral – their usual spot when the weather is fine, as it is today. The air feels fresh and the light is very clear. The trees in the square are verdant. People keep passing by: shoppers and office workers on their lunch breaks.

'Interesting morning?' Sasha asks. She takes a small bite of her baguette.

'Not really,' Shona responds. 'I've been on my own the whole time. And I don't have much work to do at the moment, so it hasn't exactly been thrill packed. How's the museum?'

'Fine,' says Sasha. 'I did a couple of tours for parties of schoolchildren, which I quite enjoyed. Oh, and we all had a bit of cake, because it's Gaynor's last day. Have I told you about Gaynor? She's a specialist in Egyptology, but she's chosen to give up work to have children. I think that's quite brave. I admire her for it.'

'Doesn't she enjoy working that much?' Shona asks, removing a crumb from her coat with delicate fingertips. Her nails are painted dusky pink to match her top.

'Oh no, Gaynor loves her work,' says Sasha, earnestly. 'She does far longer hours than she needs to because she enjoys it so much. She's extremely well respected in her field. But she didn't want a stranger taking care of her baby.'

'Right,' Shona replies. A small frown mars her white brow.

'Is that cream cheese in your sandwich?' Sasha asks, eyeing Shona's lunch with concern.

'Yes,' says Shona. 'I love it.' She continues eating enthusiastically.

'Well, so do I – but it's very fattening.'

Shona shrugs. 'I'm not really bothering about all that any more.'

'Pardon?' There is a quizzical look in Sasha's black eyes. Her lips are painted a subtle brambly colour.

'I just mean...I don't see why I should have to be on a permanent diet.'

'Doubtless you don't need to diet,' replies Sasha, with a half envious smile. 'You're lucky enough to be naturally slim and naturally very pretty.'

'No,' says Shona, slowly. 'I don't think you understand. I've been thinking...well, Callum doesn't diet, does he? Or Steve, or any man I've ever known. So why do so many women feel they need to?'

'Women tend to put on weight more easily,' Sasha points out. She glances at her sandwich as if it has just lost some of its appeal. 'Also, how a woman looks is usually very important to her. Much more so than for a man. It's part of...female identity. I think it's a very positive thing for someone to consciously take responsibility for what she eats. When a woman chooses to diet, she's taking care of her body. It shows that she respects herself.'

Shona seems to be about to reply, but she is distracted by three young executives who wander past, casting friendly glances in the girls' direction. Sasha's dark hair is lustrous in the spring sunlight, but Shona's draws their eyes like a flame.

'Mm! He had a nice smile, that fair-haired one!' Sasha

comments, when they are out of hearing. 'Pity he was only interested in your legs.'

'Shona scowls.'

'Hm?' says Sasha, confused.

'I'm fed up with men only being interested in my legs.'

An expression of slight irritation drifts across Sasha's dark, attractive face.

'You should count yourself lucky. Most girls would give anything to look like you.'

'Most girls,' says Shona swiftly, 'have their priorities wrong.'

With some difficulty, Sasha muffles her annoyance. Shona keeps on eating her sandwich, apparently oblivious.

'Do you have a new dress for the ball?' Sasha asks eventually, her voice light.

'Um…no. I haven't really thought about it, to be honest,' Shona replies. 'It's this Saturday, isn't it?' She turns guileless eyes to Sasha, made up very subtly with shades of fawn.

'Yes!' says Sasha, rather astonished. 'Don't you have anything to wear, then? You'll have to get organised!'

'I suppose I will,' says Shona. She smiles. She is wearing just a hint of lipstick. 'It'll be interesting to meet Josh, won't it?'

Sasha pulls her downy scarf closer about her throat. 'Yes. Becca seems really serious about him. I'm very pleased she's found someone she likes so much.'

'How about you? Is there anyone on the horizon?' Shona asks. 'You're going to the ball with Chris, aren't you?'

Sasha raises a dark eyebrow. 'I think it's you he's interested in, Shona.'

'Me?' Shona turns and looks at Sasha, her wide eyes a clear azure, her pink lips slightly parted in an expression of innocent surprise. 'Why would he be interested in me?' The soft curves of her cheeks are tinged with rose.

Sasha sighs. 'Because you're gorgeous, of course.'

Shona's blush deepens a degree. 'No, I'm not! And Chris
– I mean, I sometimes imagined…but I never really thought
that he…we've hardly even had a proper conversation. Chris
is *your* friend!'

'Yes,' says Sasha. 'He's my *friend*.'

'But he doesn't *know* me!'

'Since when was that an issue?' A slight breeze blows a
strand of dark hair across Sasha's face. She smooths it out of
the way. 'This isn't really a revelation, is it?' she continues,
smiling a dry, blackberry-coloured smile. 'It practically goes
without saying that anyone male fancies you.'

There is a long silence. Slowly, the girls finish off their
sandwiches. Sasha folds her empty paper bag in four and
drops it in a litter bin.

'Sasha,' says Shona, after a while. 'Why does Frances call
Chris, "Kit"?'

Sasha looks mildly amused. 'She still calls him that? Kit
dates back to my first year.'

'Did Frances know Chris then?'

'Yes. Don't you talk to your flatmate?' Sasha asks, but her
half smile implies that she rather doubts Shona does. 'Frances was doing a history option that year. She was in the same
tutor group as Chris and myself. Kelly and the two Sarahs
were in that group, too.'

'So that was when Chris and Frances became friends?'
Shona prompts.

'Yes. You know how quiet and studious she is, but she
really warmed to him. And he made a big effort to make her
feel included. He used to bring her along when the rest of us
went out. We all used to call him "Kit" at that stage…I can't
remember why. I think maybe it was Frances' name for him

in the first place.'

Shona gets up to put her rubbish in the bin, exhibiting her legs to full advantage for the benefit of a passing pair of businessmen.

'I like your shoes,' says Sasha, looking at Shona's smart black patent leather heels. 'I could do with some like that.' She tilts her oval face up to look at Shona, and the sunlight illuminates her olive skin. 'Would you like some chewing gum?' she inquires. 'It's that new tooth-whitening one.'

'No, thanks,' says Shona. She takes a seat again and crosses one leg over the other. 'Someone said something about Chris' sister and his mum the other day,' she says. 'Something about...how they'd been through a lot.'

'You *do* seem interested in Chris, all of a sudden,' says Sasha, a white spark of amusement in her black eyes.

'In Frances, actually,' Shona responds. 'Do you know anything about Chris' family going through a lot?'

'Oh, yes. That would have been Chris' youngest sister Emma. She went through a bad patch after Chris' dad left his mum for a woman half her age. Emma became very insecure. I think she developed some sort of eating disorder. That was why Chris took a year out. His mum was very depressed and Emma was ill, so he went back to live at home. He got a job at the local supermarket.' She turns to Shona, with a sad smile. 'That's when the history bunch all sort of went their separate ways. I used to see Kelly and Sarah Rice around, but we didn't used to go out like in the first year. And Sarah Tanner switched to sociology.'

'But Chris and Frances kept in touch?'

'I think she used to write to him, while he was living at home.' There is a pause. 'Why all these questions?'

'I'm just curious, I suppose,' says Shona.

As she speaks, a fine rain begins to fall, dampening her

legs, speckling the paving stones and beading Sasha's hair with tiny pearls.

'Oh, no, this is going to make my hair all frizzy,' says Sasha, ruefully. 'Let's take shelter quickly! Do we have time to look around the shops, or do you want to get a quick coffee?'

Shona steps lightly along the hallway on bare white feet. She is wearing Japanese-style pyjamas in pink silk. There is a purple blossom embroidered on one side of her pyjama top. Soft waves of red hair drift about her shoulders. It is almost midnight, but a feeble light is visible under Frances' door. Shona stops and knocks.

There is a small sound from within. It is hard to say what it is…it could have been a voice, or it could just have been the creaking of a chair. Tentatively, Shona turns the handle. Gently, she pushes the door open.

The door moans ghoulishly as it swings back on its hinges. Inside the room, it is murky, almost too dark to see. There is no sign of Frances, but the door seems to have encountered some obstacle and will not open fully. Rather timidly, Shona steps inside the room and peers around the door.

Sitting cross-legged on the floor in a stagnant pool of yellow light, there is Frances Freak. She is hunched over a book, and surrounded by sheets of paper cramped with spidery writing. As she looks up, the light on her face turns her skin a sickly yellow.

'Um, hello,' says Shona, her mouth blooming into a smile. 'I was just going to ask if I could have a bit of your milk for my coffee.'

It is now possible to see a little more through the sepulchral gloom. The tiny room is crowded with books: books on shelves, books on the floor, books on the desk…and it is cold. Shona shudders slightly.

Frances sits in ominous silence.

'I always have a coffee before bed,' Shona explains, nervously. She caresses the soft, delicate pink material of her sleeve. 'It doesn't seem to keep me awake.'

The room smells of dust. There is a plant on the desk, but it seems to have recently given up the struggle of remaining alive in these unpropitious conditions.

'Of course,' says Frances, almost in a whisper. Darkness fills the pits of her eyes. 'Of course you can have some of my milk.'

Shona couldn't at all have been blamed for dashing from the room at this point, throwing a brisk, 'Thanks,' over her shoulder. But instead, she takes a step further inside.

'Who's this?' she asks. She is looking at a small, framed photograph propped on the desk. Shona picks it up and moves closer to the light. The picture is of a slight, smiling, fairylike girl who could almost, but not quite, have been a younger, happier Frances. 'It looks like...*you*,' says Shona, unsurely.

Frances laughs, and the sound is like the rustle of dead leaves.

'That's my sister. Harriet.'

'She's kind of pretty,' says Shona, examining the photograph closely. The girl is wearing a short, pastel-coloured sundress made of a flimsy material.

'I think she's more what my parents were expecting,' says Frances, cryptically, hollowly.

'Well,' says Shona, replacing the photograph. She looks aimlessly around the narrow room. 'Well...I'll leave you to your,...studying.'

Frances nods, and her gaze drops once more to the hefty tome on the floor in front of her.

'Frances?'

She looks up, her skin jaundiced again in the lurid light.

'You don't want a coffee or something, do you?' Shona asks, her voice warm and sweet as nectar.

A spectral smile flits across Frances' cold lips. 'No,' she says. 'Thank you.'

Shivering in her insubstantial pyjamas, Shona floats out of the dingy chamber. She bursts into the bright, spacious corridor with a soft sigh of relief.

Thursday is another fresh, sunny day, but Shona is confined to the office. She is tapping rapidly away at the keyboard, her loose hair flowing freely over her shoulders, when a woman comes in.

'Goodness!' says the woman. 'That's one of Elspeth's offerings, I assume.'

The woman is probably in her late twenties or early thirties. She has short, neat hair and glasses. Her only item of jewellery is a plain gold wedding ring, and she is wearing jogging pants and a rather elderly sweater.

'Hello, Claire,' says Shona. Her hair shines poppy-red as she looks round to discover the reason for Claire's exclamation. 'Oh yes, Elspeth's been on one of her early morning rambles. She thought the office environment would benefit from a bit of…natural magic, she said!'

'They *are* lovely,' Claire responds, going closer to look at the mass of ferns and wildflowers thrust haphazardly into a large jam jar. She adjusts a bunch of grasses with short, rather stubby fingers.

Shona has resumed her typing. She looks out of place in the office, today. She is wearing a peasant-style short-sleeved blouse, its chaste white belied by the half inch of cleavage it reveals. The smooth curves of Shona's arms are blushed the faintest pink by the recent good weather. She is wearing a long, loose skirt, the colour of summer skies.

'How are you, anyway?' Shona asks, looking up, a sunny smile breaking over her lovely features. Her mouth is delicate as a flower, and when she moves her legs, her skirt rustles like a breeze through the trees.

'Fine, fine,' says Claire, briskly. 'It's been non-stop this morning, though.' She takes a small pile of papers from the pigeonhole marked CLAIRE and detaches a note that is paperclipped to the front. She peers myopically at it before dropping it in the bin and tucking the papers inside a cardboard folder she is carrying. 'First of all, of course, I had to take the children to school, then I had to go to the supermarket and the post office and the bank and the butchers. Then I went back home, and I was half way through hoovering the house before I realised that what I really ought to be doing was washing some clothes for the weekend. But I managed to get all that finished and clean the kitchen before it was time to leave.'

'I don't know how you can be so efficient,' says Shona. Her gaze dances about the room like a blue butterfly. 'I expect you're going to be pretty busy this afternoon, as usual?'

'Yes. I'm going to go through the personal counselling file because a lot of it's out of date,' Claire says, in her quiet, bland voice. The faint indentation of a frown seems permanently fixed between her eyes. 'And there are some minutes I need to type up from last week,' she continues. 'I don't really expect to finish all that today, because there's a PTA meeting this evening, so I'll have to get away promptly. My sister's got the children till eight, poor thing.' Claire's eyes rest briefly on Shona's pretty, girlish face. 'Well, I'd better go and see what kind of state the meeting room's in,' she finishes, and goes through into the next room.

'What's with the whole "country maiden" thing?' Shona

says, softly, as the door swings shut behind Claire. As she looks up from the computer screen a spiral of hair tumbles out of place. Her pink mouth curves in a small, sweet smile as she tucks the curl coyly behind her ear. 'Coyly?' she says, her tone of voice acquiring a feisty edge. '*Feisty?* How can you make out I'm so flirty when I'm just being totally normal? And for your information,' she continues, 'I'm wearing what I'm wearing because it's a warm day and this was the coolest outfit I could find, not because I want to look like a peasant girl who's hoping to get deflowered shortly. I was even foolish enough to think that wearing a long skirt might be some sort of handicap to you. Stupidly, I thought I was dressed so simply and modestly that you couldn't possibly pretend I was trying to provoke sexual fantasies in anyone.'

As Shona concludes her heated little monologue, Claire comes back into the office.

'Not talking to yourself, are you?' she asks, gently, with a smile.

'I do, you know,' says Shona, 'sometimes. Sometimes things don't seem to count unless they're spoken aloud.'

Claire eyes her with maternal concern, but she doesn't say anything.

'How're Ben and Holly?' Shona asks, with sudden, spirited interest.

'They're both fine. Well, Ben has a cold, but he's over the worst of it. Holly really enjoyed her birthday party.'

'Did Ben get his hamster?'

'Yes, he did, on Saturday. He picked out the biggest, boldest one. I think he's going to call it Brownie, but he keeps changing his mind.' Claire sees something of her own tenderness reflected in Shona's attentive expression, and says, 'You should come round and see the children. They keep on asking when you're going to baby-sit again.'

'I'd like to,' says Shona, simply. 'They're lovely children. Holly's so friendly and talkative. And Ben's really imaginative. Last time, Ben and I spent hours playing with his toy zoo after Holly was in bed. We had great fun!' The two women exchange a sympathetic smile.

'Will you have children, eventually?' Claire asks.

'I should think so,' Shona replies, her smile becoming radiant. 'More embarrassed than radiant,' she mutters, too quietly for Claire to be able to pick out the words. 'How long till Richard gets back now?' she adds.

'Sixteen days,' says Claire, fondly. 'But I'm ever so excited already! I've got it all planned out – what I'm going to wear when I go to meet him, what I'm going to cook him for dinner…I never thought I'd be such a doting wife. But I miss Richard *so* much when he's away.' Behind her glasses, Claire's eyes are shining with affection. 'Word of advice, Shona – don't marry anyone who's likely to go into the navy.' Claire gazes dreamily into the air for a moment, but then her expression becomes solicitous. 'How's Callum?'

'Much the same as usual. Busy with exams, though. So I've not seen too much of him,' says Shona, her voice low.

'Ah, you know what it's like, then,' says Claire, kindly. 'You must be missing him. It doesn't get any better over time, I'm afraid. But of course everything's going to change for you two very soon, isn't it? When Callum's course finishes. I don't suppose you'll want to stay on here after the summer, will you, seeing as Callum will be living down in London?'

'No, I think I'll be moving on to something else. I don't think it would be worthwhile for Elspeth to keep me on for more than about eight hours a week. I'll be sorry to leave, though,' she says, regretfully. 'I've really enjoyed working here.'

'We'll be sad to see you go,' says Claire, with a little sigh. 'I hope you'll keep in touch.' She sits down at a small table in the corner, and deftly begins to go through the contents of a large file. Shona draws a similar file towards her and begins to leaf through the pages with the same quiet efficiency. She makes a lovely picture sitting there, motionless, her eyes downcast, her long lashes almost brushing her cheeks.

'Oh, Claire, I tried out that recipe you gave me,' says Shona, after a while. 'It's really tasty, isn't it?'

'It always goes down well, that one. What did Callum think?'

'He didn't have any. He wasn't around.' Shona leans gently forward to reach for a pen and her skirt whispers softly about her ankles.

'That's a shame. Because he likes Italian food, doesn't he? You'll have to make it again. I could bring in the whole recipe book if you like, and you can borrow it. It's all Italian dishes.'

'That would be wonderful,' says Shona, appreciatively. 'Thank you.'

'And if you find any more muffin recipes you must let me have a copy,' says Claire, 'because Holly really loved those chocolate chip ones.'

'Yes, okay,' says Shona, with a smile. 'I'll do that.'

The two women return to their tasks and resume their harmonious silence. As they do so, the light from the window intensifies. Shona's slender hands, carefully turning over a page, are turned to pure white. Her head is bent forward over her work, her face hidden. In the warm shaft of sun the hair which veils her face is touched with gold...the rich rose gold of Claire's single ring.

'Seventeen Ash Lane,' says Callum to the taxi driver as he

takes a seat in the front. 'Just off Rotherway Road.'

'Yeah, I know it. Opposite the chippy, isn't it?'

As he clambers into the back of the taxi with Steve, Chris wonders how Callum can seem so relaxed in clothes that were surely designed to make the wearer feel straitened. Certainly Chris feels far from comfortable...he cannot think how to arrange his limbs. And his bow tie won't sit straight. Whatever he does, it reverts to the same ridiculous diagonal position.

Another thing Chris can't understand is why they're taking a taxi at all. It's only a fifteen minute walk to the house Sasha shares with the other girls. But he supposes it's all part of the obligatory extravagance of going to a ball. Or perhaps it's on account of Steve's feet, which don't seem to be suited to the confinement of an ordinary pair of shoes. Chris finds it very odd to see Steve without his enormous army boots. He hadn't really considered them to be detachable. A picture of Steve in pyjamas and army boots drifts unbidden into Chris' mind. It doesn't seem implausible.

The taxi driver darts a shrewd sideways glance at Callum.

'You three students?' he asks, his tone somehow managing to convey both deference and contempt.

'For another two weeks,' says Callum, affably.

'So where are you off to tonight? Some sort of celebration?'

'The end of term ball.' Callum shrugs, as if to distance himself from this admission. 'It's a bit of a drag, but what can you do? The girls like it.'

'Bit of a palaver,' the taxi driver agrees.

'I'll say,' Steve mutters. He has taken off one of his shoes and is massaging his foot. 'Dressing up like a bunch of bloody penguins.'

'Still, if the girls like it...' says the taxi driver, whose name, Chris notes from the identity card on the windscreen, is Martin.

Callum is nodding, as if he and the driver have established a deep understanding. 'Might turn out to be worth it. Humouring a woman tends to have its rewards.' Nothing in Callum's broad and lopsided grin suggests that he remembers the events of Tuesday afternoon.

By this time they are very near their destination. Chris is beginning to feel concerned about whether the taxi driver is going to turn at the right place, but he can't quite persuade himself to say anything.

'This is the one,' says Callum, suddenly, cheerfully, and rather late.

'So it is!' Martin exclaims, as he wrenches the steering wheel round and takes the corner at a formidable speed. 'That came up quick. I was thinking it was the next one. Which house is it?'

'Anywhere here is good!' Chris almost yells, shaken out of his silence. The taxi driver swerves alarmingly towards the pavement and screeches to a halt.

'This do?' says the taxi driver. 'You don't want me to wait, do you?'

'No, the girls will still be getting ready,' says Callum. 'They'll have been getting ready all afternoon, but they still won't be finished till the last moment,' he predicts, 'not if I know Shona. No, we'll be better off calling another taxi later on.'

'That'll be four-twenty, then,' says the driver. 'Cheers,' he says, as Callum hands him a fiver.

'Cheers,' says Callum, climbing out, and the other passengers also disembark.

When Steve rings the doorbell, there is silence. Then, after a moment, squeals can be heard from within, and the sound of people rushing about. After thirty seconds or so a blurry pinkish shape appears through the frosted glass and rapidly descends the stairs. Lizzie opens the door, damp, giggling and wrapped in only a towel.

'Goodness me, Miss Matthews,' says Callum, with a disarming grin. 'Do you usually answer the door in this...state of undress?'

'What d'you think you're playing at?' Steve demands. 'Haven't you seen the time? Go and get dressed!'

'Unless of course you're going out in that rather fetching towel?' Callum asks, raising an eyebrow slightly.

Without saying a word, but still giggling, Lizzie flees back upstairs. The men troop into the lounge.

'We better make ourselves comfortable,' says Callum. 'I reckon we're in for a long wait.'

Steve doesn't reply to this, but he does sit down. Irritably, he grabs hold of the fluffy pink cushion which is sharing his seat, and tosses it onto the floor. He removes both shoes without undoing the laces, and morosely begins to massage his feet again.

'What was that?' Chris asks, suddenly. 'Was that the doorbell?'

'Could be,' Callum replies. 'Could be Becca's boyfriend.'

Steve gives a sort of explosive snort and growls something under his breath. It could have been, 'This'll be a laugh,' but Chris cannot be sure.

Callum goes to answer the door, and after a couple of moments of inaudible conversation, he returns with a tall, friendly-looking man of about twenty-five, who is also dressed in a dinner suit. His long, fair hair hangs loose about his shoulders.

'This is Josh,' says Callum. 'Josh, this is Chris. The one with his foot in his lap is Steve.'

'You're the one who's with Lizzie?' Josh asks Steve. Steve grunts in acknowledgement. 'And you're the history student?' Josh says, turning to Chris. 'History was always my favourite subject at school.'

Chris is rather taken aback. He has been forced to admit many times that he studies history, but this is not the reaction he's learnt to expect. He's more used to having people grimace and start avoiding him, so now he isn't sure how to respond. Josh seems about to add something else, when Steve unexpectedly speaks up.

'Well, that's a fine head of hair you have there, Josh,' he says, with a sort of smirk. 'You can chat with the girls about hairspray and curlers.'

Chris cringes inwardly, but Josh grins. 'Always something to fall back on, when the conversation lapses.'

Steve stares at him. 'Don't you ever cut it?' he asks.

'Occasionally. I can give you the name of my hairdresser if you like, so you'll know who to avoid?'

At this, Chris almost laughs aloud, something that he rarely does and which at this moment would have been most impolitic. Callum, he notices, is also looking rather amused. It is quite a novelty to see Steve looking discomfited...even more so than seeing him without army boots. However, Steve is saved from replying by the sound of someone on the stairs.

'Surely they're not ready?' says Callum, incredulous. 'We're not even *late* yet. It's probably Lizzie wanting to flaunt her bath towel again!'

But it isn't Lizzie, it's Sasha. Sasha looking stunning in the quintessential black dress, its neckline plunging between her breasts in a deep V-shape. The thick velvet embraces her narrow waist and the soft curve of her hips. It clings about her thighs, before sweeping towards the floor.

Callum is the first to find his voice.

'Good evening, Sasha,' he says, suavely. 'You're looking very lovely tonight.' She acknowledges his words with a small, velvety smile. 'Not that you don't always, of course, but particularly tonight.'

Meanwhile, Sasha's lustrous black eyes have turned towards Josh, who seems eager for her acknowledgement.

'You're Becca's housemate? I'm Josh,' he says, and offers her his hand. Her slim, dark hand is swallowed up in his larger, fairer one. She smiles her soft smile once more before crossing the room to stand with Chris.

'Hello,' says Chris.

Steve doesn't say anything, but he appears to have cheered up considerably.

Soon after Sasha's impressive entrance, Lizzie bursts into the room, swiftly followed by Becca. Lizzie's hair is elaborately arranged, some piled on top of her head, some hanging down in coy ringlets. A small tiara is embedded amongst her blonde curls. She is wearing a strappy, backless dress of flamboyant fuschia, and is looking particularly buxom. Becca is dressed in pine-green satin, which cleverly offsets the bright gold of her hair. The dress fastens behind her neck, leaving the smooth brown skin of her back exposed and enticing. A bracelet set with peridots is twisted round her upper arm.

All of this is too much for Steve.

'Get a load of that!' he exclaims with relish, looking from Sasha to Lizzie to Becca. 'Total chickfest!'

Lizzie toys with one of her ringlets, giving Steve a flirtatious look from under more than usually curly lashes. Becca meets Josh's eyes, her mouth tempting, ripening in a smile.

'Becs, you look gorgeous,' says Josh, taking her by the hand. 'What a cool hair-thing!' He brushes her smooth brow with light fingers, then touches her hair, coaxed back from her eyes and clasped in place with a green glass hair clip.

'Well ladies, you're all looking beautiful,' says Callum gallantly, 'and if your respective partners can spare you, I should like to borrow each of you for a dance later on. But where's my partner? Not in a flurry over a broken nail, I hope? Not had a disaster with the curling tongs?'

'She's nearly ready,' says Lizzie, with a coquettish little toss of the head that makes her tiara sparkle.

At this moment the door glides open and Shona appears. Everybody turns to look, and there is silence. Silence, that is, except for Chris' rapid, ragged breathing. He feels enveloped by her perfume, which is heavy and sweet, like incense. He feels almost as if he is seeing a vision, and his heart is leaping so violently within him that he finds it hard to believe its movements aren't outwardly visible. He feels that surely any moment everyone will notice, everyone will turn and stare at him as he stands there sweating, trembling almost. But of course they don't. Because they're all staring at Shona, too, awestruck...rapt.

From the sculpted hollow of her alabaster neck, to the tips of her gleaming shoes, she is draped in gold. She stands motionless, the sumptuous material glimmering, her bare arms white and beautifully shaped, as if carved from ivory. Her hair is moulded to her head and formed into burnished waves. Beneath gilt eyelashes her eyes are a rich, opaque blue, like lapis lazuli. She seems distant, inviolable and impressively tall.

'Well, I almost feel I should applaud,' says Shona, startling everyone. Her finely-chiselled lips, too, are painted golden. 'What a clever little performance! All I did was pick up an old dress from a charity shop, at the last moment. All I did was throw my hair up, slap on a bit of — admittedly fairly unusual – lippy.' She grins, rather crudely. 'And yet you've managed to turn me into…I don't know quite what…a precious statue? A work of art? Very impressive, indeed. Congratulations. The only little detail you seem to have overlooked is that perhaps I don't want to be a piece of elephant's tusk. Perhaps I don't want to be…an effigy. Who knows, strange things *do* happen maybe I'd actually quite like to be a human being for a change? A person? A woman, even! Not an *icon*!'

Shona stops talking, but no one moves, no one speaks. What is she talking about, this beautiful lunatic? Who is she talking to? Doesn't she know who they are, where she is? Lizzie's eyes are wide and shocked in the midst of her sparkly make-up. There is a fervent, almost desperate look on Callum's face. His gaze is fixed with everyone else's, on the figure standing rigid in the doorway, resplendent in her rich attire, her features exquisitely cut but strangely impassive. Chris feels his heart still battering against his ribs, beating with all the ardour of a votary.

Then, abruptly, Shona begins to pull the grips from her hair.

'What are you doing that for?' Lizzie gasps. 'It looked fantastic!'

'Changed my mind,' Shona explains, breathlessly. 'It was too…lifeless!'

As she speaks, her hair comes pouring down over her marble shoulders, glowing hot red like molten gold.

'Does marble speak?' Shona asks, her voice suddenly full of wrath. 'Does gold?'

Callum is approaching her, his face flushed.

'Do you want to come outside for a minute, Angel?' he murmurs. 'Can we have a talk?'

'No,' says Shona, her hair a bright blaze around her head.

'Shouldn't you be ordering taxis? Shouldn't you be introducing me?' she nods in Josh's direction.

'Yes, of course,' says Callum, fairly calmly. 'This is Josh, who I'm sure you've heard plenty about.' He gives Josh an apologetic look. 'Josh, this is my girlfriend, Shona.'

'Very pleased to meet you,' says Josh courteously, taking the cool white hand Shona offers him.

'Right, I'll ring the taxi company,' says Callum, managing his lopsided grin. 'Do you want to brush your hair before we go, darling?'

'I suppose I'd better see if I can brush the hairspray out.'

She turns to go, her figure tall and imposing. The folds of her gown flash as she walks past Callum, through the door.

When Callum and Shona have left the room, the others exchange bewildered glances. Becca turns to Josh.

'I'm sorry about Shona,' she says, in an undertone. 'She's not usually like this. She's not usually...arrogant. But she's been ill lately, and she's probably still not feeling well.'

'I don't think that was arrogance,' Josh replies, slowly.

'Oh!' says Becca, raising an arch brow. 'No, well, you wouldn't. Men have a way of overlooking Shona's little faults – I can't think why.'

'That girl wants her head looking at,' Steve is saying to no one in particular, loudly enough so that it is almost certainly audible from the hallway. 'It's a shame, because she's a stunner, an absolute stunner. No offence to you other ladies, because you're all good-looking girls,' he adds, leering rather obviously at Sasha...and not at her face either, Chris notes. He wonders if Steve has been drinking already.

Chris turns to Sasha himself, feeling that it is now absolutely imperative that he thinks of something to say. He wonders if he should tell her how nice she looks...but it is bound to sound silly. There is a sort of hollowness inside of him, distracting him, adding to the awkwardness of an already uncomfortable situation. And the hollowness, he realises, has to do with Shona. It is only to be expected, and yet it is painful to him, that Shona can appear in a room in all her unapproachable beauty and disappear again without so much as acknowledging him.

'The taxis are going to be here any moment,' says Callum, coming back into the room. 'Ladies, can I fetch anyone their coat?'

Chris manages to recognise Sasha's coat, obtain it from Callum and help her put it on. There, he has now performed one small part of his duties. Coat-fetching he can just about manage. He notices that Josh has quietly presented Becca with a single red rose...he wonders whether that would have been an easy way of being a decent partner for Sasha, or whether it would have been a breach of etiquette. Would she have taken it to mean he had serious romantic intentions towards her?

Shona has just returned from upstairs, as dazzling, as flawless as ever, her hair now rippling lavishly about her face, glinting like rubies and copper and bronze. And both taxis have arrived, Callum is saying. So, in a flurry of door-holding and grateful acceptance of male arms, with much ceremony, frequent compliments and many gracious female smiles, the company leaves for the ball.

Chapter 5

Connecting

It is midday on Sunday, the day after the ball. Ellen has just arrived at 17 Ash Lane in chic black trousers, a clingy black top and a tweed jacket. There is a green silk scarf wrapped twice around her head and her hair has the deep shine of a fresh chestnut.

'I feel a bit overdressed!' she comments, as she enters the kitchen and looks round at the other girls. Becca is sitting cross-legged on a dining chair, wearing tartan pyjamas in muted colours. She looks unusually defenceless...rumpled and soft and drowsy. Lizzie has a cosy white towelling bathrobe on, which is hanging open to reveal a sliver of smooth leg and a pale pink nightie with a teddy bear on it. She is combing her hair carefully with a wooden comb, her expression solemn and ingenuous. Her cheeks are round and smooth, her nose pert and her hair almost the colour of buttercups. Caroline is wearing pyjamas of plum-coloured silk. The matching negligee has been casually abandoned, draped over the back of a chair. She is sitting on the work surface, her feet resting on the surface opposite. Her usually neat hair is tousled and her neck looks long and white. She is eating a banana in a slow, indulgent manner that is somehow not quite consonant with her otherworldly expression.

'Where's Sasha got to?' Ellen asks, chattily. She is wearing large wooden earrings in the shape of leaves.

'Still in bed,' says Caroline, with that subtle and intriguing lisp. 'She didn't pull. She's just being lazy.' She smiles, but it is somehow synthetic.

'Typical,' Ellen replies, her eyes practically violet this morning. They are a very changeable pair of eyes, chameleon-like, almost kaleidoscopic. It is generally felt that they are blue, but in some lights they look almost black. To confuse matters further there are small flecks of brown in them, or, according to Ellen herself, green. 'You've got to tell me about the ball,' Ellen says, turning to Lizzie and Becca. 'I bet it was a good night. Was it?'

'Yes, it was…' Lizzie's words suddenly dissolve in helpless giggling. 'It was hilarious! I was wearing – I had – it suddenly *broke!*' Lizzie manages to say, before becoming completely inarticulate.

Ellen looks to Becca for help, a comical expression of bafflement on her face.

'Lizzie had this very elaborate backless, strapless bra on,' Becca explains. 'And half way through the raspberry roulade it just sort of *collapsed!*' At this point Becca too is almost overtaken by laughter, but she manages to add, 'she practically impaled herself on her own underwire!'

Lizzie is wriggling her sparkly silver toenails helplessly. 'And Steve goes…Steve goes…' she stops giggling with an effort, swallows, and says, '"How the mighty have fallen!"' Nevertheless, she has to repeat this three times before Ellen and Caroline can make out all the words. Becca, meanwhile, is doubled up in an agony of mirth, and seems likely at any moment to fall off her chair.

Ellen and Caroline exchange bemused glances.

'I guess you had to be there,' says Caroline, and returns her attention to the neglected banana.

'But why did he say that?' Ellen asks.

'I don't know!' says Lizzie, still unable to control her laughter. 'I guess he just ...' She indicates her ample bosom.

'He was quite drunk,' says Becca. 'It was just the way he said it, in this dead serious voice,' she goes on, but accidentally catches Lizzie's eye and the two of them burst out laughing once more, Lizzie's laughter a silvery giggle, Becca's rich and low. Tears glisten in Becca's hazel eyes. She clutches her friend's arm for support.

'Stop, stop!' cries Lizzie. 'Let go! Stop laughing before I wet myself!' But this hardly helps to speed Becca's recovery.

'What did everyone wear?' Ellen asks. 'If you can stop laughing long enough to tell me! Sasha never showed me her dress. It was black, though, wasn't it?'

'Oh, yes, it's a lovely dress,' says Lizzie, calming down a little. 'Long and sleeveless with a V-neck. Ever so slinky.'

'Very sexy,' Becca agrees. 'Steve certainly seemed to think so,' she adds, with a faintly suggestive inclination of the head.

'I bet Shona looked lovely,' Ellen says, smoothing a chocolate-coloured tress back under her scarf.

'Oh, it was sickening,' Becca responds.

'She had a *gold dress*,' Lizzie tells Ellen in a voice full of yearning. 'And gold shoes! She looked really amazing.'

'You can imagine how striking it was,' says Becca, 'all that gold, with that gorgeous hair of hers.'

'What about the men?' Caroline asks. Her tone is innocuous, but an impudent smile is twitching at the corners of her mouth.

A small, confused frown appears on Lizzie's childlike face.

'Yeah, they noticed all right,' says Becca. 'Of course.'

'No,' says Caroline impatiently. A carnivorous glint is apparent in her pale, leaf-green eyes. 'I mean how did the men look? Did they put in any effort? Were they all in DJs?'

'Yes,' says Lizzie, 'they all were. Oh, Callum's so gorgeous in a dinner suit!' she adds, with a little sigh.

'You could almost forgive him for being Callum, couldn't you?' says Becca. She fingers the soft material of her sleeve. Her nails are still painted a snakey shade of green from the previous night. 'Josh looked fantastic too, of course. He can certainly carry off a tux.'

With this, Becca untangles her long legs and gets to her feet. She rubs her eyes, sleepily, endearingly, and then begins to root through cupboards, in search of a cereal bowl.

'I hope Steve's not too hung over,' says Lizzie anxiously, twisting a long strand of blonde hair round a small, tapering finger. 'He needs to revise today.'

'I was forgetting the boys had exams,' says Ellen. 'It's a funny time to hold the ball, right before their finals!'

Becca shrugs her narrow shoulders. 'Seems a bit daft, but that's when they always have it. That's the science faculty for you.' She shakes a Frosties packet vigorously over her bowl, but it seems to be empty.

'Right,' says Caroline suddenly, and slings her banana skin across the room. Ellen ducks, but she has no need to. The banana skin soars over her head and lands neatly in the bin.

'Right,' Caroline repeats, 'I'm going to get dressed because Tony'll be round at any moment.'

'Tony?' says Becca, despairing of the Frosties and reaching for the bread. 'I'm still on Simon.'

'Simon?' Caroline wrinkles her small nose. 'Eeugh.' She

slips swiftly off the kitchen surface, landing with elfin grace on bare feet. 'See you all in a minute or ten.'

'Or twenty?' suggests Ellen, taking in Caroline's unbrushed hair, her naked face, considering what will be necessary in the way of choosing clothes and coordinating jewellery.

'Or twenty,' Caroline admits, as she heads for the door. 'At least.'

'I don't know!' says Ellen, when Caroline is gone. 'Some of us would be happy with *one* man and she gets through several a week!' There is a warm light in her violet eyes…half teasing, half serious.

'Harsh, isn't it?' Becca agrees, nibbling on a piece of dry toast. She is standing at the window with her sleeves rolled up, letting the sun warm her silky, honey-coloured skin.

'But I couldn't be like Caroline. Could you?' says Lizzie. Her rose-pink lips are parted just slightly. 'What's going to happen when she meets the man she wants to settle down with? It's okay if you're a guy…girls sort of expect you to have been with other women. But if you're a girl and you've slept with lots of men…guys don't like that.'

'I know what you mean,' Ellen says, slowly. 'She's bound to find someone she wants to stay with eventually.'

'Men,' says Becca, who is now gnawing on a rather hard biscuit, 'are very odd. We just have two categories for them: are we interested, or are we not. Whereas they…they put us in all sorts of complicated groups and subdivisions. There's the women they'd go out with, the women they'd live with, the women they'd marry, the women they'd sleep with…' She pauses to get another biscuit from the barrel. 'The women they'd sleep with after a couple of pints,' she continues, 'the women they'd sleep with after four or five, the women they'd sleep with if they were really desperate and she put a paper bag over her head and promised not to tell anyone...'

'Ellen,' says Lizzie, suddenly concerned, her eyes growing rounder than ever. 'We're not being very hospitable! You haven't even been offered a drink.'

'Ah, she knows where the kettle is,' says Becca, with a grin. The huskiness of her voice is somehow disarming. 'I'm going to have a shower now, but I'll bang on Sasha's door and see if I can make her come down.'

As Becca leaves the room, Lizzie is already filling the kettle up, chattering away as she does so.

'Would you like orange juice?' she is saying. 'Or pineapple even?– I think I have some pineapple juice left. Did you have breakfast? Are you hungry? There are yoghurts, if you like. Or toast, or grapes, or apples.'

'Bit of a wuss, that Josh,' Steve is saying, as he ascends the stairs to Shona's flat. 'Bit of a pretty boy.'

'He was okay,' says Callum, 'but he does let Becca walk all over him. She opens her big mouth and starts wittering away, and he just sits back and takes it. But he'll get bored of her nagging and her opinions soon enough.'

'What I want to know,' says Steve, 'is who that was with the lovely Jenny Steele. And how he managed it.'

'Don't you know him? That's Rob Morrish,' Callum replies. 'Or "Superstud" as some little brunette I once met in the union bar kept insisting. He was a mate of mine, years ago.'

'Bit of a ladykiller, is he?'

'You might say that,' says Callum. 'He shagged every girl in Shipton Hall the year I was there. Or so he said. More of them than would like to admit it, anyhow. I was always asking him how he did it, but he reckoned it was just a gift he had.' He grins at Steve. 'Hell of a gift though, being able to charm the knickers off any girl you meet.'

'Lucky bastard,' Steve agrees, as they reach the top of the stairs.

Shona opens the door swiftly and lets them in. Her legs seem endless in those provocative denim shorts of hers. She is wearing a little T-shirt in bold pixie green, which ties in a knot at the front, leaving her taut stomach bare. She looks spring-fresh and slim as a sapling.

'Hello, Angel,' says Callum. 'We thought we'd drop round and see if you wanted to come to the pub. We needed a break from revising.'

'Mind if I use the facilities?' asks Steve. 'While you two are chatting?' Without waiting for an answer he disappears into the bathroom.

'That's a stroke of luck,' says Callum and attempts to kiss Shona, placing his hand on the warm, naked skin of her back. But Shona shies skittishly away, twisting teasingly out of his grasp. She takes a pace backwards and stands eyeing him from under the flirtatious curl of her lashes.

'Look, Shona,' says Callum, 'we need to talk. I'm still ever so worried about you. It'd make me feel much better if we got you to a doctor. Just to chat things through. Just so he can check you're okay.'

'My doctor's a woman,' says Shona, irrelevantly. 'But Callum, I've told you, I'm not going to the doctor's.' She gives him a wayward look and then looks away sulkily, her lips full and seductive. 'There's nothing wrong with me.'

'But it won't do any harm to get you checked out, will it, Angel? Just to set my mind at rest.'

'If you're going to nag me then you can leave right now,' she replies, snappishly.

Callum raises his hands as if to defend himself. 'Okay,

okay,' he says. 'But try listening to yourself, Shona. You're being very temperamental lately. I think if you saw the doctor you might find that it's something hormonal.'

Just then, Steve rejoins them, interrupting the conversation.

'Shall we sit down?' Callum suggests. 'While we decide what to do?'

Callum opens the lounge door, but to his surprise he finds Chris in there.

'You too?' says Callum, taking a seat.

Chris nods. 'Yes. The American Revolution gets a bit wearing after a while.'

'Same problem with fluid dynamics,' says Callum. 'We were thinking of going to the pub. Are you interested?'

'Yes, but I'm a bit busy...tied up. I've got some cookies in the oven.'

'What about you, Shona?'

Shona is sitting on the floor, her arms wrapped around her long, folded legs, her chin resting on her knees. There is a mischievous look in her big blue eyes. 'I think perhaps I'll wait around here and see if I get offered a cookie,' she says, giving Chris a tantalizing smile.

'Looks like we wasted our time coming round then,' says Callum.

Shona registers his disappointment with coquettish satisfaction and then turns alluring eyes on Steve. 'Where's Lizzie?' she inquires.

'She's at a keep-fit class,' says Steve. 'With bloody Caroline. This is the second time they've been. Not that she'll keep it up, not Lizzie. I keep telling her so.' He rubs his nose vigorously, and then adds, 'she's not too fond of exercise – rather more fond of cakes and ice cream, which is where the problem comes in.'

'What do you have against Caroline?' Shona asks. Her hair, tied becomingly back with a scarf, is a rich, glowing russet.

'Caroline,' says Steve emphatically, 'is a slut. Can't keep her legs, or her mouth, closed.'

'But what's that to you?' Shona wants to know. 'Why are you so concerned about Caroline's sex life?'

'Because she's suddenly so chummy with my Lizzie,' Steve answers. 'What are people going to think of Liz if they see her out and about with that tart? And what do they talk about? What sort of stories is a dirty bitch like that going to tell? Lizzie doesn't want to be friends with that sort of girl.' Steve frowns, fiercely, regretfully. 'I don't even know why I let Lizzie share a house with her.'

'Lizzie's a bit of an innocent, isn't she?' says Callum, who has always had a certain fondness for her. 'It would be a shame to spoil that.'

'Innocent?' says Shona. 'What do you mean by that? I think she knows what sex is by now. I'm sorry, you two, but you can't have it both ways.' She casts an insolent look at Steve as she says, 'You can't screw a girl for months and expect her to remain all maidenly ignorance.'

'Well, aren't we tetchy today?' says Callum. 'You want to be careful about taking sides with girls like Caroline. People might think you share her...habits. Here you're among friends, but elsewhere people might get the wrong impression.'

'People always get the wrong impression,' says Shona, sullenly. 'I am hemmed in by people's wrong impressions.'

There is a pause. Everyone seems to be avoiding each other's eyes.

'How can you demand such contradictions of us?' Shona says, vaguely, her gaze vacant. Her mood seems to have changed again…her white limbs look fragile and her lips pale and soft as a new bud.

Callum is weighing up the relative merits of escaping to the pub, or waiting around in the hopes of broaching the subject of the doctor's with Shona again. He has just decided to leave, but to return later without Steve, when Shona raises her head. There is a mischievous look in her eyes, and her broad smile is almost lascivious.

'So, Frances,' she says. 'It's a terrible thing to admit since I've lived with you nearly a year, but I only have the haziest idea what your thesis is on. Could you tell me a bit about it? You may be able to educate some of us ignorant scientists.'

There is another lengthy pause. Frances is so taciturn that at times she is almost invisible, but there she is, coiled on the sofa next to an unfortunate Chris. He is squashed against the arm, sitting as far away from her as he can without appearing rude. For once, Frances isn't wearing that revolting cardigan. Instead, her arms and legs are lost in the folds of a long, loose greenish shirt, making her seem narrow and limbless. Her eyes are blank as beads and her dull skin is scaly.

'It's about eighteenth-century women's writing,' says Frances, slowly, smoothly. The sibilant sound of her voice seems to contaminate the silence. 'Novels and plays and poems written by women in the eighteenth century.'

'Were there any?' asks Callum, with a roguish grin.

'Yes,' she says. A hand appears from within her shirt, and glides across the sofa. It makes its stealthy way towards the coffee table, slithers underneath and emerges holding a book. 'This is one,' she says. 'By Eliza Haywood. Her novels were very successful.' She darts Callum a devious glance, and says, 'Most eighteenth-century novelists were women.'

'I find that hard to believe,' says Callum. 'Why have we never heard about them? I mean, people still read books from that time and all of them were written by men. People still read *Gulliver's Travels*. That was around then, wasn't it?'

'Yes, everyone's heard of Swift and Pope and Johnson and Defoe,' Frances concedes.

'So if women were writing in the eighteenth century then they can't have written anything very good. Otherwise people would still be reading it,' says Callum, reasonably. 'So I don't know why you want to study it. Why not write a thesis on something that's stood the test of time?'

A subtle look flickers in Frances' eyes and she slides the book towards him. 'Borrow it,' she says.

'What?'

'Read it,' she says, her voice cold.

'No thanks,' Callum replies, jocularly. 'I've not read the standard stuff yet. To be honest, I'd rather read the classics than something obscure.'

'Makes sense,' Steve chips in. He has been looking rather bored. 'If you want to read you might as well read something decent.'

'So,' Frances hisses. 'You won't read eighteenth-century women's writing because it's no good. And you know it's no good, because no one reads it. Isn't that a bit...circular?'

Callum looks at Frances: her scrawny body under the green skin of her shirt, the venomous set of her meagre lips, the cold-blooded look in her eyes. A thin strand of lank hair has come loose and is snaking down the side of Frances' face and into the front of her blouse. The thought of anything snaking into Frances' blouse almost makes him shudder, it is so repellent.

'That's so unfair!' Shona gasps, opening her eyes to their full, startling extent, their colour Mediterranean. 'Doesn't she deserve any *respect*? She has feelings, I'm sure.' Sitting as she is, Shona's shorts have eased their way up to reveal a further few inches of tender, white thigh. She has bitten her lips to a deep, voluptuous red. She turns shameless eyes towards Chris. 'Chris…Kit…haven't *you* read it?' she asks.

Chris looks at Shona, surprised, then at Frances' book. 'No,' he says. He doesn't seem to know what else to say.

'Well, give it here, Frances, I'll read it,' says Shona.

Callum looks amused. 'You don't *read!* he says. 'Not anything longer than *Cosmopolitan,* anyway.'

'Well, maybe I should,' she replies. 'I'll make a start as soon as you're gone,' she adds, rather cheekily.

'All right then, Angel,' Callum replies, matching her playful tone. 'We'll let you get on with it. I'll be round later to check how you've got on, and if you've made it past the first chapter you can have a gold star.'

Shona drifts into the office after her lunch break on Wednesday, her lovely face wan as a waning moon. Her eyes are watercolour blue and her mouth is mournful, a subdued pastel mauve. Her hair is plaited, but loose strands waver distractedly around her head. She is wearing a pale and flimsy blouse, reminiscent of pink sweet peas; her long, loose skirt is a noncommittal shade of lilac. She looks a little like a pressed flower: pretty, but crushed and brittle – her colours slightly faded.

Claire is already in the office, poring over the contents of a large black ring binder. She is wearing jogging pants again, and a tracksuit top that doesn't match. When she hears Shona enter, she looks up from her work, her plain face genial.

'Are you all right?' she asks, pushing her glasses up her nose. 'You're looking a bit peaky.'

'Oh, it's nothing,' Shona replies quietly. Her sylphlike figure seems insubstantial, as if a strong light would shine straight through her. She sighs. 'I've just got a few things on my mind.'

'Do you want to tell me?' Claire asks, viewing Shona with solicitude.

Shona presses delicate fingertips to her pale forehead. 'It's Callum,' she says, hesitantly. 'Well, it's not Callum, it's me,' she corrects herself quickly, her tone distressed. 'It's just that...there are things he expects of me, which I'm not sure I'm going to do...But I haven't told him so. And there's something he's been trying to persuade me to do...' She gazes into the distance for a long moment, and then goes on, 'I don't want to do it, but when someone's going on and on at you, in the end you just have to give in.'

'You *have* to?' Claire asks, seriously.

'Well, in the end it's the easiest thing.'

'But do you have to?' Claire asks again, gently.

'I guess not. I *choose* to, because it's easier.'

'Mm,' says Claire, with an understanding nod.

Shona smiles, weakly. 'I'm not talking about some bizarre sexual act. Nothing like that.'

'No,' says Claire, in a reassuring tone. She pulls her tracksuit top more comfortably down over her jogging pants. 'Anything else?'

'No. Yes. I don't know.' Shona wanders over to the window and gazes out at the hard blank face of the building opposite. The sensitive line of her throat is silhouetted against the sky. After a while she turns back to Claire and says, 'I'm just very confused because, well, maybe Callum's right and I'm wrong. Maybe everyone else would agree with Callum. In which case I would have to do what Callum wants.'

'You would have to, would you?' Claire says, her voice kind.

'I would choose to, then. I think I would. Maybe I

wouldn't.'

'What you do *is* your own choice though, isn't it?' says Claire earnestly. She twists her wedding ring thoughtfully on her finger. 'Even if someone says "This is logical" or "This is right and that would be wrong." It's your responsibility to decide whether to accept what they say, or to choose to do such and such a thing even though its *not* logical, or its *not* right.'

'Yes, but…I hate feeling like I'm on my own…I really think everyone else would take Callum's side. And I can't stand up to everyone else. I can't cope completely on my own.'

'You can't, or you won't?'

'I can't. I mean, I have been, but…it's not getting any easier. I feel like giving up.' Shona plucks helplessly at the thin material of her blouse. 'I suppose that means I *won't* cope. That I've decided not to. Or that I'm tempted… tempted to give up coping.'

'Mm,' Claire agrees. 'Does that help at all, knowing that?'

'Knowing it's all up to me and what I do is my own fault? That I can't blame anyone else?' Shona smiles slowly, the doleful depths of her eyes lightening just slightly. 'Yes, weirdly. It does help.'

Shona turns her shy smile briefly on Claire and then sits down in front of the computer. She watches the small coloured jigsaw pieces of the screensaver floating about on a black background, occasionally colliding and fitting together. The jigsaw pieces are identical to those that appear in the 'Jigsaw' company logo.

'How are *you*, anyway, Claire?' Shona asks, pushing the mouse around absent-mindedly with a shapely hand. She is wearing a ring of silver filigree. 'Have you made much progress with that wedding dress design?'

'I've done some sketches,' says Claire. 'I was asked to do something unusual, so that's given me a lot of scope.'

'But all your designs are unusual!' Shona exclaims, but she sounds tired…strained.

'Yes,' Claire agrees. She contemplates Shona, concerned. 'But this time I've thrown off all inhibitions,' she goes on. 'I'm doing the groom's outfit as well. Probably something in velvet, something really vivid.' Shona nods, wordlessly, and Claire adds, 'I was hoping to get the bulk of my ideas down on paper last night, but Carrie from the band came round with a bottle of whisky!'

'Oh dear!'

'It was good stuff as well, a really nice malt. She's not ashamed to exploit my weaknesses, that Carrie,' says Claire. She stares down at her battered trainers, adding, 'It was about two when she finally left, rather the worse for wear!'

'Have you done any gigs with the band recently?' Shona inquires, finally opening a file entitled *HousingInfo* and scrolling down to the bottom of the document.

'Not since the beginning of May, but we've got something coming up in a couple of weeks.'

Shona attempts to add something to the text on her screen, but gives up after half a sentence. She leans back in her chair, letting her arms hang limply over the sides. As he tilts her head back against the headrest, a small red curl slips out of place and settles on her forehead. 'Has your friend written any new material?'

'He has. He's working on something with a "contemporary feel" because he's decided everything he's done in the past sounds like second rate Duke Ellington!' Claire says. 'There is a vocal part to it, which I think is going to be quite…challenging. Apart from anything else it's very low, even for me.'

'I really must come along and hear you some time,' says Shona, with an effort. She seems completely enervated. 'You'll have to give me the dates of your next few gigs.'

'I will,' says Claire. 'I'd like you to come.' She closes the ring binder and stands up. 'Just popping next door.'

Shona responds with a fleeting smile, an absent look in her beautiful eyes. The breeze from the closing door sends quivers through her thin clothing, sets it trembling against her skin. She looks as if a stronger gust would snap her spine.

'I'm ever so grateful for the lift,' says Lizzie to Sasha, who is brushing her sleek hair briskly before they get out of the car. 'It'll probably be starting to get dark by the time I've done my shopping.'

'It's no problem,' Sasha says, slipping her brush back into her bag and opening the door. 'You shouldn't be wandering the streets on your own at this time. Anything might happen.'

Lizzie nods, her clear eyes wide. 'I know it's only a short walk, but Trant Lane scares me even in broad daylight. All those bushes at the side of the road. Anything could go on in there and no one would see.' A shudder passes through her body.

Sasha locks the door of the little Fiesta and the two girls cross the car park side by side, Sasha dark and exotic, Lizzie blonde and angelic. As they go through the doors they are greeted by a dazzle of bright lights, a gust of warm air and the metallic racket of supermarket trolleys.

'Warm in here,' Lizzie comments, removing her denim jacket. She is wearing a strappy pink top with flared jeans. There are large daisies sewn on near the ankle. 'Grab us a basket, please?'

A silver bangle slides down Sasha's slim arm as she reaches down for a basket. She is wearing a sleeveless black top with black trousers. The outfit shows off her admirable figure, and a flame-coloured scarf provides a flash of colour at the throat.

'Right, I need some shampoo,' says Lizzie, heading for the relevant aisle, 'and either a conditioner that'll actually work or one of those hot oil treatments,' she adds, over her shoulder.

She quickly finds the haircare section and stands cuddling herself as she surveys the large range of options before her. The radiance of her hair seems to illuminate her fair skin, her pretty mouth, her small, freckled nose.

Sasha's attention has been diverted by the facial products. 'This is quite interesting,' she says, examining a small bottle. She purses her succulent lips, which are painted a dark reddish shade, like a tropical fruit.

'Which is that?' says Lizzie, glancing across as she reaches down a small tub of intensive conditioner. 'The tea tree cleanser? That's very good for blackheads.'

'No, it's the shine control two-in-one cleanser and toner.'

Lizzie drops the tub into her basket, and then picks a bottle of hair dye off the shelf. 'Do you think this would suit me?' she asks Sasha, showing her the picture.

Sasha's discerning gaze sweeps over the smiling woman on the packet and then over Lizzie. 'That looks very similar to the colour it is now.'

'Do you think I should go for something darker?'

'Maybe something a little warmer,' Sasha advises. 'Oh, while we're here, I need to get some —' she turns around to find a young man stacking shelves under a bold sign which reads: 'Feminine Hygiene'. 'Oh,' she says.

'Oh!' says Lizzie, and giggles.

'I'll pop back and see if he's gone when you go to the tills,' says Sasha. 'It wasn't important, anyway.'

'Okay. Lets find the bread, then. I need bread and rice cakes.'

'What will you do about meals when you move in with Steve?' Sasha asks, as they go off in search of bread. 'I can't see him coping on salad and rice cakes!'

'I don't know,' Lizzie answers. 'He gets a lot of pizzas delivered at the moment. I'll probably cook one thing for him and something else for me, because I really don't want to put more weight on.'

'It's going to seem very strange, when you move out,' says Sasha, whose striking figure is attracting some attention.

'And when Shona moves in with Callum,' Lizzie adds. 'Down south. I wonder if she'll come back and visit?' They have found the bread aisle now, and Lizzie is stuffing loaves into her basket. 'Wasn't Shona funny at the ball? She didn't seem well. She seemed rather...confused.'

'She seemed rather conceited,' says Sasha. 'I think she's decided she's so gorgeous she can say whatever she likes, regardless of whose feelings she's trampling on. She doesn't seem to realise how lucky she is.'

'Do you think so?' Lizzie looks at Sasha, surprised, her face artless as a cherub's. 'Callum seems to think she's ill. It can mix you up if you're feeling ill, can't it, sometimes?'

'I think Callum thinks she has psychological problems.'

'Really? Poor Shona,' says Lizzie. 'I wonder if she's seen a doctor about it?' Her brow crumples momentarily in concern. 'And poor Callum!'

'What else did you need to buy?'

'Diet coke. And some peppers. Oh, and I'm supposed to be getting a chocolate mousse for Becca. Let's do that now, before I forget.'

The girls head towards the back of the store and find the cooling cabinet stacked full of temptations. There are

fromage frais and crème caramels, vanilla creams and full fat
yoghurts, mini trifles and fruit fools. Lizzie is looking at a
multi-pack of dark and sumptuous mousses.

'These ones are the ones she usually gets, but I thought
she said she wanted one with cream on top.'

'This one has cream,' says Sasha, picking up an indulgent-
looking carton of fluffy cream and chocolate goo.

A middle-aged man in an anorak is looking at margarine.
He notices Sasha and Lizzie poring over the chocolate des-
serts.

'You naughty girls!' he says, with a wink. 'You'll be sorry
when you're forty!'

Shona is sitting alone in the kitchen, her pale forehead supported by her fragile hands, her hair like glowing embers.
The phone has been placed on the table in front of her.

'When I was seven,' says Shona aloud to the empty room,
'I went to stay with my cousins in Cornwall.' Her voice, as
she says this, is dejected and she doesn't lift her head. 'The
only thing I remember about it, is the day a sparrow flew in
through the dining room window and got trapped inside the
house. The dining room was attached to the lounge, you see,
and there was a window at each end...and the sparrow kept
flying between the windows, thumping against the glass and
falling down.' She is quiet for a moment. Then she continues,
in still more hollow tones, 'Because it's in a sparrow's nature
to fly. It can't stop trying, even when if finds itself in a glass
cage. In the end it hurt itself so badly that my uncle was able
to catch it and take it outside. They told us it got better and
flew away, but I knew even at the time that one of the cats
probably got it.' She slides her fingers into her shining hair
and resumes her former silence.

Dim, greyish sunlight is coming in through the kitchen

window and reflecting dully in the plates and glasses on the draining rack. The intermittent sloshing of the washing machine interrupts the quietness of the evening. The only other sound is Shona's breathing, which is so soft it is barely audible, but uneven, as if she is on the verge of tears.

'Is something the matter?' Frances has skulked silently in and caught Shona unprepared.

Shona lifts her head. Her face is perfect, but her eyes look hurt. 'No…nothing much.'

Frances waits, poised for more information. Her hands, gripping her bony elbows, are thin and spidery. Her hair isn't tied back and is unbrushed and matted as cobwebs. She is watching Shona intently.

Shona's hand flutters towards the phone in a vague gesture. 'It's just depressing when your friends don't seem to have time for you any more.'

Frances does not respond immediately. Her thin lips twist and there is a scheming look in her eyes. At last, in a low, furtive voice, she says, 'Would you like some of Kit's hot chocolate? He left it here by accident.'

Shona looks at Frances, startled. 'Wouldn't he mind?'

'No,' she says. She is crouching on the floor, prying into various cupboards. 'He likes you,' she adds slyly, glancing up at Shona sideways. 'A lot.'

Now Frances has found two mugs, which she pushes onto the kitchen surface. Shona gets to her feet, her hair ruffled, her eyes still with that injured look. She takes the milk from the fridge and fills the two mugs. She is wearing a downy, pale blue cardigan and well-cut jeans, which show off her trim thighs. Her hand seems to quiver as she touches the microwave timer.

'I'm sorry about the other day,' says Shona, as she watches the two mugs revolving in the microwave's bright interior. 'It wasn't that I wanted to put you on the spot about your thesis.'

'Have you read any of the book?' Frances asks, in an undertone. Her hands keep twitching, guiltily.

'Yes. Some. I'm enjoying it, actually. I sort of expected it to be like Jane Austen, but it's not, is it?' She looks at Frances, her head on one side, her eyes bright and credulous. 'More happens.'

Frances is silent, but there is a look of predatory satisfaction on her face. Shona is leaning against the kitchen side, her expression remote, unguarded. She traces her collarbone absently with a slender finger. Her throat looks white and vulnerable.

'Frances?' Shona says, suddenly. She sounds almost frightened.

'Yes?'

'Would you say I need to see a doctor?' A hectic flush has appeared on her otherwise pale cheeks. 'About my mental health?'

'Why would you think that?' Frances asks, in her whispery, insinuating voice.

'Callum thinks so.'

Frances starts shovelling hot chocolate powder greedily into the mugs. Her fingernails are bitten and ragged. 'I would've thought you'd know more about it than Callum,' she says, not looking at Shona. 'Working for Jigsaw. Would you like cream?' She moves across the room with alarming speed and starts rooting around in the fridge.

'He thinks I should see a doctor because I told him I hear a voice,' Shona tells Frances' skinny back. 'A voice that...narrates. Which makes me feel trapped in my own head. Suffocated.'

Frances emerges from the fridge slowly, like a creature

from its lair. She is holding a large spray can. Cream is exuding from an orifice at the top.

'Frances?' says Shona, her voice timorous. She looks helpless, like the injured bird she remembered, or a fair damsel in a tale of chivalry. Everything in her expression, her quaking voice, her slender, delicate body, is crying out for rescue.

Frances nods, her hair straggling down the sides of her unlovely face. 'I think everyone hears that voice.'

Shona's eyes grow wide and her defenceless mouth opens, wordlessly. She stares wildly at Frances, the damsel suddenly cornered by a hideous monster. '*You* hear it?'

Frances nods. She avoids Shona's eyes, keeping her own little pinched ones focused on the cream she is splurging into the mugs.

'What, you hear *that?*' Shona asks, hysterically. 'You heard a voice just then, talking about little pinched eyes and splurging cream?'

'Yes.' Frances pushes up her sleeve and makes a violent attempt to scratch her arm with her bitten nails. She cringes slightly at the ugly rasping sound this makes.

'Callum doesn't,' Shona retorts. She buries her hands in her dark red hair and continues to stare at Frances, waiting for an answer, a frenzied look in her eyes. Frances, however, doesn't reply. 'Why doesn't he hear it?' Shona asks, desperately.

Ignoring her flatmate's agitation, Frances is sprinkling chocolate powder over the two mounds of cream. 'It isn't in men's interests to admit they hear the voice,' she says at last. She sounds hesitant. 'Even to themselves.'

'You're telling me *everyone* hears it? Becca and Lizzie? Steve? Chris? My parents? People on the street? *Everyone?*' The pitch of Shona's voice is rising uncontrollably.

Frances shoves one of the mugs towards Shona. She holds the other in one hand and dips a scrawny finger in the cream.

'I'm dipping a scrawny finger in the cream,' says Frances, a devious look on her face. 'A devious look on my face. Apparently.'

Shona stares at Frances, stunned. Frances' cunning little eyes appear over the rim of the mug as she sips her drink, watching Shona's confusion over the mountain of cream. Shona's soft, moist mouth opens and closes mutely. Her huge, woeful eyes are more eloquent. They are liquid, a profound shade of indigo, the long black lashes damp.

'But Frances,' Shona says, finally, her voice trembling. 'If everyone hears the voice then why don't they ever mention it? Why don't they *argue* with it?'

'I don't think they notice it,' says Frances slowly, pitilessly. 'They hear it, but they don't notice that they're hearing it.'

There is an expression of horror on Shona's face as she watches the words creep from Frances' mouth. Shona shuts her eyes, screws up her beautiful face and shakes her head, as if to dislodge the thoughts which have pierced her mind like fangs. It is as if she hopes that when she opens her eyes, Frances will have crawled away...retreated into some dark and distant corner.

'I thought I'd drop by,' says Becca, breezing into Shona's flat, 'because we haven't had a proper chat in ages.' Her sandy hair is falling into her eyes, so she flicks it out of the way. There is something captivating in her unpremeditated movements, her relaxed stance, as if she is unaware of her own good looks. Her sky blue vest-top clings comfortably to her slim body and her capri pants end half way down her smooth, tanned calves. She has clean white pumps on, and a hooded sweatshirt is slung over her shoulders. 'You're not busy, are you?'

'No, I'm not doing anything that's not mundane!' says Shona, blithely. Her hair is the hue of a hot sunset and has been flung into a loose arrangement on her head and clasped in place with a wooden clip. Her eyes are a clear aquamarine. 'You don't mind if I just finish cleaning the oven, do you?' she asks, padding into the kitchen on bare feet. 'It won't take long.'

'Of course not,' says Becca, 'though I don't know why you're doing housework on such a gorgeous day.' She pulls her sweatshirt from her shoulders and drapes it over the back of a chair. Then she strolls across the linoleum and casually puts the kettle on. 'Guess what? I just ran into your boss.'

'Elspeth?' says Shona. She has a short, wrap-around skirt on, with a pattern of red and purple flowers. When she crouches down in front of the oven it rides up a little, teasingly exposing an extra two inches of her lovely legs.

'I think so – the one we met when we were Christmas shopping. She's amazing, isn't she?'

Shona smiles dazzlingly, like the sun reflecting off water. 'Yes.'

'We had a great long conversation waiting in the queue at the bank. I want to know where she gets all that energy from!' Becca, with her buoyant smile and lively expression, doesn't look as though she lacks energy herself. 'She was telling me about a new drama project she's set up for people with mental health problems and local teenagers. But you probably know all about it.'

'Not really,' says Shona, closing the oven door and straightening her long legs. Underneath her wide-necked T-shirt she seems to be wearing a bikini top. A stripy strap is visible at the neckline where the T-shirt is starting to slip off her shoulder. 'Elspeth's involved in so many different projects it's hard to keep track of them all. And I barely see her, really. She's hardly ever in the office.' She sits down sideways on one of the kitchen chairs and her skirt slides sensuously up her thighs once more.

'She was saying they're doing a production on the theme of identity,' says Becca, her husky voice warm. 'There's going to be a series of monologues and a dance based around mirrors, and at the moment they're experimenting with masks. Talk about infectious enthusiasm!' Becca continues. 'I'm not at all arty and I don't know anything about mental health, but now I wish I could join in! She must do so many people such a lot of good.'

Shona's head is flung back as if she is basking in the sun, her face illuminated. 'My shoulder's gone all stiff,' she says, incidentally. She stretches her arms luxuriantly. 'Elspeth set Jigsaw up single-handedly, you know,' she tells Becca. 'She used to be a social worker, but she gave it up when she managed to get funding to launch Jigsaw as an information service. Then about a year later she applied for the grant to start forming new advocacy groups – because she saw there was a need for that.'

'That's pretty cool,' says Becca. 'Do you want a coffee?' she adds, unselfconsciously helping herself to some.

'I'm all right, actually. How's Josh?'

Becca follows Shona through into the lounge, coffee in hand. 'Josh is fantastic. I'm beginning to think he *likes* the completely uncensored me. Which is pretty unusual in a man.' She takes a seat next to the window where the sun can warm her already bronzed shoulders. Her hair looks sun-bleached. 'Shona, I've just noticed you're not wearing makeup! I've never known you to go without.'

'No…' Shona replies, slowly. 'I've sort of decided I won't put makeup on if I don't feel like it.'

'Good for you,' says Becca, a little surprised.

'I started wondering why I feel I have to try and be perfect in the eyes of everyone,' Shona confides. The summer sunlight echoes around her delicate collarbones and shadows gather in the hollow of her throat. 'It's a terrible thing, trying to be something in the eyes of everyone, instead of just *being*.'

'That's deep,' says Becca. She sounds amused.

'I thought you'd understand,' says Shona, unsurely, the set of her lips becoming a little petulant. 'It's very hard to get out of the habit of seeing yourself through everyone else's eyes. It gets to be part of how your mind works and you do it whether or not anyone else is there,' she adds, fretfully. 'I'm not even sure how I look through my own eyes. Or how anyone else – or anything else – looks through my eyes.'

'Part of me wants to say, "You are one mixed up chick!"' says Becca with a grin. 'But I know what you're on about. It's a female thing, to focus on how you look and what other people think of you, instead of having ambitions to *do* things, to *achieve* things. I try not to fall into that, but I know I do, all the time.' Becca passes a long, tanned hand through her hair, letting the pale gold run slowly through her fingers. 'I mean, at work gender discrimination is rife. Equal opportunities is a laughable concept. But I don't spend half as much time worrying about that as I do worrying about my skinny arms and flat chest.'

'Lift and separate,' says Frances, suddenly. She is perched like a gargoyle in the darkest corner of the room, her thin nose buried in a book.

'What?' Becca stares at Frances with a kind of horror.

'Lift and separate,' Frances repeats, sombrely, her eerie voice seeping out of the shadows. She raises stony eyes. 'It's a male strategy for weakening women. Exalt an ideal form of femininity and women's energy is diverted into trying to embody it. Women end up competing with each other, instead of taking a united stand against oppression.'

A funereal silence descends. The weight of Frances' presence seems to crush the glowing summer day.

'You know what Frances,' says Becca, eventually. 'You're funny. And I don't only mean peculiar.'

'Do you want a coffee or something, Frances?' asks Shona. 'I might have one myself, after all.'

At 16.48 a train arrives at Casewich station and Shona, red hair rippling in the breeze, alights. She is wearing the same short skirt and T-shirt as she had been earlier, but now she has added strappy sandals and a denim jacket. She barely glances across the platform, which is Victorian, its woodwork and metalwork painted a nostalgic shade of green. Instead, she walks swiftly under the hanging baskets spilling over with nasturtiums and moves towards the exit, a light bag over one slender shoulder. Casewich is generally thought quite a pretty little station, but the effect is rather compromised by the yellow, plastic litterbins and a large advertisement for haemorrhoid cream.

In the car park, Shona heads straight for a curvy silver car, her long legs drawing the gaze of a group of youths who are smoking in the corner of the car park. Her skirt flutters provocatively around her thighs as she opens the passenger door.

'My goodness, what *unusual* nail varnish,' says the woman in the driving seat as Shona gets in, eyeing her painted toes with something which does not appear to be unqualified approval. 'How lovely to see you.' She deposits a kiss on Shona's smooth cheek before starting the engine.

This woman is quite obviously related to Shona. Her hair is the same deep red colour, although it is cut much shorter and meticulously styled. Her profile, her nose and something about her mouth are reminiscent of Shona, but her face is altogether less remarkable and her skin does not have the taut, glowing quality of youth.

'How are you, dear? You said on the phone you'd not been feeling too well?'

'Oh, that was nothing much. I'm fine now.'

'Just feeling a bit down, were you?'

'Mm.'

'And how is Callum? Is he looking forward to starting his new job?'

'I suppose so. But he's busy with exams at the moment.'

'Of course! Well, I hope they go well for him. Tell him I was asking about him.' She glances quickly at Shona with a stretched, lipstick smile.

They have now reached a neat little cul-de-sac full of large, modern houses. The car turns into a driveway, drawing up next to a sizeable, black BMW.

'Don't the roses look pretty?' the older woman comments, gesturing towards the front garden as they get out of the car. 'They're doing much better this year.'

'Lovely,' says Shona, her hair shimmering in the brilliant sunlight.

The other woman walks across the driveway, smoothly, gracefully. She is wearing cream trousers, a powder blue blouse and beige mules trimmed with sequins. Her figure is still trim, but standing next to Shona as she opens the front door, she looks rather short. 'We've had the hall repapered, as you can see,' she says. 'It's rather nice, don't you think?' They walk through the coffee-coloured hall and into the lounge, where Shona settles herself on the large leather sofa.

'Your father's in his study,' says the other woman. 'He was very pleased to hear you were coming home for the weekend, but I shouldn't disturb him at the moment. Would you like a drink?'

'Yes, please. Coffee, please.'

With a brief, bright smile, the other woman disappears.

'"Shona tentatively perches on the corner of the hard leather sofa," you should have said,' says Shona quietly to herself. 'My mum's hair never used to be the same colour as mine,' she adds, '"thoughtfully." It was always a bit lighter. But now she dyes it to cover the grey.

'She lapses into a meditative silence.'

Shona's lovely eyes drift caressingly across the wall opposite her, passing from photograph to photograph. The biggest one is of a pretty, sweetly smiling Shona, aged eight –

'It's a really saccharine smile. I hate that photo.'

– in a long, green dress with pearly buttons. Her face was a little chubbier in those days, but she is still recognisable. It is a studio portrait, printed very large on canvas.

'Horrible.'

Lower down is a portrait of a less childish and even more beautiful Shona – just her head and shoulders, this time. She is wearing sparkly earrings and what seems to be a black evening dress.

'It is a black evening dress. I wore it for the sixth form ball.' Shona rises to her feet to examine her image more closely, her heels sinking into the deep carpet. 'That's the most recent photo they have of me, of those they thought fit to display. That's probably the one they show to their guests. "And this is our daughter…"'

Just then the lounge door opens and Shona's mother comes in, with coffee on a tray.

'There's a few bits I need to do for dinner, dear. Will you

be all right?'

'Oh yes,' says Shona with a pretty smile. For a moment she is startlingly like the eight-year-old in the photo. 'I might just pop up to my room.'

'Well, don't take your coffee up there, will you?'

'Okay.'

'As soon as her mother has left, Shona abandons her coffee in the lounge and slips upstairs.' Her step is light, and her hair bobs gently against the denim of her jacket, soft copper against coarse cloth. When she arrives at her bedroom door, she rests a white hand hesitantly on the handle. There is a small wooden plaque with her name on it, decorated with pressed flowers.

'"Decisively, Shona turns the door handle and walks boldly into the room. She shuts the door carefully behind her." So this is my room!' she exclaims, with sudden ardour. 'Very tasteful in pastel blue. Not *my* taste, though.'

Shona's face is pure white in the blaze from the window as she crosses the bedroom. She stops in front of a round wall mirror. It is framed in dark wood, with small white roses painted on.

Shona's limpid eyes meet the limpid eyes in the mirror and she gazes at her reflection, which gazes back, rapt. Her warm red hair is echoed warmly in the circular glass, and her rosy mouth is doubled. There are two flawless faces, two white throats…two identical Shonas, like a pair of lovely twins.

'My parents gave me this mirror for my tenth birthday,' says Shona, gazing into the eyes of her equally beautiful sister. 'Which basically means my mother did. I don't think Dad ever had any part in choosing my presents. It used to hang here…' Shona touches a nail lower down the wall, 'until I got too tall.'

Slowly, Shona removes the mirror from its place and hangs it on the lower nail.

Then she takes a chair and sits in front of it.

'It was when I turned ten that the room was redecorated,' Shona goes on. 'I desperately wanted it to be pink, but my mum said it wouldn't go with my hair.' Shona smiles wryly and the mirror girl's shapely lips curve playfully in imitation. 'She never *would* let me wear pink or red. So she was probably a bit affronted by what I'm wearing today.' Shona fondles the thin cloth of her skirt, gently fingering the red and purple flowers.

'Funny to think it's been empty so long,' says Shona, still admiring her alluring twin. 'This mirror.' Then she stands up and replaces the mirror on the higher nail. 'I used to hate my hair,' she announces, pulling a wavy lock over her shoulder and examining its reflection. 'People called me Ginger.' The other girl looks back at Shona, her beautiful eyes touched with melancholy. 'And I used to long for big, brown eyes, like my best friend Jodie. Right up until I was seventeen, when Jodie told me she heard some boy say I had sexy eyes. But I was never sure whether it was a joke.'

Reluctantly, Shona turns away from her likeness. She looks around the room, her eyes a lucent blue, verging on lavender. It is quite a large room, and very tidy. There is a wardrobe, a chest of drawers with several china ornaments on top, and in the middle of the room a small bed with a frilly coverlet.

'Those are my dolls,' Shona says, pointing at a huge, glass-fronted cabinet filled with elaborately dressed porcelain dolls. 'Not that I was allowed to play with them. See that one, in green with black hair? That's Clara. She was my favourite. I wanted to *be* her.'

Shona tilts her face upwards to look at the dolls on the

higher shelves and the light catches the exquisite line of her jaw. 'I always thought that red-haired one was the ugliest. Mum wanted me to call her Shona, because of her hair...but I called her Eliza, because I didn't like the name.' Shona giggles to herself, her mouth growing more enticing. 'Actually I used to call her Ginger, but only in secret.' She smiles, and the curve of her cheek becomes childlike and endearing.

'Oh yes, the cabinet. Dad made that. He doesn't often do that sort of thing...he isn't exactly the handyman type. But he made that for me. He thought I'd be really pleased, and so did Mum...so I tried to be.'

There is a pause as Shona gazes through the glass at the dolls in their hats and lacy dresses, their fur-edged coats, their ruffles and bows.

'And there in the cabinet I see my own reflection, trapped.'

She is staring, not at the dolls, but at the ghost of herself in the glass.

'Yes!' she says. 'The ghost of myself.'

Shona reaches up and unfastens the cabinet doors. She opens them wide.

'That's better,' she says. 'Now I'm going to go and drink my coffee, while it's still vaguely warm.'

Chapter 6

Detaching

'It's probably nothing,' says Lizzie for the tenth time, smiling weakly. Her lips are painted a bright cherry red. 'He probably wants to come over and...' Her voice falters. 'I don't know. He sounded so *funny* on the phone.' She is wearing a summer dress and her hair is in plaits, tied at the ends with pink ribbons. Her pretty face is round and looks very white.

'I expect there's some perfectly ordinary reason why he wants to talk to you,' says Sasha reassuringly, her dark skin glowing as if she is lit from within. She is dressed simply in black and is wearing a pendant with a feng shui symbol on it. 'Try not to worry too much.'

'Oh, I know, I know I shouldn't,' says Lizzie, timorously. 'But I get so frightened. What if he's met someone else?' She opens her china-blue eyes wide and gazes helplessly at Sasha, then at Shona, who is sitting across the lounge, looking svelte in blue jeans. Her legs are crossed elegantly at the knee, her red hair draped like fox fur over her shoulders.

Sasha lays a comforting hand on Lizzie's dainty white

one. 'Come on Lizzie, you know he loves you. It's *you* he cares about.'

'But you remember what happened before Christmas?'

'I know that was awful for you,' Sasha responds, in a voice soft as summer rain. 'But that's all in the past now.'

'But *why* does he do it?' Lizzie asks, distractedly playing with the yellow curls at the end of one of her plaits.

'Sometimes it's very hard for us to understand men,' Sasha replies. The smooth satin of her trousers contrasts intriguingly with the soft, dull black of her top. 'You must remember that they're different to us, physically, mentally and emotionally. It's more difficult for a man to stay faithful. It's something they have to work at.' She presses Lizzie's hand, gently. 'I'm sure he *wants* to. I'm *sure* he doesn't want to hurt you.'

'It's more difficult for a man to stay faithful?' repeats Shona, sharply. There is a hungry look about her voluptuous mouth. 'In disbelief,' she adds, more quietly.

'Yes Shona, there are biological reasons for that.'

'What are you saying?' Shona's huge eyes are lined in black, making them seem dark and artful. 'Testosterone makes men randy, so it's okay for them to betray the women who love them? Is it also okay for them to *kill* the women who love them, because testosterone makes them more aggressive?'

'Shona, please try to calm down,' says Sasha, evenly. 'There's no point in anyone getting upset, because we don't even know why Steve's coming round, yet.' She turns to Lizzie, whose delicate feelings are beginning to crumble. 'Don't cry,' Sasha says in a soft, coaxing voice. 'It'll *ruin* your makeup.' Indeed, tears would have been disastrous, because Lizzie's eyelashes are stiff with mascara.

'Lizzie is under *no* obligation to look pretty for Steve!'

Shona snaps, viciously.

'Clearly the sensible thing for her to do is to hold herself together so that she and Steve can talk things over calmly.' Sasha looks at Shona with eyes that are deep, dark and still as a midnight lake. '*You* may choose to have public tantrums, but most of us like to stay under control.'

'Under *whose* control?'

'I don't know what you're talking about, but I do know that this isn't helping Lizzie. I think perhaps you'd better go.'

'And like a lake her eyes don't *see*, but merely reflect,' says Shona, slowly, deliberately, like a stalking predator. 'Why can't you understand what's going on here?' she asks, more fiercely. 'Why don't you *look* instead of regurgitating self-help books? Can't you see that there are more important things than how attractive you are to men?' She glares at Sasha and her expression is savage, her eyes touched with carnivorous glee. Her body is lithe and tense under her jeans and her flimsy blouse.

Sasha takes a long gentle breath in and then expels it slowly, like a restful breeze.

'That's all very well for you to say,' she replies serenely, her gaze direct, her head poised on her graceful, olive neck. 'You can afford to say that women shouldn't diet or wear makeup, because you're beautiful without doing either. And you can afford to make fun of the men who adore you and the women who envy you, because whatever you do the men keep on adoring you and the women keep on envying you.' The light throws a cool sheen on Sasha's near-black hair. Her eyes are lustrous as she continues, 'But for the rest of us it's different. If we don't take care about how we look then we get no respect from anyone – and we certainly have no chance of finding a man. Maybe you don't appreciate Callum, but for most women finding love *is* important. Maybe the most important thing of all.' Sasha's gaze is calm and steady, but the look in her nocturnal eyes is slowly becoming more challenging. 'You don't know how lucky you are,' she tells Shona. 'Perhaps you should try empathising with the rest of us, instead of upsetting Lizzie and picking fights with me.' She squeezes Lizzie's hand sympathetically. 'I think you ought to leave us in peace, go back to your flat and try to re- alise what a spoilt little princess you are.'

Desperately, Shona tears her gaze from Sasha's. She is chastened, her skin white, her big, muted eyes downcast.

'I'm sorry, Lizzie,' says Shona, quietly, hesitantly. 'I don't mean to make things harder for you, but I just think...I just think it's important to recognise what Steve's doing to you, before Sasha starts making excuses for him. Sometimes the way Steve treats you isn't right or fair; and I think it's more important to deal with that than to keep your mascara intact.'

Lizzie looks up at Shona with glassy eyes. 'I know you're only trying to help, Shona, but...'

Shona raises her eyes from the floor and there is still something bloodthirsty flickering there, a craving lingering in the midst of the innocent blue. It is as if she wants to shriek deranged words that will tear at Sasha's throat, to gorge her- self, to rave and babble.

'Well, I'll go home then,' she says, hiding her lunatic mal- ice behind her lovely face. 'I really hope it's a false alarm, Lizzie. Call me if I can do anything to help.'

Without speaking to Sasha again or glancing in her direc- tion, Shona stands up, her red hair raging about her head, her sensual mouth a deep, bloodstained crimson. She seizes her jacket by its fur collar and dashes from the room.

Steve stands in the doorway of Callum's lounge, staring with mild bewilderment at the confusion of books and papers chaotically dispersed across the sofa.

'Working hard, Chris?' he says jocularly, rasping his hand back and forth across his chin.

'Mm,' says Chris, who is kneeling on the floor, shuffling the papers around. He manages to smile rather nervously at Steve, but all the while there is a look of deep concentration in his eyes. His friendly face is looking slightly haggard.

'Siddown,' says Callum, appearing behind Steve. 'Ah,' he says, noticing his badly-placed housemate. 'I see the problem. Last minute panic, is it, Chris?'

Slowly, Chris realises that the other two are intending to sit on the sofa.

'Yes,' he says, dismayed. He looks agitatedly about the room, for no reason that Steve or Callum can fathom. Then, suddenly, he pounces on a large, stripy mug of something that is probably hot chocolate. He drains it hastily. Then, fortified, he returns to the sofa and begins to gather his work together.

Callum seats himself casually on the sofa's arm. 'I hear you committed another indiscretion,' he says to Steve, with a rakish grin.

'Yeah well,' Steve responds, rather uneasily. 'You know how it is.'

'Who was it then?'

'Some bird at someone's party,' says Steve, evasively. 'I didn't *screw* her. We just got off.' He sits down heavily in the only armchair, resting a hand on each of the arms. They are large hands and powerful, with a big gold signet ring on one thick finger.

'I don't s'pose Lizzie was too happy?' says Callum.

'Nah. And I had to tell her, because there were people she knew. It would've gotten back to her.' He shrugs.

Chris, having piled up his belongings at one end of the

sofa, sits down. He puts a pad of paper on his lap and stares at it helplessly, biro in hand.

'It was just one of those things,' explains Steve, scrutinising Chris' face from across the room. 'I went out on a bit of a whim and, you know, I'd had a few beers and she was a good-looking girl. Sometimes,' he says, striking the arm of the chair emphatically, 'you just can't help yourself. Isn't that right, Chris?'

Chris looks up and laughs awkwardly.

'She *was* pretty hot, though,' Steve assures his audience. 'A blonde.'

'Can't go wrong with a blonde,' says Callum, somewhat to Chris' confusion.

'And she had a cute smile,' Steve goes on. He runs a hand over his short hair.

'Very nice, too.'

'And a pierced lip,' Steve adds, 'Which I wasn't sure about.'

'Bet that was...a bit weird.'

'Yeah...' says Steve, musingly. 'A bit weird.'

A few moments of silence pass, during which Chris painstakingly writes *Main Topics* on his pad, Callum looks out of the window and Steve discovers the remote control behind a cushion.

'Anyhow,' says Callum, finally. 'Last exam, tomorrow.'

'Not for me,' says Chris, aggrieved.

'How many more have you got left?' Callum asks.

'Three.'

'Ah well. Come out for a beer tonight. Forget about it.'

An expression of agony crosses Chris' face. 'I can't,' he says, in strangled tones.

Steve has just switched the TV on. 'You're gonna have a load of packing to do after tomorrow,' he tells Callum, his eyes on the screen. 'When are you moving out?'

'When I've found a place in London. A few weeks, I reckon. Shona's contract finishes at the end of June, so she'll be able to come down right away.'

'Lizzie says she's going to visit,' says Steve, 'once you're set up in your little love-nest. She's got it all worked out. She thinks she's going to be doing a lot of shopping, but I think different.'

Callum grins. 'It's probably dangerous to have Shona living that near London. I can just see her blowing my wage packet on designer handbags.'

'Have to watch that,' Steve agrees.

Chris is rapidly coming to the conclusion that he needs a quieter working environment, but that even more urgently he needs a hot chocolate. He collects his most necessary notes together and takes them through to the kitchen, leaving Callum and Steve discussing the football results.

When Shona arrives at the office on Wednesday morning, she finds Elspeth sitting in front of the computer. Her smile is manic, her nose is sunburnt and her hair stands out around her face in a frizzy orange mane.

'I *am* pleased to see you, Shona,' she says, boisterously. There is a thin film of sweat on her forehead. 'You'll be able to tell me what format I ought to be saving this in. I want to send it to the City Centre Arts Committee as an attachment.'

Shona casts silver-shadowed eyes over the image on the screen. Her lipstick is dark red and glossy. 'JPEG is best,' she says, coolly.

'I can't *imagine* what we're going to do without you,' Elspeth declares loudly, fiddling with the computer. 'You've been an absolute treasure. To think, now we have email, we have our own *beautifully* designed web page and we can access all our records at the touch of a button. Our users can even read the newsletter on-line! And it's all down to your hard work.'

'It's been a privilege to work here,' says Shona. Beneath her shiny maroon skirt her legs are bare. She is wearing an embroidered blouse, just thin enough so that the lace of her bra can be glimpsed underneath. 'I shall miss it.'

'Gracious! It's been a privilege to have you. A woman of your abilities!' Elspeth says, baring her teeth in an alarming grin. Her thin arms are protruding from a dress that is roughly the colour of congealed blood. She is wearing a long chiffon scarf in a nauseous shade of green.

'What a lovely scarf,' says Shona, suddenly. 'I love that deep lime colour. It's great with the russet of your dress.' The sun is shining through her hair, glinting off the fine, coppery threads.

'You like those wonderful autumnal shades, too?' Elspeth says, vaguely. She types something into the computer in a frenzied fashion, stares at it fiercely for a moment and then deletes it. 'I'm in such a muddle this morning,' she says, wildly. 'Shona, have you any idea when the next CCA meeting is? It's gone right out of my head.'

'I think it's next Tuesday. June the second,' says Shona, calmly. She fingers the silver chain which encircles her slender neck. 'By the way, thank you for reorganising the filing cabinet. I came in on Monday morning and it was done! It's great – everything's so much easier to find now!'

'Blissful, isn't it…not having to search through this,' Elspeth gestures expansively, 'chaos.' Then, without warning, she leaps to her feet, scattering papers onto the floor. 'Is that the time? I must skedaddle!' she exclaims, 'Or I shall be late for my group at St Hugh's.' She plucks at the material of her long, shapeless dress, which is sticking to her skin. 'Isn't it sultry?' she says. 'Don't you just *long* to go barefoot in this weather?'

She doesn't wait to hear Shona's response, but prances gaily out of the room clutching her raffia-work bag.

'My last exam – ever!' cries Chris, drunk and jubilant. There is a small quantity of sweet, brown liquid in the bottom of his mug, which he swills around vigorously and then downs in one.

Becca is sitting cross-legged on the floor. 'Hey! Go easy on the Baileys!' she says in her sweet, throaty voice. 'There's not a lot left!'

'I think that was the last of it,' says Shona, who is draped across an armchair, her pink silk negligee spread out beneath her like a bed of rose-petals.

'Was it? Oh, no!' Becca reaches for the bottle and holds it up to the light. Optimistically she upends it, but only a meagre couple of drops drip into her wine glass. 'What are we going to do?'

Shona shrugs. 'Buy some more?' She has just come out of the bath and is dressed in pale blue pyjama bottoms and a white vest-top patterned with blue flower-buds. Chris is trying to keep from looking in her direction; her delicate white flesh makes him feel giddy. Or perhaps, he comforts himself, it is only the alcohol.

Shona's suggestion does not meet with much enthusiasm from any quarter. No one seems at all eager to move.

'What about that vodka?' says Frances suddenly, her voice leaking thinly from within her enormous cardigan.

Shona looks puzzled. A few curls of hair cling damply to her neck and her exposed shoulders. 'What vodka?' she asks.

'The vodka you found in the cupboard when you moved in,' says Frances. She looks squat and stunted, huddled on the sofa. Her hair is stringy and unkempt.

'Oh...' Shona stands up and goes through into the kitchen, releasing a sweet, floral scent into the air. Chris drags his mind reluctantly away from the thought of the warm body beneath her thin pyjamas.

'Jus' think,' murmurs Chris to no one in particular, when he has recovered from Shona's departure. 'Now I'm not a student I can get my own place; I can get a rabbit...' A hazy look comes into his light brown eyes. 'I could have it running loose around the house. Train it to use a litter tray, like a cat.'

'Or you could just get a cat,' says Becca, unsympathetically.

Chris meets Becca's eyes a little blearily. She is wearing bootleg jeans and a shirt checked in shades of fawn and chocolate. It ties at the front, revealing her smooth, golden stomach in a way Chris cannot help but appreciate. 'But I like *rabbits*,' he says.

'But what are you going to do for money?' Frances asks, squashing her ugly features into a frown.

'How will you afford to keep this rabbit of yours in carrots?' Becca adds, brushing her honey-blonde hair from her eyes.

Shona has just returned, half a bottle of vodka in one hand, and half a bottle of coke in the other. She looks inquiringly around the room.

'I dunno. I'll get some...job,' says Chris, managing with an effort to keep his mind on the conversation and off Shona's lovely face and big, dizzying eyes.

'Anyone for a vodka and coke?' Shona asks. Her mouth looks soft as a flower. 'Kit? I'm afraid the coke's rather flat.'

'I'll just have a vodka,' says Chris, carefully avoiding her eyes 'When Frances has finished rinsing my mug.'

'I'll try a vodka and coke,' says Becca, helping herself.

'Frances?' says Shona, indicating the vodka bottle as Frances comes waddling back into the room in large, furry slippers. Frances bobs her head up and down on her scraggy neck, and accepts the proffered vodka.

'I should get yourself a nice rich girlfriend and keep house for her,' suggests Becca, returning to her conversation with Chris. 'One who likes rabbits.'

Chris feels this is no bad idea, particularly if the girl in question had Shona's long-lashed, soft blue eyes; but he doesn't think it politic to say so.

'What's your ideal man like, Frances?' Shona asks, to everyone's surprise.

'Blind,' says Frances, abruptly.

Shona considers this for a moment. 'Mine too,' she says, with a startling smile.

'This is terrible,' says Becca, sampling her drink. 'Ugh, I'm not convinced this even *is* vodka. Mind if I try some of yours?' she asks Chris. She takes his mug and sips it warily. 'Definitely tastes funny,' she concludes.

'I don't think the vodka's too bad – it's mainly the coke,' says Shona. 'Perhaps someone should go to the shop on the corner.'

'Perhaps *someone* should,' Becca replies, raising an eyebrow.

'The Open All Hours shop would have some orange juice or something,' Shona persists. She is absent-mindedly scrunching her wet hair with one hand, her eyes a dreamy blue.

'But it isn't,' says Frances. Her skin looks rough and greyish.

'What?' asks Becca, baffled.

'Open all hours.'

'Isn't it?'

'No. In fact it's hardly ever open,' says Frances with a sort of trollish leer. 'Some days it doesn't seem to open at all.'

Chris sips his drink thoughtfully, wondering if he should volunteer to go to the shop in spite of this new information. Shona nestles deeper into her armchair, curling her white feet under her. She rests an elbow lightly on the armrest and places her finely-shaped jaw on her hand.

'Becca,' she says softly, 'There's a voice in my head that narrates. It's like another person who watches me all the time. Do *you* hear that voice?'

Becca meets Shona's eyes with a steady hazel gaze. 'Well,' she says, a peculiar smile on her shining, plum-coloured lips. 'Not quite the way you do, perhaps. But certainly I know what you mean.'

'Do *you*?' Shona has turned suddenly to Chris. 'Kit?'

'Um,' Chris accidentally meets her eyes, then, panicking slightly, looks away. 'I don't – I mean, I'm afraid I don't know what you mean.'

'For instance,' says Shona, something tigerish in her tone, 'when you walk into a room with a woman in it, does a voice in your head describe her?'

'A voice in my head?' Chris repeats, avoiding her painfully blue gaze.

'Does it *assess* her?' asks Frances, turning her misshapen face towards him, watching him intently.

'Her appearance?' adds Becca. She leans forward over the coffee table. 'How attractive she is?'

Even staring at the pattern of the carpet, Chris can feel the glare of three pairs of unblinking eyes upon him, staring at his face. Those eyes seem alien and unfriendly; he feels suddenly lost and alone.

'Does it get in the way of you listening to her? Feeling for her?' he hears Shona say. The words sound indistinct, as if his head were muffled in pillows. 'Is she something to be looked at, not someone who does the looking? Is she something to be thought about, not someone who thinks?'

The words churn in Chris' brain. He can make no sense of them.

'A voice in my head?' Chris repeats.

'Hollowly,' says Shona.

'Monotonously,' says Becca.

'Playing for time,' says Frances, in an insidious whisper.

'No,' says Chris, trying to speak firmly. 'There's no voice in my head.'

With relief, Chris feels the three pairs of eyes withdraw. He hears a creak as Frances shifts her position on the sofa, a dull clink as Becca stands her wine glass on the coffee table. After a few moments he risks a glance at Shona. She is gazing into the distance, her face very pale.

'Well, I guess I'd better get back,' says Becca after a while. 'Work tomorrow, and all that.'

'I'll show you out,' says Shona, unfolding her legs and walking across the room, her footfalls soft. Chris looks up again to catch a last glimpse of her as she disappears. Her skin is glowing gently like the petals of a moonlit lily.

When Becca and Shona have left the room, Kit turns to the hunched, repugnant creature beside him.

'What are you trying to *do* to that poor girl?' he asks.

'What do you mean, Kit?' the creature answers, shrinking into the sofa.

'You know what I mean,' says Chris. He doesn't raise his voice, but he is angry. 'She wouldn't have come out with those things if you hadn't got your claws into her. You've taken advantage of her illness...confused her.' He thinks, with a pang, of how Shona has changed over only a few weeks. 'She needs to see a doctor, but instead of helping you've convinced her that her delusions are reality!'

'The voice she hears *isn't* a delusion.' The reply comes in a low hiss. '*I* hear it.'

'I know what you mean by that,' Chris replies, swiftly. 'You're trying to make her believe that her "voices" are somehow the same thing as your conspiracy theories. You're *using* her.' He turns to look at the wretched Frances Freak, but her little eyes evade his. 'Don't you have any pity?' he asks. 'When I think of how she looked, all white and wan, that misty look in her eyes…thinking she's stumbled upon some sort of profundity, when really you're just encouraging her to talk nonsense…gibberish!'

'Don't you listen to anything she says?' Frances Freak says, slyly. 'She's screaming out for someone to understand, but all you can see is what she looks like. All you're interested in is her pretty face, her fantastic body.'

'Ah, so that's it!' exclaims Chris, suddenly comprehending. He almost wants to laugh at Frances' pettiness. 'You're jealous because Shona's beautiful and I can't help noticing.'

There is a flash of fury in Frances' usually dull eyes. '*Of course* I'm jealous,' she admits, resentfully. '*Of course* it hurts to see you gazing at her adoringly when you can hardly bear to look at me. But that isn't the point.' She hides her eyes behind a scaly paw. 'You don't know anything about Shona. You may know the length of her legs and the precise shade of her eyes. You may be able to guess her bra size, for all I know,' she adds, in a vindictive tone. 'But you don't know how she thinks, because you're too busy looking to listen.'

'Frances,' says Chris, growing frustrated, 'I'm going to go home. Will you *please* think about the effect you're having on Shona and whether it's fair…or moral.' He fixes her with an earnest gaze and tries to make his tone persuasive. 'You're unbalancing her mind, Frances! This is serious. Please think about what you're doing.'

'Kit, I'm not doing anything to her!' Frances practically
screams. 'Can't you get over your need to make a victim of
her, if you can't stop making a monster of me?' She looks
back at him with her creased, hostile eyes. 'Why don't you
talk to her yourself?'

Chris feels something alarming happen to his heart. For
an instant he pictures himself talking gently, seriously, to a
vulnerable and melancholy Shona, her white hand clasped
protectively in his, her eyes bright with tears.

'Why don't you?' Frances Freak repeats.

Abruptly Chris dismisses the vision. It is not something
that would ever, could ever, happen. Girls like Shona scarcely
noticed his existence.

'Oh no,' Frances wails. 'It's because she's so gorgeous,
isn't it? You won't talk to her because you don't think of her
as human. She's practically a divinity to you, isn't she?' she
says, cruelly, bitterly. 'She is unapproachable; she exists on a
different plane!'

'Stop *twisting* everything,' says Chris, a little desperately.
'I'm not going to argue. I'm going home. But you think
about how you're damaging Shona. What would Callum
think if he knew what you were doing? Or think about it
from her parents' point of view. From the point of view of
anyone normal!'

'Why can't *you* think about it from *Shona's* point of view?'

'I said I'm going,' says Chris, with determination, and
leaves Frances Freak to fester alone.

She says nothing as he walks out, but remains unmoving
in the corner of the sofa. Her neck is bent; her hair drips disconsolately over her face; but beneath this greyish shroud the
look in her eyes is perverse and unrepentant.

Tears shimmer in Shona's blue eyes as the bright knife slices down. Salty droplets tremble on her dark lashes and then course over her flawless face, falling onto her creamy hands, the tabletop, the mutilated onion. A yellowish light streams though the window, turning her hair the colour of paprika.

'It's so...*stifling*, having that voice in my head. I can't hear myself think. About a month ago I got so frustrated I started screaming in the street.'

With deft fingers, Shona selects some mushrooms from a paper bag and begins to chop them. The knife just misses the tips of her nails each time, the shell-pink and the white reflecting in its blade.

'It was partly because of those builders on George Street. I had to go past them on the way into town.' She looks up, lingering tears still giving a tragic appearance to the pale contours of her face. 'It was the way they were looking at me. And the horrible feeling that...I'm not my own property. That any man who wants to can *look* at me like that. Like he doesn't even need to hide the fact he's taken me into his mind against my will, where he's using my body for his sordid fantasies.'

Shona picks up a scarlet pepper and makes an incision near the top. She cuts swiftly around the stalk and removes it, and then begins to dice the red flesh.

'But the worst of it, that time on George Street, was that I couldn't *get myself back*. I stood there, right next to the main road, and screamed, but I still couldn't get the voice out of my head. But what really made me want to scream myself into unconsciousness was that the voice wasn't telling me I was a mess, that I looked ridiculous, as I must have done. It was telling me I looked beautiful and dramatic.'

'Shona...' says Frances, who is standing over her, watching darkly as she prepares the vegetables.

Shona pops a small piece of pepper into her mouth, which is the deep, rich colour of wine. 'Mm–hm?'

'Don't wish yourself unpretty,' says Frances, the whispery tone of her voice making the words sound menacing. 'It doesn't make things any easier.'

'Doesn't it?' says Shona, slashing a courgette. 'I don't think you realise how much I'd love to...go unnoticed.'

'I get hassled by those builders too.'

Shona manages to refrain from outright laughter, but she cannot help looking surprised as she stares at Frances' pinched, unattractive face, her murky eyes.

'They probably shout the same comments at both of us,' says Frances. Her hair is dark with grease and she is still wearing her oversized cardigan. 'Only they're rather less sincere when it's me they're victimising.'

'How do you mean? What do they say?'

'The usual thing,' says Frances, evasively, failing to meet Shona's eyes. 'They yell, "Hey, gorgeous!" and then they all laugh. Or, "Fancy a bit of that, Kev? I reckon she's up for it."' She winces, her small eyes almost disappearing among the black shadows of her eye-pits. 'Sometimes it's a bit more graphic.'

'How about just, "Frances winces"?' says Shona, confusingly, as she sets the onions simmering in a wok. Her hair keeps tumbling over her face, so she throws it up swiftly and haphazardly in a velvet band she had round her wrist. Curling red tendrils escape, caressing her neck and teasingly stroking her cheeks. She tosses a chopped chilli into the wok.

'Do you want a glass of this?' she asks, indicating a bottle of red wine.

'With my beans on toast?' Frances hisses, twisting her bony hands.

'Says Frances, amused.'

'No thanks.'

'Frances glances quickly at Shona, an expression of half convinced gratitude on her face,' says Shona, a lunatic spark in her eyes.

Rather wildly, Shona throws the other ingredients into the wok, more of her fiery hair coming loose as she does so. She is wearing cropped green trousers and a wide-necked blouse in a particularly piquant shade of red.

'Frances?'

'Yes?' Frances Freak replies, groping around in a cupboard and eventually emerging with a chipped plate.

'Do you *like* that cardigan?'

Frances looks down at the grimy greyish garment. Her spindly, black-trousered legs poke out ridiculously from under the cardigan's bulk. 'I like the way it covers me up.'

'What do you mean?' Shona asks, with a smile that is cinnamon-sweet.

'I mean that it keeps most of me hidden,' Frances Freak replies, dismally. She shoves a dank strand of hair behind a squashed-looking ear. 'It limits the amount of me that people can despise, because it limits the amount of me they can see.'

'Everyone's ears look like that,' says Shona, for no apparent reason. 'Except that Frances' have a bit of a point. Which I think is rather cool, actually.' She whirls the fizzing, spitting ingredients swiftly round the pan and shakes in some herbs. 'But you don't like the cardigan itself?' she asks. 'You don't like how you look in it?'

Frances' scrawny face contorts into an ugly grimace. 'No.'

'You're really not fond of Frances, are you? Is it because she won't play to the camera?' Shona asks, apparently addressing the empty air. Below the embroidered hem of her trousers, her feet and a portion of smooth shin are naked. 'Or is it because she knows exactly what you're up to?' Her ankles are slender, her creamy feet remarkably pretty.

'Foot fetish!' says Shona. 'Interesting. But Frances, isn't what you do just as bad as tarting yourself up in shoes you can't walk in and clothes that are too tight to be comfortable and too skimpy to keep you warm? In both cases you're letting yourself be controlled by other people's opinions.'

The wide neck of Shona's bright blouse is sliding seductively down over one white shoulder. The kitchen windows are beginning to steam up, giving the bluish-lilac sky outside a fuzzy texture.

'When you wear that cardigan you're not expressing yourself, you're defending yourself,' Shona continues, shaking the wok violently. 'Aren't you just as trapped as the woman who tarts herself up to please men?'

Frances' skeletal hands reach into the microwave, from which she removes a bowl of stagnant orange beans. She slops them onto a couple of pieces of underdone toast.

'Shona,' she says, eventually. Her voice sounds flimsy. 'I never said I had all the answers. At the moment I'm just trying to do…what's easiest.'

It is Saturday morning and Frances Freak is hurrying towards the dust and dinginess of the rambling old university library. Before she ensconces herself among the books, however, she needs to collect some notes from her office, so she dives into the Arts Building and scurries up a narrow staircase.

Professor Hudson almost bumps into her on the stairs. He is a kind and erudite man, considered somewhat verbose by many of the students, but liked in spite of it. Today he isn't wearing his customary jacket and cravat, but instead is dressed for the weekend in chinos and a short-sleeved shirt.

'Well, hello Frances,' the professor says, genially. He has a tendency to address students formally, as 'Mr Thompson' or 'Miss Smith,' for example, but in Frances' case he has always made a generous exception. 'What brings you into the department so early on a Saturday morning?' he asks, with a smile. 'I should have thought that at such an hour last night's undoubted alcoholic indulgence would still have you confined to your bed!'

Frances Freak sniggers, awkwardly. She doesn't seem to know what to say.

'Your commitment is very refreshing,' says Professor Hudson in congratulatory tones. 'Remind me, Frances; your subject is the eighteenth century – am I right?'

'Eighteenth-century women's literature, yes,' she says in an almost inaudible hiss.

'I thought that was it,' he answers, nodding. 'I hope you don't mind me saying that I do feel that's rather a pitiful waste of your talents. I would gladly have taken you on to do a PhD on Shakespeare. That piece you wrote on *King Lear* was exceptional.'

Frances fidgets uncomfortably under Professor Hudson's twinkling blue eyes. Her pallid, sun-starved skin and her severe hairstyle give her the appearance of a small, wizened librarian.

'But why is studying eighteenth-century women's writing "a pitiful waste"?' she asks. There is a testy, irritable look on her face.

'It is rather a specialist area, you must admit,' says the professor, resting his briefcase on the banister. 'Very few people read either the literature or the research that's published on it. Whereas if you had chosen a more mainstream subject I think you have the potential to produce some very important work.'

As the professor finishes speaking there is raucous laughter on the stairs below.

'He's my fancy man, I already told you!' a voice says, and there is more laughter. Almost at once a cleaner appears, smelling of smoke and breathing audibly as she climbs the stairs. She is wearing brash red lipstick and carrying a vacuum cleaner. Frances shrinks back against the banister as the cleaner passes them.

'I don't think of my research as "specialist",' Frances responds, once the cleaner has clattered through the swinging door at the top of the stairs. Her small, embittered eyes rake the professor's cheerful face. 'It's about the emergence of the novel form. I would have thought that was mainstream,' she says, argumentatively.

'Of course, but to limit yourself to women's writing is a serious mistake if you're looking for a broad readership,' the professor explains. 'When you're trying to produce scholarly research it's important not to be seen as partisan.' He passes a hand over his thinning hair. 'Why is it that our female post-graduates so often seem to retreat to the peripheries of the subject?' he asks. 'It really is exasperating. I'm all for having more female professors, but it seems that the most intelligent women deny themselves that opportunity by concerning themselves only with the obscure.'

'Surely that's a vicious circle,' says Frances, curtly. She thrusts her sharp nose in the air. 'Who decides what's "obscure"?'

But the professor is looking at his watch anxiously. 'I'm sorry, Frances; much as I'd like to continue this discussion, I'm going to have to dash off. I only came in to pick up some work – my wife will be wondering where I've got to!'

Professor Hudson smiles warmly at Frances despite her prickliness. He takes the remaining steps two at a time and strides away, swinging his briefcase.

Annoyance glitters in Frances' colourless eyes. She continues up the staircase until she reaches the swinging door, which leads into a long, murky corridor. She opens the second door on the left; something like a smile, but less friendly, touches her pale lips.

'Hello, Deborah,' she says.

The girl in the office looks up. She has big brown eyes and freckles. Her light brown hair falls half way down her back in a smooth, shining sheet.

'Hey, Frances,' she says. Her accent has a slight American flavour. 'How are your eighteenth-century women?'

'I think I'm finally getting somewhere. Have you heard of...'

'Yeah, mine's going well, too,' says Deborah. She is wearing a white vest with steel blue jogging pants. A heart-shaped pendant hangs from a gold chain round her neck. 'I'm leaving Simone de Beauvoir for the moment. I'm trying to concentrate on contemporary feminists. Actually, it would really interest you. I've got an article you'd definitely want to read.'

'Okay,' says Frances, abruptly.

'Actually I've not got it on me at the moment. Or I have, but I'm going to need it.' She flicks her hair over her shoulder. 'You didn't just run into Roy Hudson, did you? He was lurking about a few minutes ago.'

'Yes; he was telling me his theory about...'

'I hate that guy. He must've blinked and missed the last three decades. He has no respect for women, absolutely none. He's the worst of them all, except Sarah Hegwin,' she says, contemptuously. 'She wants to lose about four stone from the look of her, but she eats a Mars bar half way through tutorials almost as a matter of course! It's disgusting.' Deborah stands up to reach a book off a shelf, displaying her own lean, toned body. Her bare arms are tanned a warm brown. 'You know, I thought no one would be in on a

Saturday morning, but Patsy's been in as well,' Deborah comments. 'I guess you haven't seen her new hair colour?'

'Is it still blonde?'

'Or thereabouts. It looks *grey*. And she's like, "Oh, do you like my hair?" and I'm all, "Yeah Patsy, it's gorgeous." She just doesn't have a clue, does she? I don't know how she ever got on the PhD course.' Deborah plucks a sheet of paper out of the printer and skim reads it, hand on hip. 'Right, I've got to go now, actually. I'm going jogging with my friend. We've been doing regular jogging and weights and we're on this really strict diet as well. It's good. I've lost three pounds already. See you!'

As Deborah leaves the room, the cleaner comes in, dragging a black plastic sack behind her. Deborah rolls her eyes at Frances over the cleaner's rounded shoulder and then disappears.

'Hello, Maureen,' says Frances.

'It's all right, dear, I'm not going to disturb you,' the cleaner responds. 'The carpet doesn't need doing right now, does it?'

'No, I think the carpet's fine.'

'Then I'll just take the bins.'

Frances reaches a waste-paper bin from under the desk and hands it to the cleaner. Then she opens a drawer and squints at its contents, looking for the notes she'll need in the library. She riffles through the papers with skinny hands, the fingertips purplish-grey, the nails bitten to the quick.

'Did you get your essay finished in time?' Frances asks.

'I did,' the cleaner replies. 'Bit of a bugger though, that Spenser, isn't he? Give me a nice bit of Shakespeare any day!'

Chris is wishing he hadn't come. Why had he let Callum drag him round to Shona's when he could have spent the evening…quietly reading a book, for example? But instead here he is, forced to sit and watch helplessly as Shona stalks around the room in her little denim shorts, offering people drinks and smiling her painfully beautiful smile.

'What are you having, Kit?' she asks softly, coming to a halt in front of his chair. He cannot think which is more problematic, to stare at her unfeasibly long legs, or to gaze directly into the perilous depths of her eyes. Confused, Chris attempts a compromise; but that is even worse.

'I'll have a beer, please,' Chris says finally, opting to look fixedly over her right shoulder.

'I thought Lizzie and Steve were coming with you?' Shona says, as she passes him a beer.

And now she's talking to me, Chris thinks, dazedly, entirely failing to comprehend her words, much less to compose an answer.

'They're just outside,' says Callum. 'I don't know what they're doing, but they've got quite lovey-dovey since Steve's little escapade.'

She wasn't talking to me! Chris tells himself, and suddenly it seems that the worst thing Shona could do is ignore him.

'You have all the sensitivity of a pneumatic drill, Callum,' says Becca, dryly. Her amber eyes rest lightly on Callum's lop-sided grin. 'Don't look so bloody pleased with yourself,' she says. 'It wasn't a phallic metaphor!'

'Your long-term relationship hasn't mellowed you, then,' Callum responds, still grinning. 'How long's it been now? Over a month. That must be some kind of record.'

Steve and Lizzie have just arrived, Steve looking more than usually cheerful, Lizzie looking pretty in a pink sun-dress. Her ponytail band is ornamented with a large silk daisy and there is a faint blush on her cheeks.

'Where's Josh?' she asks Becca, dimpling.

'Not sure,' Becca replies unconcernedly, viewing Lizzie through the gold mesh of tousled hair which has fallen over her eyes. 'But I'm meeting him later.'

'How are you, Liz?' Shona asks. She has sat down and is snuggling into an armchair, her legs curled up, auburn waves rolling over her shoulders. She is wearing a cosy-looking fleece, but Chris thinks that he can almost detect tiny raised bumps on the exposed flesh of her legs. Taking firm control of his mind, Chris refrains from imagining himself warming her in his arms.

'I'm okay,' Lizzie replies. 'Do you like my new dress?'

'It's pretty,' says Shona.

'Very cute,' Becca agrees, adjusting her clingy sage-green T-shirt. 'So, you three,' she says, turning to the three men. 'How does it feel to have finished your exams?'

Steve grins at the welcome reminder that his days in academia are over. Callum stretches his legs out in front of him and says, 'I'm knackered, actually. I've hardly slept since Tuesday night. And when I do sleep I keep dreaming about going to London.'

'What is it, Frances?' Shona asks Frances, who is perching on the sofa, dressed in the inevitable cardigan. She looks at Shona and smirks.

'Smiles, self-consciously,' says Shona. A bright spark of hair falls over her face.

'I dreamt something very strange last night,' Frances says. Her face has a ghoulish pallor and her eyes are shining luridly. She looks not so much like a creature who would have dreams, as one who would inhabit them.

'Which is how you see all women,' says Shona.

'We're the figments of men's imaginations,' Frances replies, leering in Shona's direction.

'Exchanging a confidential smile with Shona,' says Shona.

Callum is gazing at Shona in dismay; Steve and Lizzie are staring at her in confusion, Chris in horror. Chris feels that he is watching a calamity occur in hideously slow motion, but that he is powerless to prevent it. A gruesome vision of Shona deteriorating, fading, turning into Frances, appears before his tortured imagination.

'Tell me your dream, Frances,' says Shona. She is grinning unrestrainedly, her lips glistening red.

Frances looks feebly back at Shona, but remains mute.

'Go on,' Shona insists.

'Unless it was really dodgy,' Becca qualifies, raising an eyebrow.

'You were in it, Kit,' Frances says hesitantly, turning pale eyes on Chris. Chris feels a vague sense of alarm.

'Wahey!'

'But it *wasn't* dodgy, Becca!' says Frances, cringing further into the sofa.

'Oh,' Becca replies, huskily. She sounds disappointed.

Chris watches Frances' scrawny face with a feeling of foreboding, as she considers what to tell her audience. He doesn't want to hear what she is going to say. He doesn't want to feature in Frances Freak's dreams, and he wants Callum and Steve to hear the details even less.

'Kit was in a sort of ruined gothic mansion,' says Frances, twisting her thin hands, 'doing research for his exams – in the dream you were still doing exams, Kit – and I was with him.'

Embarrassed, Chris looks across at Callum and Steve. Steve looks bored; Callum is obviously busy thinking up something amusing to say.

'So what happened?' Becca prompts.

'Well, for a long time we were walking around in the grounds. There was ivy everywhere, and statues that had fallen over; and there was a forest at the end of the garden. Kit was telling me that there was a beast that came out of the forest at night. It was a wolf, I think. Or something.'

Lizzie's eyes have grown round and credulous, like the eyes of a small child listening to a bedtime story. 'What then…?' she breathes.

'Kit was telling me to be careful not to go near the forest because of the beast, when I realised that he didn't know who I was. He thought I was *you*, Shona.'

Callum and Steve have to stifle their laughter. Chris thinks he hears Steve mutter, 'That's likely!'

'Go on,' says Becca.

'For some reason it was really important that he shouldn't realise his mistake. So I put my hood up to hide my hair.' There is more sniggering from Steve and Callum's side of the room. 'I was wearing a sort of old-fashioned, dark-coloured cloak.' Frances pauses to pass a dry tongue-tip over her thin lips. 'Then Kit…went off somewhere, and I quickly went into the forest to hide, so that he wouldn't find out I wasn't Shona. That's all I remember.'

'Freud would have fun with that,' says Becca, her voice rich as mocha.

'Obviously, unconsciously she wants to be Little Red Riding Hood,' says Callum, grinning boyishly. 'You read too many stories, Miss Freak.'

There is a short silence. Callum is still grinning to himself. Chris sips his beer thoughtfully, wondering if there is any possibility of escaping in the near future.

'Is that a *new* top, Becca?' Lizzie asks, chirpily. 'I've been thinking about getting one of those. Was it from Fawleys? Obviously I'd want one in a different colour,' she adds, in reassuring tones. 'That colour's lovely on you, but on me…' A little shudder passes through her body.

'They have a nice one in a sort of dove grey,' says Becca, fingering the soft material where it meets her tanned skin.

'Or maybe the baby blue one...'

'They're at it again!' says Callum, swigging his lager.

Steve is rooting around in his earhole. 'Did you see the football?' he asks.

'Nope.'

'We had that film on, didn't we?' Chris points out. He tries to remember the title. '*Living Dangerously*. With Cara Fezzon.'

'Ah, she's hot!' Steve responds, with enthusiasm.

'You should've seen her in this,' says Callum. 'There's this fantastic shower scene.' He places the lager bottle on the coffee table, so as to be able to use both hands in the forthcoming explanation. 'First of all you see her through the shower door, which is glass and all steamed up,' he tells Steve, using his left hand to represent the glass, and waving the other to signify the condensation. 'Then the camera pans round,' says Callum, his right hand metamorphosing into the camera, 'and comes in closer–'

''Scuse me,' says Becca. Her wide mouth is painted a succulent plummy shade. 'Do you think we want to hear about your cheap thrills?'

'Talking of great shower scenes,' says Callum teasingly, grinning at Becca.

'Ignoring Becca,' says Shona, toying with a red curl.

'There's an even better one in *The Second Star*,' Callum finishes.

'Examining it for split-ends, actually,' Shona murmurs.

'That's Stephanie Peak, isn't it?' says Steve. 'The one with the tits.'

'Says Steve, crassly, a great clumsy smirk spread across his face,' Shona says. 'And Callum is practically slavering at the mere thought.'

'Natalie Peterson has got to be the best, though,' Callum asserts. 'She's gorgeous. Chris likes her, don't you Chris?'

'Callum continues, mercilessly,' says Shona. 'There is a sort of deliberate cruelty beneath…beneath…'

'Beneath his amiable manner,' Frances says.

'Yes,' Shona agrees. 'He's more…brutal than you'd think.'

Shona's legs are distracting Chris from the thought of Natalie Peterson. She has unfurled them and placed her feet on the floor. There is something defenceless-looking about Shona's bare feet…something intimate about seeing them uncovered. And her legs… Her legs are like no other legs Chris has ever seen. They are smooth and slender and the skin glows gently.

'By the way, everybody,' says Shona, reaching for her vodka and orange, 'I think Frances has an announcement.' She takes a sip of the drink, cool liquid against her soft lips, the glass held lightly in her slender fingers.

'Natalie Peterson's okay,' Steve concedes, having given the matter careful thought. 'But she's a bit skinny.'

'Granted, she does look a bit rough in that latest one she did,' says Callum.

'Hello?' says Becca, loudly. 'Would you lot care to shut up and listen?'

Startled by Becca's aggressive tone, the men halt their conversation.

'It's just that it's my birthday next Saturday,' says Frances, her voice reluctant and almost inaudible. 'And Shona's persuaded me that I ought to go to Justine's. So if anyone wants to come, we'll be leaving about eight.'

'And if you come beforehand,' Shona adds, 'we might have some food.'

'Jolly good,' says Steve. 'Ah, but what about that girl on the shampoo ad? The one on the beach. She's just got this little bikini on, and her body...' Steve gives a low whistle. 'Mind-blowing!'

'Why do you think it's okay to see women as bodies?' Becca inquires, rather caustically. Her eyes are like yellow flame.

'What you mean,' says Callum, resuming his grin, 'is that you don't like the thought that other women might be better looking than you. Obviously...'

'Don't tell me what I mean!' Becca interrupts. She looks up at Callum fiercely, from her cross-legged position at his feet.

'What do *you* think, Kit?' Shona asks Chris. Something inside Chris leaps nervously. Shona has addressed herself directly to him, and now she is looking at him, her lovely, dark-fringed eyes upon his face. He tries to think of a suitable response.

Callum raises amused eyebrows. 'What's with the new nickname?' he asks. Chris feels his cheeks warming and hopes it isn't too obvious in the dusky light.

'Why can't women be people, even if they are good-looking?' Shona asks, losing interest in Chris. She is combing her hair with her hands, drawing her slender fingers over its copper harp-strings. 'Copper harp-strings?' Shona adds, to the further confusion of those listening. 'That's a bit whimsical!'

'You're not making any sense, Angel,' Callum remarks, cheerfully.

'I think Shona's pointing out that you're objectifying women,' Frances hisses. 'You don't see anything other than how they look. I think she means that you're not concerned with what they think or feel or say.'

'*I* think Shona can speak for herself,' says Chris, furious with Frances for putting her words into Shona's lovely mouth; for pretending to be Shona's friend, for trying to *possess* her.

'Certainly she can,' Frances answers. 'Maybe she should, if anyone's willing to listen.'

'In the ownership sense, or the demonic sense?' says Shona, to everyone's confusion. 'I suppose the demonic sense would be appropriate, since I'm just a body – an empty shell.'

'What *I* think,' says Steve, 'is that all this Women's Lib stuff has gone way overboard. If a bloke isn't allowed to say he thinks a woman's good-looking any more…'

'Excuse me,' Frances interjects, giving Steve a malevolent look. '*Is* anyone willing to listen to Shona?'

'Is anyone willing to listen to *me?*' Steve demands. 'Or aren't men allowed to talk any more? This is *way* overboard.'

'Exactly,' Callum agrees. 'I mean, no one complains if a woman fancies a film star, or if she covers her walls in pin-ups! It's not about *equal* rights any more, it's about women getting everything their own way!'

'Will everyone listen to Shona!' Frances Freak virtually shrieks.

'She's not trying to say anything, Frances,' Chris points out. He risks a glance at Shona, who is placidly folding three bright ribbons of her hair one over another in a long plait.

'You want to make sure you don't hold any doors open for this lot,' says Steve to Callum. 'Better not hold any doors open for Shona, or you'll get a right bollocking.'

'"Frances feels a sudden urge to shake Kit very hard",' says Frances, her eyes cold as pebbles in her pallid face. '"She also understands perfectly why Shona wanted to scream in the street. However, she masters…er, she mistresses –

arrghh! She gets the better of these impulses, because she understands that they would all be counterproductive. So she sits still, silent and apparently docile. And that is counterproductive as well.'"

'You know, Steve,' says Callum, 'I'm very tolerant of other people's opinions. But if she stops shaving her legs…'

Steve and Callum both start laughing.

'Shut up! *Shut up!*' shouts Becca, shocking everyone into silence for the second time that evening. 'Now listen to Shona.'

'I wanted to explain,' says Shona, weakly.

'Strong but vulnerable,' whispers Frances.

'That it hurts to hear you assessing women's appearances so casually. I guess it is an issue, for me at least, that we don't want it rubbed in our faces that other women are better looking. It hurts when you feel inadequate.'

'Come on, Angel…' Callum begins, but he is interrupted.

'Shut up!' Becca snarls.

'And it is an issue,' Shona continues, timidly, 'that…well, for instance, you might hope that because Steve's in a relationship with Lizzie he wouldn't be so interested in other women. You might think that even if he was, he wouldn't talk about it in front of her so shamelessly.'

'Hey!' says Steve, annoyed. 'What gives you the right to go telling me…'

'*Shut up!*' Becca yells.

'No, I bloody won't. I don't have to take orders from you! And I don't have to listen to Shona lecturing me!'

'Aren't you going to let her finish?' says Frances, her voice rising to a wail, her face bloodless as a banshee.

Chris wonders if it is obvious to everyone, or only to him, that Shona is simply performing a speech prepared in advance by Frances.

'I'm not going to let her tell me what to do!'

'We didn't come out tonight to get yelled at, or to be told off,' Callum points out, looking first at Becca, then at Shona. 'We thought we'd have a nice social evening. Have a few drinks. Why do you have to spoil it?'

'Wailing banshees, indeed,' says Shona in waspish tones. 'Nothing but cheap tricks and outright lies.'

Callum stares at her, disturbed, not knowing who she's talking to or what she means. She looks back at him, her large eyes pellucid, oblivious to his concern. 'She meets Callum's irascible green eyes, unflinchingly,' she continues, nonsensically.

Callum turns to Chris and then to Steve, to see if they are as perplexed as he is. Both of them look confounded.

'What do you reckon, Steve?' Callum asks. 'Shall we go back to the Lion?'

'No point sticking around here, that's for sure. Come on, Liz,' says Steve, getting to his feet.

'You coming, Chris?'

Steve strides towards the door and Callum follows, with Chris not far behind. Lizzie trots obediently after them.

'Smiling apologetically over her shoulder,' says Shona.

'You do realise your girlfriend's gone completely loopy,' says Steve to Callum, as the door shuts behind them and they head for the stairs.

As Callum applies the handbrake, Shona comes out of the front entrance and treads lightly along the garden path, between rows of white and purple pansies. She is dressed in fluid blue and lilac, and she is wearing a straw hat.

'Hello, Gorgeous,' says Callum cheerily, as she sits down in the passenger seat. 'So, where do you want to go?'

'I don't know,' says Shona, from underneath her hat. 'It

was your idea to meet up.'

'We'll find somewhere to go for a coffee, then.'

'I don't really fancy that,' she says, temperamentally. 'Shall we go for a walk in the park?'

'What park?'

'The one near where I work.'

Callum is a little surprised by this. He doesn't generally frequent parks and Shona has never before shown any inclination to do so. 'If you like,' he says amenably, nonetheless.

The drive to the park takes only a few minutes, and since Shona seems content to sit in silence, Callum doesn't disturb her. He draws up not far from the heavy wrought iron gates.

'I quite often come here in my lunch hours,' Shona remarks, as Callum locks the car up. The gauzy material of her blouse flutters around her body in the faint breeze.

'I didn't know that!'

'Why would you?' Shona asks. 'And her voice is bleak,' she adds in an undertone. Callum gives her a quizzical look, but says nothing.

On a warm Sunday afternoon the park is at its busiest. Callum and Shona walk past sunbathers, picnickers, excited dogs, intrepid sparrows and children of all colours and sizes on bicycles, tricycles, roller-skates and scooters. In the middle of the park a group of students try to play cricket using a coke bottle for a bat. A football game goes on to one side, without any apparent concern for the couples sprawled on the grass nearby. A small boy weeps disconsolately over a dropped ice cream.

'Why did you want to meet up, anyway?' Shona asks, suddenly.

'I wanted to see you, of course!' Callum answers jovially, in spite of her abruptness. 'And anyway, I reckon we've got a lot to discuss. Like whether you're coming flat-hunting with me.' He grins at her disarmingly. 'Can you take time off this week?'

Shona comes to a halt and turns to look at Callum. The expression on her lovely face, shaded coolly under the brim of her hat, is one of disbelief and amazement.

'I don't mind if you want me to sort it out,' Callum assures her, hastily. 'You can just join me when you've finished work. When does your contract finish? At the end of June?'

Shona doesn't answer his question, but just gazes at him, her perfectly formed lips strawberry red and slightly parted. An old man with a toothbrush moustache gives them a curious look as he walks slowly past.

'Callum,' Shona says at last. 'Haven't you noticed that we've barely seen each other for the last four weeks?' The expression in her shadowed eyes is inscrutable. 'How can you imagine I'm going to move in with you? Why would you think I'm going to give up my flat and move hundreds of miles away from my friends to follow you to London?'

'What are you talking about?' Callum asks, bewildered. 'This is what we planned! We discussed this!'

'No,' says Shona, her voice cruel and even. 'We never discussed this.' Without warning, she turns away from his searching eyes and continues walking along the path. Callum follows, quickly. 'I'm not sure we ever really discussed anything,' Shona continues. 'But I suppose what you mean is that you assumed I was moving to London with you and I didn't protest.'

'Shona...' Callum starts speaking anxiously.

'Let me finish,' says Shona, irritably. 'At the time you first assumed I was going to London I did actually intend to. But since then...everything's changed between us.'

Callum looks at the tall, slender girl walking beside him, her face partially hidden by the hat, her hair frisking about her shoulders in the slight breeze. He watches her skirt rippling around her ankles as she walks.

'Oh, Angel,' he says, gently. 'This has been a difficult time for both of us, but especially for you. You haven't been well,' he says, his voice becoming sad, 'and I admit I haven't looked after you as well as I should have – as well as I could have if I hadn't had my finals.' Swiftly, eagerly, he captures her warm, white hand and holds it as they walk. 'I know you need me to look after you. I will take better care of you in London, I promise.'

'I need you to look after me?' Shona echoes, her smooth cheeks very pale.

'Yes, Shona. You need someone to take care of you, and not every man would be patient with you, after some of the things you've put me through. But I know you're not well and I want to look after you, because I love you.'

Again, Shona is silent. A dog of dubious parentage dashes past them, chasing a ball, its long fur streaming out behind it. A German Shepherd starts to bark and joins in the pursuit.

'You know it's the truth,' says Callum, ardently. 'You know I love you.'

Shona keeps her head down, so that he cannot see her expression. Slowly, she disengages her hand. 'I don't think you even know what the words mean,' she says, faintly.

Callum looks at his girlfriend in bewilderment. 'Angel, I said I'm sorry. It will all be different in London.'

'I'm *not going* to London,' she says, stubbornly. 'Absolutely not. There is no way, no chance, no possibility. I'm staying here.'

'Are you telling me you want to end our relationship?' Callum asks, shocked.

'What relationship?' says Shona, helplessly. The words fall like teardrops into the placid afternoon.

They are just passing into the shade of a tall oak tree. Callum steps into Shona's path so that she has to stop and face him, small patches of light shimmering on the folds of her skirt. He expects her to look down so that her expression is hidden, but instead she removes her hat and stands bareheaded before him. Her skin looks very tender, very fair. Her cheekbones, her jawbone, her collarbone all look very delicate, and her mouth looks very soft. But her eyes, in that defenceless face, are defiant. Callum looks at those defiant eyes and feels angry. Angry that she can be so calm while he is panicking, angry that she seems to be playing with him. 'We haven't broken up, Shona!' he reminds her. 'It's normal for one party to inform the other party if they want to split up!'

Shona stares at him for a moment longer. 'Oh, did I forget that little formality?' she says, her tone satirical. 'Somehow I thought you'd catch on, eventually...but obviously not.' She smooths a rebellious tendril of hair back into place. 'Well Callum, please consider yourself dumped. I hope that's unambiguous enough for you.'

Without further elaboration, Shona turns and walks back towards the park gates. The sunshine ignites her hair as she leaves the shade of the tree, the breeze fanning it into a violent blaze.

When Shona arrives back at the flat she goes straight into the kitchen and tosses her hat lightly onto the kitchen table. She finds lemonade in the fridge and pours some into a tumbler. Her cheeks are reddened, her skin glowing slightly. She stands at the window for a while, sipping from the glass, cooling her fingers on its icy surface.

'In other words,' says Shona, 'I'm hot and sweaty and I smell.'

She meanders into the lounge, her flimsy clothes drifting

around her, and settles on the arm of a chair.

'What's this you're listening to?' she asks Frances Freak, who is contorted into a ball on the sofa. Her sharp nose hovers over the pages of a book.

'Bill Evans,' she answers.

'Oh,' says Shona. '"Blankly." That means nothing to me, I'm afraid. What are you reading? Is it work?'

'No, it's just for fun.' Frances raises the book so that Shona can read the title.

'I haven't heard of that, either.'

'It's good,' she says, squinting at Shona. 'At least – I like it. It's written as a diary.'

'Books like that kind of irritate me,' says Shona, airily.

'Do they? I like the immediacy.'

'Not "airily". "Shona confides" would be more like it. Or, "Shona confesses".'

'Maybe because I've always kept diaries,' Frances mumbles to herself.

Shona's gaze floats over towards Frances. 'Have you? Do you keep one now?'

Frances nods. Her empty eyes are intent on Shona's perfect face, as if trying to drain her unspoken thoughts.

'Excellent! I have thoughts!' Shona cries.

'Only so that I can be a psychic vampire,' says Frances, with a sneer.

'That was a smile,' says Shona.

'A sardonic smile,' says Frances.

'Smiling again, more shyly.'

Frances doesn't respond. Her scrawny face is vacant and she is picking at her pale lower lip with skinny fingers.

'What were you trying to say yesterday, when Callum and the others walked out?' Frances asks, abruptly.

A cloud passes over Shona's sky blue eyes. 'I was going

to say...I was thinking...Do you think they see *all* women that way, Frances?' She hesitates, her vivid lips hovering a few millimetres apart. 'Because that would mean that to them – to Callum and Kit and Steve, who I thought of as *friends* – to them I'm just a body, not a person.' Shona shifts her position on the chair's arm, and the fine material of her blouse gently resettles itself around the slope of her breasts, the hollow of her waist. 'That makes me feel so lonely.'

She looks wide-eyed into the distance; then her misty gaze falls on her empty glass. 'Do you want a drink?' she asks. 'Oh, you've already got one. What is that?'

'Wine,' says Frances. 'I thought I'd start early. I had a depressing morning. There's more in the fridge. Have some.'

'I think I will,' Shona responds. 'Thank you. My morning was okay, but I think this afternoon's been gruelling enough to do as an excuse.' She breezes out of the room, her hair a haze of red.

When Shona returns shortly after, the narrow stem of a wine glass between her delicate fingers, she finds Frances' cold eyes upon her once more.

'What are you after, you vampire?' Shona inquires.

Frances doesn't answer at once. A sort of twisted smirk is growing on her face.

'A grin,' says Shona.

'I was wondering why your afternoon was gruelling,' hisses Frances.

'Oh,' says Shona. 'Well.' She fondles a soft curl of hair, drawing the shining red threads out straight, and then letting it spring back. 'I split up with Callum.'

Frances watches Shona playing with her hair. 'Did you?' she says, unsympathetically.

'Mm,' Shona murmurs, smoothing the long curl back behind her ear. 'You don't seem surprised. *He* was.'

A breeze blows in through the open window, lifting the curtains and setting the pages of a magazine flapping, till it overbalances and slips from the windowsill.

'I never understood why you were going out with him in the first place,' retorts Frances. She sets her book down next to her. 'Was it just that he's gorgeous?'

Shona's eyes widen. 'You think Callum's gorgeous?'

'Of course. Don't you?'

Shona looks at Frances' ridiculous face, her pasty skin and drab hair, her emaciated limbs and drab clothes. Amusement glimmers in Shona's large, soft eyes. 'Well, he's not bad-looking. But I wouldn't exactly say gorgeous!'

'Those lovely green eyes and long black eyelashes!' wails Frances, whose eyes are colourless and her lashes invisible. 'That irresistible grin! And the way his hair falls in his eyes! And all you can say is, "he's not bad-looking!"' She gives her flatmate a look of disgust. 'What are you, a woman of stone?'

Shona is staring at Frances in fascination. 'You totally fancy him!'

Frances is midway through a gulp of wine when she hears these words; she chokes convulsively and her face darkens to puce. 'I do not,' she splutters, indignant. 'I wouldn't touch him with a bargepole.'

Shona's smile sparkles and laughter begins to bubble up in her throat.

'I mean it! I think he's horrible!' Frances moans. 'But physically he could hardly be improved upon.'

Shona begins to shake with laughter. She tries to speak, but she is giggling too much.

'Stop laughing at me! Every woman with *eyes* thinks he's gorgeous! I may be beneath his notice, but that doesn't stop me noticing *him*. I only wish it did!'

Shona smothers her mouth with a white hand, but she

cannot hide the merriment in her eyes. She presses her soft red lips together and her laughter subsides, though a little smile still hovers about her moist mouth. 'Don't you think he's a bit skinny?'

'Skinny?' Frances repeats, outraged, clasping her own skeletal hands together. '*Skinny?* Hardly. Slim, perhaps.'

'His legs are skinny. Have you seen his legs?'

'There's nothing wrong with his legs!' Frances almost shrieks.

'He has knobbly knees!'

Frances glares at Shona. 'Looks reproachfully at Shona.' A weary sigh escapes Frances' faded lips. 'What I hate about the bloody narrator – apart from the way I'm sure he exaggerates my...physical monstrosity – is the way he takes the humour of everything I say. He obliterates the ironies and the self-mockery. He makes me seem harsh and unfeeling when really...it's shyness.'

'Frances, you're not physically monstrous,' says Shona, soothingly.

Frances stares at her dully. She rubs the purplish stain under her right eye. 'You still haven't explained why you were going out with Callum, if it wasn't his looks.'

A smile hovers around Shona's moist mouth.

'Well? Why was it?' Frances insists.

Shona strokes the stem of her wine glass with a long finger. '"Thoughtfully." I don't know, really.'

'She looks confused.'

'I *am* confused. It was just...because he asked me out, I suppose.'

'But why did you say yes?' Frances demands. 'And why did you stay with him for two years?'

Shona doesn't answer for a while. She uncrosses and re-crosses her slim legs beneath her long skirt, which rustles gently. 'Well, he did what boyfriends are supposed to do,' she says, at last. 'He told me I was beautiful and sent me lots of flowers. I suppose that made me feel I was worth something.' Her voice fades to the softness of a faint breeze.

Shona looks up to find Frances' pale, curious eyes fixed on her. Something in Shona's face alters almost indiscernibly; there is a deeper vulnerability in the shape of her cheek, the softness of her mouth. She tears her eyes from Frances' intrusive gaze.

'Frances, I was thinking about your birthday,' she says, hastily. When she goes on her voice sounds fresher, brighter. 'Do you have anything to wear? Because I might go into town some time this week and look for something for myself, so…if you wanted we could go together.'

'Actually, I've already got something to wear,' Frances answers, coolly.

'Oh.' Shona runs a hand over the undulating surface of her hair. She smiles. 'Well, you know if you wanted a second opinion…or want to borrow make-up or anything…'

'I wouldn't use make-up, because of my eczema.'

'Or if you wanted to use my curling tongs…'

There is a brief silence. Frances Freak picks up her book and stares at the back cover. Bewilderment blends with the bright blue of Shona's eyes.

'I know you're trying to help,' Frances says, without looking up. 'But I really don't want the ugly duckling treatment.' She opens her book and begins looking for her place, turning the pages slowly. 'I would rather be laughed at for being who I am than for trying to be what I'm not,' she adds, thinly.

'Right,' says Shona. She fingers the light material of her skirt, her eyes troubled.

Frances doesn't even glance up. She twists her splindly legs into a tighter knot and begins to read again.

Chapter 7

Beginning

A newspaper lies on the table, spread open on the jobs page, but Chris has abandoned his seat in front of it in favour of pacing around the kitchen. He takes three steps over to the fridge, spins round rapidly and takes three steps back to the doorway, where he turns again. Pacing, Chris decides, really doesn't help in a room of this size. Instead of promoting bold steps and expansive solutions, it seems to limit his thoughts and increase his frustration. Irritably, he resumes his seat, sitting down so heavily that he almost tips the chair backwards, and slamming his elbow on the table in the process.

GAs, RSWs, RPNs, NQTs...no wonder he can't find a job, he can't even understand what the advertisements mean. Community Services Coordinator, Development Officer, Domestic Assistant, Recycling Technician...why do all the job titles sound like euphemisms? It's hopeless, hopeless...he can't concentrate long enough even to read a complete advertisement. Defeated, Chris buries his face in his large, knobbly hands.

'I'm just not used to having to be this self-motivated,' Chris tells himself, but he knows that's not it. 'Being on my own in the house is lonelier than I thought,' he tries, but that's not the problem either. 'Bugger,' says Chris, more fiercely. 'I've got to sort this out.'

With sudden resolution, Chris leaps to his feet. Should he…change his shirt or something? Comb his hair? No. Better to seem casual about it.

Maybe she won't be in. What would he do then? Trying to feel resolute, Chris strides into the lounge, ignoring how shaky he suddenly feels. His hand hovers over the telephone receiver, but instead of picking it up he tears a piece of paper from the phone-pad and puts it in his pocket, together with a pen. If she isn't in, Chris concludes, things will be very much easier.

What now? Nothing; he should just go round there quickly, before he changes his mind. Keys? – In his pocket. Jacket? – No, it looks warm enough. Money? This only occurs to him as he's shutting the front door. Well, it might have been a good idea. Maybe they'd go out. If things went well. Or maybe he should buy wine on the way? Or flowers? No…it'd look like he was trying to be Callum if he turned up with flowers. Anyway, it was too late now. He'd left his wallet behind.

Chris stands outside Shona's flat, willing himself to press the buzzer. He silently orders his hand to do so, but instead it places itself nonchalantly in his pocket and will not move. Chris considers the possibility that perhaps he just needed to get out of the house; perhaps the walk has done him good; perhaps if he went back home he would find he could concentrate on applying for jobs now.

'Hello! What's wrong with you?' It is Frances Freak's whispery voice. Her thin arms are full of books and the wind is plastering strands of greyish hair across her face.

'Oh! Hello. Nothing. What do you mean?'

'Your hair's sticking up and you look out of breath.' Frances fumbles around in her pocket and eventually finds her keys. 'Are you coming up?' She doesn't wait for an answer, but shuffles inside without looking at Chris directly. As he follows Frances up the stairs, Chris notices that her jeans are too long. There is a dirty rim around the bottom of each leg, where she keeps treading on the hem.

'Is Shona in?' Chris asks, as they go into the flat.

'Doesn't look like it,' says Frances, depositing her books on the coffee table. She gives him a suspicious look, but just says, 'Do you want tea? There's no hot chocolate unless you brought your own.'

Chris isn't sure whether to be relieved by Shona's absence or not. 'I'll make the tea,' he says, attempting a smile. 'Because you make terrible tea.'

'So you're always saying.'

Chris goes into the kitchen, trying not to think about anything other than making tea. He fills the kettle and takes a couple of mugs from the draining board. Clean crockery is one of the luxuries of not living with Callum.

Chris jumps as he realises that Frances has somehow crept in without him noticing. She is watching him narrowly, standing in her usual hunched posture, her hands dangling limply. Her neck is bent forward and Chris can see the tendons jutting out under the stretched skin.

'So, Frances,' says Chris, trying to sound jocular.

'So, Kit,' she responds, her eyes small and shrewd.

There is a brief silence. Chris fiddles with a teabag. It is becoming obvious to him that until he explains his presence they are going to stand around in awkward silence.

'So, Frances,' he says again. 'I actually came round...for a reason.'

'Yes?'

'Yes.'

With a frantic gurgling, the kettle comes to the boil. Chris waits until it switches itself off, and then pours water into the mugs, almost managing to scald his hand with the steam.

'You'll probably laugh at me,' he says, prodding the submerged teabags with a teaspoon, willing himself to get it over with. 'But I was going to ask you out.'

Chris hears no gasp of joy, no exclamations of surprise. There is such a long silence that in the end Chris is forced to look up. Frances hasn't moved, except that now she is frowning. As Chris watches, she wrenches a strand of hair out of her eyes and wedges it behind her ear.

'You were going to ask me out,' she repeats flatly. He isn't sure if it is a question.

'Yes.' He turns back to the mugs, fishing the teabags out one at a time and dropping them carefully into the bin. Suddenly Frances Freak's arms are around his waist.

'Kit – you don't have to do this,' she hisses into the back of his shirt.

'No, Frances, I *want* to.'

'No, you don't,' she says, abruptly letting go of him and retreating across the room.

Chris turns round and looks at her, huddled against the work-surface, her grubby cardigan clenched in her small fists. 'I never noticed your eyes,' he says, suddenly. 'They're silver. Silver-grey.'

'Kit?' she says, and her eyes slide evasively away from his.

'Yes?'

'I know you don't see me as girlfriend material; and I'm

not even sure I see you as boyfriend material.'

Chris tries to ignore the emotional jolt this gives him. He concentrates on putting milk in the tea. Then he says earnestly, 'The thing is, Frances, whenever I don't see you for a few days…it's awful. You're the best friend I have and I didn't even realise it till now.' He hands her a mug of tea. 'Here – take the handle – it's hot.' He picks up his own tea and takes a tentative sip. Then he risks a glance at Frances. 'Hey, don't smile at me like you think I'm daft!'

'You are.'

'I'm not! I'm being serious. I haven't appreciated you as I should've.'

Frances keeps on smirking. 'You *are* daft. You're nicer to me than anyone.'

Chris replaces the milk in the fridge and then positions himself opposite Frances once more. She doesn't seem to intend to sit down, so he doesn't either. He cradles the mug in his large hands, his brow crumpled thoughtfully. 'I cook you meals and I make you endless hot chocolate, yes,' he admits. 'I stay up till the early hours talking to you, when it suits me. But in all of that I've never treated you with the slightest respect.' He looks troubled; the expression in his eyes is very frank. 'I don't stand up for you in front of other people – sometimes I won't even listen to what you want to tell me.'

'You know, Kit, next time you ask someone out, you might want to get me to give you a few tips,' says Frances, resuming her thin-lipped smirk. 'By the way, this tea's dreadful.'

'Your cheap teabags,' says Chris, with a slight smile. 'But Frances, I'm trying to say that I want you to be…permanent. You're a much more remarkable person than I've wanted to realise…to admit,' he says, seriously. Then suddenly he exclaims, 'You've never smiled like that before!'

'You've never said anything like that to me before.'

Chris grins happily in response. 'So you see, now? You understand? You agree?'

Frances' eyes slip away again. She stares stubbornly at the linoleum.

'I see that you think better of me than you used to,' she says, eventually. 'I understand that you don't want to lose our friendship.'

'And?'

'And that makes me extremely happy.'

'But?'

'But…I don't see that it has anything to do with…us having a romantic relationship.'

Chris realises that he is starting to get a headache. In his imagination, being turned down by a girl had always presented itself as unpleasant, but fairly straightforward. He wonders, as a patch of dull pain positions itself next to his left eye, how Frances is managing to make it seem so complicated.

'I don't think people take their friends seriously enough,' Frances announces, oblivious to Chris' discomfort. 'You could be as committed to me as a friend as you could to me as a girlfriend. And I think that's what you want: a committed sort of friendship.' She smirks again. 'You don't have to deny it. I *know* you don't fancy me.'

Chris looks up and meets her eyes. 'She says, with the sort of smile which could change his mind.' He massages his temple gently.

'Good grief, don't start flirting with me,' says Frances. 'That would just be bizarre. Do you have a headache? I'll get you a tablet. Let's be normal now, can we?'

Whatever her employees thought of Elspeth's cardigan, they couldn't plausibly pretend they hadn't noticed it.

'That's...very unusual,' Claire says, and the word 'unusual' is hardly adequate.

'It is, isn't it?' Elspeth answers, beaming daffily. 'Absolutely gorgeous, isn't it? It's all done with natural dyes – onionskins and beetroot and suchlike. This part,' she gestures at a broad stripe of lurid green, where the cardigan's hem sweeps the floor, 'is nettle!'

'Gorgeous,' Shona echoes, rather hollowly. She is wearing a tasteful little plain black cardigan and a skirt in a glowing emerald shade.

'The sleeves are amazing,' says Claire, still transfixed by Elspeth's strange attire. 'Like batwings. Those textures are lovely.'

Elspeth, however, has stopped listening. Her mind is already elsewhere. 'Claire, are you still counselling Rachael Simmonds?' she asks, twitching her hands in the air for no evident reason. 'She phoned yesterday and asked for you, but I felt *sure* she'd finished her sessions.'

'No, she still comes every now and again,' Claire responds, adopting her small, practical smile. 'She just books a session when she wants one. Actually she's interested in helping put the newsletter together. Just in a voluntary capacity.'

'Oh, that's fantastic! She's lovely, Rachael, isn't she? Absolutely lovely.' Elspeth looks dazedly around the room, and seems to notice Shona for the first time, sitting at the desk.

'My goodness Shona, I almost forgot to congratulate you!' she cries, as if astonished at her own negligence. 'I've only just heard your news!' Shona flinches slightly as Elspeth suddenly throws her arms about her and plants a loud kiss in the vicinity of her cheek. 'Bless you, flower, don't look so confused. I mean the news about your *doctorate*, darling! I had no idea you were planning a return to academia!'

'It's all been rather last minute, actually,' Shona murmurs.

'But how exciting! I'm so delighted for you! What made you decide to do it?'

Shona leans back in her chair, daunted perhaps by the volume at which Elspeth finds it necessary to conduct her inquiries. She rearranges her lovely legs, the lace rim of her skirt gripping her creamy thighs. 'It's been wonderful working for Jigsaw,' she says carefully, 'but I've really missed studying. I enjoyed it so much in my fourth year. I think I would have applied to do a PhD straight away if I'd thought I was good enough.'

Elspeth precedes her response with a theatrical gasp. 'Goodness me, didn't you get a first class degree?' she says.

Shona re-ties her hair band, her deft fingers twisting it swiftly round her long ponytail. Her hair burns like a hot coal next to Elspeth's dull carrot-colour. 'Well, yes...but that seemed like a bit of a fluke at the time. I only did maths because I liked it, you see. I never felt that I was very good at it.'

'Then it's to be hoped this doctorate gives you a bit more confidence!' Elspeth exclaims. She pushes a hand through her frizzy hair, leaving a large orange clump standing on end. 'Your parents must be *terribly* proud.'

'I don't know,' says Shona with a small smile. 'I think my mother would rather see me keeping house impeccably for a well-salaried husband.'

'Surely not!' cries Elspeth. She begins to rustle melodramatically inside a plastic bag. 'I brought these in as a sort of celebration. They're absolutely divine!'

With a flourish, Elspeth produces a green glass bottle and a paper bag containing what appears to be a number of small, misshapen cakes.

'This is ginger cordial,' Elspeth explains. 'With ginseng and all *sorts* of wonderful things in it. My friend Demelza makes it herself. These are...which ones were these now?' She gazes into the paper bag in stupefaction. 'These are mandarin and carob slices, from the Organic Café. I hope you don't mind them squashed!' She lets out a peel of laughter.

'They look wonderful,' says Claire, with more tact than accuracy. She pushes her glasses up her short nose.

'This is very kind,' Shona murmurs. She stands up, straightening her long, bare legs. 'I'll get some cups, shall I?'

'Oh yes, that would be marvellous,' gushes Elspeth. She brandishes the green bottle at Claire. 'I discovered this fabulous stuff at Demelza's winter solstice party. I must warn you it has quite a bite to it!'

A fruity fragrance drifts into Shona's bedroom, through the open door of the en suite. It is reminiscent of limes or grapefruit...a tangy, citrus scent.

Shona emerges, in her dusky pink negligee. Instead of sitting down at the dressing table, she examines her face in a round wall-mirror, which has little white roses climbing around the wooden frame

'It feels like a sort of heirloom,' Shona murmurs, aloud.

She runs her hands slowly through her wet curls. Her cheeks, in the mirror, are a delicate pink from the heat of the shower.

'And my eyes are all bloodshot!' says Shona, with an abrupt laugh.

Her negligee is falling open at the front, revealing the smooth white flesh of her chest and the shadow of her cleavage. Her lips are warmed to a rich raspberry.

'I'm not going to be cute tonight,' Shona announces, to

the empty room. 'In fact, for a change, I'm going to be a dragon.'

Shona turns away from the mirror and opens her wardrobe doors. From the row of richly coloured garments, she removes a long, velvet skirt in dark red and a shining, multi-coloured top which seems to be composed of tiny squares of metal.

'Like scales, you see,' says Shona.

She lays the clothes carefully on the bed and crosses over to the dressing table. She opens one of the drawers.

'Can I "rummage around inside"? Or is rummaging not ladylike?' She peers into the drawer's depths apprehensively. 'I hope I didn't get rid of the make-up I need; I don't think I did. Oh no, look, here's the lip-pencil and the black eyeliner. And here's the powder.'

Shona returns to the wall-mirror, and begins to dab powder onto her face.

'There are flecks of gold in it,' she says. 'It's fairly subtle…but don't worry, there won't be anything subtle about my face by the time I've finished with it!' She meets her own eyes gleefully in the mirror, which are a startlingly intense colour. 'And still bloodshot. Right, let's do something about these eyes.'

Shona takes the eyeliner in her slender fingers and draws a smooth black line around each eye.

'Quite a thick black line. And don't forget to mention that I'm extending the shape of the eye upwards and outwards, at the edges. I think dragons have slanting eyes. Or they should. Oh! Mascara!'

Swiftly, Shona locates a long black tube of mascara.

'I have to do this because otherwise my eyelashes will look orange against the black,' she says, applying mascara deftly. 'And that wouldn't work. Right, now for the fun part.'

Shona takes the lip pencil and begins to draw a dark red line around the black line of her right eye.

'I think if I smudge it in slightly…and extend the tail of the eye a bit…yes. That looks good to me. Quite startling!'

With a look of insane satisfaction on her lovely face, Shona repeats the process, desecrating her other eye.

'Desecrating? No. I think it looks great. But I'm going to need some eye-shadow to finish off with. Let's see…yes, this is what I want,' Shona mutters to herself as she searches in her drawer. 'Now I'm going to put the purple stuff here, on the outside edges of my eyelids, almost up to the eyebrow. And then this orange eye-shadow – which I never thought I was going to use in my whole life – I'm going to put a bit on the rest of my eyelid…and blend it slightly with the purple. And I'm going to put a tiny bit underneath, as well. These eye-shadows are quite glittery, which I think is good.'

She pauses to survey her reflection for a moment. She looks like a very beautiful woman with two black eyes.

'Now I'm not doing anything with my lips,' she says, apparently unperturbed by what she sees in the mirror. 'Otherwise I shall look like a clown.' She stares at herself a moment longer. 'When my hair dries it will be quite a flamey colour, which will work well with the dragon theme, I think. Oh, now I'd better do my nails.'

Oblivious to the oddness of her appearance, Shona goes back to her drawer of make-up and begins looking at nail varnish.

'Red or purple would work,' she says. 'Or gold. But I think black would be best, really. It's more like talons.' She eyes her nails, critically. 'I'll have to see if I can file these into more of a point before I start.' She glances at her watch, which is lying on the dressing table. 'And I'll have to hope no one arrives while my nails are drying. It's ten past seven already!'

In another part of the flat, Frances is also getting ready for the party. For possibly the first time in her life, she is standing in front of the full-length bathroom mirror, looking her reflection up and down with evident satisfaction. And indeed, strange to say, a certain transformation does seem to have occurred in the appearance of this unpromising girl. Her pale skin seems to have acquired a new lustre. Instead of her ragged cardigan, she is wearing a long, flowing dress. But strangest of all, her hair, once so grey and lifeless...

'You ought to know better than to think you can flatter me into submission,' she whispers.

The illusion does not last. At closer quarters it quickly becomes clear that the dress, which from a distance was elegant, is in fact shapeless and much too large. It hangs sadly from Frances Freak's bony frame and drags on the floor behind her. Frances' skin is as dull and scaly as ever and her hair ...

'Hush,' says Frances Freak. 'Someone's arriving.'

'Harriet!' shrieks Frances, opening the door.

'What have you done to your hair?' the girl responds smilingly, as she walks in. She is possessed of a very delicate form of prettiness, with slender, fragile-looking limbs and fine, pale blonde hair. Her eyes are a soft grey, but their expression is sprightly. 'It's nice!' she says, reaching out a small, slim hand to touch a strand of Frances' hair. 'But why *green?*'

'I like green,' says Frances in her whispery voice, and the other girl laughs.

'Well, happy birthday!' she says. 'I've got some things for you. Shall we go into the lounge?'

Harriet takes a seat on the sofa and searches through her

rucksack. She is wearing jeans and a puff-sleeved, peasant-like top that displays the tender, almost translucent white of her arms. After a moment Harriet finds what she is looking for; she hands Frances a large package.

'It's from Auntie Kay and Uncle Jim,' she says. One of her teeth is misaligned, jutting out slightly in front of the rest, but somehow this makes her smile all the prettier.

'It feels like a book!' With small, crabbed hands, Frances tears the blue and purple flowery paper from her present. She stares at the volume which lies among the ragged strips of paper, an expression of displeasure on her thin, pallid face. 'The complete shorter fiction of DH Lawrence...good grief,' she says, sourly. 'I don't want that glowering at me from the bookshelf while I'm trying to write my thesis!'

'I had a feeling it'd be disastrous,' says Harriet, amused by Frances' reaction. 'There's a cheque from Mum and Dad, somewhere...' She searches in her bag once more and produces a yellow envelope. 'Mum wanted me to help choose clothes for you, but I managed to persuade her to just give you the money,' she explains, with a conspiratorial smile. 'And this is from me.'

She hands Frances a small, rectangular parcel, neatly wrapped in silver paper. Frances eyes it suspiciously before slowly unwrapping it. Inside there is a reddish case, which Frances opens to reveal a row of moonstones on a silver chain.

'Tell me if you don't want it...I know you don't really wear jewellery,' says Harriet, looking slightly anxious. 'I just saw it in a craft fair, and for some reason it made me think of you.'

'It's beautiful. I'll wear it tonight!' Frances responds, with a wan-lipped smile. 'Thank you, Harriet.'

'Cool. Now, I'd better get changed. I guess people will

start arriving soon. Woah!'

This last exclamation is elicited by Shona, who has just walked into the room with her multicoloured face.

'That's quite spectacular!' says Harriet, recovering herself. 'How cool! Was there some theme to this party I didn't know about?'

'No,' Shona and Frances say, simultaneously. Shona is staring in amazement at Frances' hair and Frances at Shona's face.

'I didn't expect that, Frances!' says Shona, her blue eyes wide in the midst of her daubed eye-sockets. 'It looks excellent! What a gorgeous willowy colour.'

Frances shifts her gaze evasively and doesn't reply. Harriet, meanwhile, is gazing at Shona unselfconsciously. 'How did you do that makeup?' she asks. 'It's fantastic!'

'Quite literally,' murmurs Frances.

'Did you go to art college?' Harriet wants to know.

A sudden, aggressive buzz interrupts the conversation and makes everyone jump.

'What's that?' Harriet asks, startled. 'Oh, the intercom. I'd better go and get ready. Which is your room, Frances?'

Harriet disappears into Frances' bedroom and Frances hovers nervously around the hallway, twisting her thin hands and gnawing her lips. Shona inspects her face in the hall mirror, her soft smile contrasting oddly with her strange makeup. Carefully, she arranges her long red curls so that some of them fall in front of her shoulders. After a few minutes there is a loud banging on the door, which Shona opens to allow Chris, Josh and Becca in.

'Shona, that make-up's awesome! And I love your top!' says Becca, by way of greeting. Her wide mouth is glossy and there is just a glimmer of silver around her eyes. She is dressed in chocolate brown bootlegs and a grey-blue jumper, strategically cropped to expose a sliver of golden-brown flesh.

'And more to the point, she's wearing that sassy, generous Becca-grin,' says Shona.

Meanwhile, Chris is looking around for somewhere to put the plastic bag of drinks he has brought. There is nowhere obvious, so he follows Josh across the room towards the undersized, green-haired creature who seems to be trying to retreat into a corner.

'Are you Frances?' Josh asks, in friendly tones. He holds out his hand and grasps her small, brittle one. 'I've never met a mermaid before,' he says. 'To be honest, I'm not really sure about the etiquette.'

Frances darts him a suspicious look. Then her thin lips spread in a reluctant smile.

'Don't worry,' she says. 'Mermaids aren't easily offended.'

'But no jokes about seafood?' Josh asks, earnestly.

'No,' says Frances, and her eyes slip away.

Chris has forgotten all about the problem of what to do with the drinks. He is staring at Frances Freak's hair, an expression of disbelief on his face.

'Hello, Kit,' she says. 'Is something wrong?'

'Frances!' Becca exclaims, crossing the room, before Chris has a chance to reply. 'What's that impish smile for?' She doesn't wait for an answer, but proffers a parcel. 'Happy birthday! By the way, you look fabulous!'

'Quite literally,' murmurs Chris.

'Your dress is so cool!' says Becca. 'I want it, and I'm not even a dress person! I love all the tiny beads.' She pauses to take a sip from a bottle she has already procured from somewhere.

'"Swig," not "sip",' says Frances. 'Becca doesn't sip.'

'Too ladylike,' Becca agrees.

'Frances,' says Chris, unable to contain himself any longer. 'Why have you dyed your hair green?'

'He asks, disgruntled,' murmurs Frances. She looks up at him with narrow, colourless eyes. 'I like it.'

'But why *green?*' Chris asks. 'Why not...I don't know...brown? Or a bit blonder?'

'Why don't *you* dye your hair blond?' Becca asks, eyeing him critically. 'Yeah. That would be pretty wild.'

'Don't you like it?' Frances hisses at Chris. 'Asks Chris, sadly.'

'Well...it's a bit weird.'

'Obviously,' says Frances.

'I don't think blond would really suit Kit.' It is Shona, who has just joined the group, her eyes ringed in many colours, her arms and shoulders bare and glowing like pearl.

Chris looks up and is so startled that for a good few moments he cannot take his eyes off her, dangerous though he knows this kind of prolonged exposure to be. He hadn't noticed her outlandish appearance on the way in, being reluctant, as usual, to meet her eyes.

'It needs to be mid-brown,' Shona announces, her chain mail top clinging at the curve of her waist, shining in shades of purple, emerald green and gold. Chris wonders what she means and then realises, to his embarrassment, that she is still talking about his hair. 'Because of his dark skin tone and his hazel eyes. His colouring isn't quite the same as yours, Becca. I think blond hair would unbalance it.'

'I get what you mean,' says Becca, letting a handful of her own honey hair trickle through her fingers. 'But I still think blond hair would be rather groovy. If he bleaches it really white...'

Chris is not enjoying this conversation. He doesn't like to be the centre of attention, and he cannot understand why his hair colour is suddenly a topic of discussion, when he himself has never given it that much thought. He wonders what Josh is making of all this, but Josh is wearing his habitual expression of mild amusement. Chris shifts his gaze to Becca and is disconcerted to find her coolly looking him up and down. He glances away quickly, but his eyes are drawn back to Shona. He finds her staring him unabashedly in the face. The vivid blue hurts his eyes and he has to look away.

'Slain by Shona's basilisk glance,' mutters Frances, barely audibly.

'Darker lashes would accentuate his eyes,' Shona suggests, to Chris' increasing discomfort. He feels that his eyes need not so much accentuating as obscuring behind a pair of very dark glasses. Silently he begs for the topic of conversation to change.

'Kit feels violated,' says Frances.

'It's because he's not used to his appearance being public property,' Shona replies. 'Open to discussion.'

'Says Shona, breathing fire,' hisses Frances.

'His hazel eyes are downcast in his dusky face,' says Shona.

'A spasm of self-consciousness momentarily contorts his features,' says Frances.

Chris stares at the carpet, his mind throbbing under the pressure of their hostile female eyes. It is only with an effort that he avoids running from the room.

'He doesn't like us pinning him down,' says Shona. 'Restricting him.'

Chris decides that the only way of coping is to concentrate on something outside of his immediate situation. He looks over Becca's shoulder and notices someone passing the doorway; someone small and slim in a silver dress.

'Maybe we should let him breathe,' says Frances.

Trying not to listen, Chris watches as the girl comes into the lounge. There is something familiar about her slight form, her luminous eyes…and then he recognises her as the girl from the photo in Frances' room. Now Chris notices Steve and Lizzie standing in the hall – they must have just arrived. They follow Harriet into the lounge and Chris sees that Lizzie's butter-blonde hair is swept up with small, glittery clips. She is wearing a white mini-dress with a little blue cardigan. Steve walks behind her, his hands in his pockets, a surly expression on his face. Chris wonders if it is safe to start listening to the conversation again.

'I'm really feeling quite boring today,' Becca is saying to Shona and Frances. 'In comparison with you two. Shona, your face is a work of art!' She grins broadly, nonchalantly, and then says, 'Talking of which – have you seen Josh's arm?'

Chris watches in mild bewilderment as Becca grabs Josh by the arm, unbuttons his sleeve and yanks the loosened cuff up his bare arm. Josh doesn't resist; there is a humorous expression in his eyes.

'See?' says Becca, brandishing Josh's arm.

Chris looks, and sees that just above Josh's elbow, black against his skin, is a pattern of interlacing strands, like Celtic knotwork.

'He painted that himself,' says Becca, to no one in particular. 'Isn't it cool?'

Chris wonders if he is supposed to respond to this. He isn't used to having to state opinions on men's bodily adornments. Steve has just joined the group and seems more ready to comment.

'That's very pretty,' he says, breaking into a laddish grin. 'Ever paint your nails, Josh? Ever put on a bit of lipstick?'

'Not often,' Josh replies, seriously. 'Although Becca sometimes paints my nails for me.'

Steve stares at Josh, unable to tell whether this is a joke. Lizzie is looking at Josh with round blue eyes.

'That's a lovely shirt,' she says, chirpily. 'Those three little buttons on the cuffs are so cute!'

'A snorting noise comes from Steve's direction,' whispers Frances.

'I like the silvery sheen on the blue,' says Shona, turning her dazzling face to Josh. Her sensual lips curve in a smile.

'Yes. It brings out the colour of his eyes,' says Lizzie, excitedly.

'Steve makes a low sound, like a growl,' Frances whispers again.

'Will you stop caressing my arm in public, now?' Josh asks Becca. 'Can I get dressed again?'

'Not if you keep on smiling in that sexy way,' says Becca, but she tugs down his sleeve anyway. 'You button it.'

As Josh fastens his cuff, Frances glances surreptitiously around the group, her small eyes shrewd and calculating.

'This is Harriet, by the way,' she says, abruptly. 'My sister.'

Harriet smiles shyly. Her hair shines with a soft glow, like the moon. Her short, silver dress displays her slender limbs and the fine bones of her shoulders.

Steve grins reassuringly at her and says, 'Hi, Harriet.'

'Lecherous isn't reassuring,' says Shona under her breath. 'You forgot to mention that Steve's eyes have already spent some time exploring Harriet's anatomy.'

'What's that?' says Steve.

'Nothing,' says Shona, opening her bright, long-lashed eyes very wide.

'Ooh!' says Lizzie suddenly. 'Presents!' She reaches into her fluffy white handbag and hands Frances a pink-wrapped present secured with a glittery bow.

'So, Harriet,' Steve says. 'You're Frances' sister. She's kept *you* well hidden.'

'Murmurs Steve, suggestively,' says Shona, more audibly.

'Gaping at Harriet with his mouth open,' says Becca. 'And talking in a particularly creepy way.'

Harriet looks from Shona to Becca; she flicks a pale strand of hair from her sea-grey eyes and smiles bewitchingly.

'Gratefully,' says Shona. 'Bewitchingness is in the eye of the beholder.'

Meanwhile, Frances has opened her present, which turns out to be three scented candles, marbled in different colours.

'That one's raspberry, that one's orange and *this* one's chocolate. And it's gorgeous!' Lizzie explains, excitedly.

'So, Harriet,' says Steve, boisterously. 'I bet you like cocktails, don't you? You look like a girl who likes cocktails.'

'You can tell that by looking at her breasts, can you Steve?' asks Becca, in caustic tones.

'Oh, Harriet, you'll love the cocktails at Justine's,' says Lizzie eagerly, her cupid's bow lips curving in a childlike smile. 'The best one tastes just like banana milkshake!'

'Something flashes in Steve's eyes,' says Shona. 'Something...aggressive.'

'What's your bloody problem?' Steve asks Shona.

'Aggressively,' says Shona. 'Don't mind what I say. I'm completely loopy, remember?' She smiles prettily at Steve.

Becca turns impatiently to Frances. 'Are you going to open our present?' she demands, in her rich, husky voice.

Frances nods obediently. She tears the wrappings from the present to reveal a large box of very expensive-looking chocolates.

'Now I know chocolate is chocolate, and gorgeous by definition,' Becca tells her, 'but trust me, these things are in a league of their own. And whatever you do,' she cautions, her hazel eyes earnest, 'don't open them when I'm around.'

'What did *you* give Frances?' Lizzie asks Shona, curling a blond tendril of hair around a small finger.

'A jazz CD,' says Shona. She shifts her position slightly and her velvet skirt undulates against her legs. 'I went through your CD collection for ideas, Frances, but I was still completely lost when I got to the shop. I had to have this really long discussion with the guy in the jazz section.'

'He was kind of cute, right?' says Becca.

'No!' Shona protests, but her cheeks grow pink. 'Well, yes...' she admits.

'With a mischievous smile,' hisses Frances.

'A wicked grin,' says Becca.

Shona is smiling voluptuously. Her eyes glow and her hair burns against her pure white skin, but she just says, 'There's food in the other room, you know, and a load of drinks.'

'Food?' repeats Becca.

'Her eyes lighting up,' says Shona.

Shona appears in the kitchen doorway, her flowing skirt redder than blood, bright hair licking her throat like flames.

'Well, this is a mess,' she says, and giggles. She leaves the kitchen hastily. 'Almost tripping over the bin,' she mutters. In the hallway, she pauses to look at her reflection. Her gaudy makeup does not look better for being slightly smudged. 'And I'm a mess, too!' she announces. 'Frances!' she calls, drifting up the murky hall. 'Frances, do you want tea or something?'

The door of Frances' room opens a crack. A slice of her pallid face appears in the aperture: a dull grey eye; a pointed nose.

'Yes,' she says. 'Please.'

The door shuts abruptly and Shona makes her way back up the corridor. Her chain mail top is lashed to her body with a leather thong, making a criss-cross pattern on her smooth white back.

'Wrapping paper everywhere,' she mumbles. 'Steve's left his coat here. These *stupid* shoes!'

By this point she has reached the lounge, so she sits down and removes the platforms she is wearing.

'She collapses into an armchair and struggles inelegantly with her stupidly high-heeled and uncomfortable shoes,' she says. 'I think you mean. That's better.'

She rises from her chair, tiny sparks of gold glinting on her face and shoulders. On bare feet, she pads into the kitchen.

'The wreckage of what once was a kitchen,' she says, filling the kettle. 'But I'm not going to worry about it till tomorrow.' She jumps, as she realises that Frances has done her usual trick of creeping into the room, unnoticed.

'Sorry,' hisses Frances.

Shona leans against the work surface, resting on a shapely arm that glows white in the fluorescent light. 'Don't you get fed up with all this 'hissing' nonsense?' she asks. 'Do you dislike your voice? Because I like it. I'd rather have yours than mine.'

'I don't know…' Frances replies. She picks at a cuticle. 'I don't think I'd dislike it if I didn't think other people did.'

'I really don't think they do,' says Shona, stifling a yawn. 'Those are very cute pyjamas.'

The word 'cute' would, to most people, seem a strange one to use of anything connected to Frances Freak. However it cannot be denied that Frances' pyjamas would be endearing if worn by someone less bony, less haggard and less sly-looking.

'Hm. How do you think, "bony, haggard and sly-looking" would translate, if the voice wasn't on a mission to undermine you? Slender, drowsy and intelligent-looking?' says Shona. There is a pause. 'How about, "Frances' slight form is clad comfortably in pyjamas; there is a sleepy expression on her small, perceptive face"?' She smiles slowly. Her cheek curves gently, white against the black background of the curtainless window. 'Yes, I quite like that,' she says. 'Anyway, did you have a good evening?'

'Yes. Very good.' Frances' voice is flat and unconvincing. 'That's my voice!' she says, savagely. 'If you're not convinced by it then it isn't my fault!'

Shona looks at her overexcited flatmate and smiles archly. 'Grins in amusement,' she says. 'Will Harriet be all right, going back on her own?'

'Yes. Her friends will meet her off the train.'

'She looks so much like you. Not like Callum and his brothers, you'd never guess they were related.' Shona fingers her neckline, where the metal scales meet her warm skin. 'Did Kit give you a birthday present?'

'Yes, this morning. It's a big notebook with coloured pages and a black velvet cover. And an ink pen.'

Shona has turned her back on Frances, and is finishing making the tea. 'What will you use it for?'

Frances smirks to herself. 'Smiles secretively,' she murmurs. 'I'm always writing things in notebooks. Thoughts and ideas.'

Shona swiftly clears the kitchen table, her white hands deftly removing half a dozen wine glasses, some dirty plates and a bowl with nothing in it but crisp-fragments. She places two mugs of tea on the table and sits down.

'Frances,' says Shona, fixing her with a hard, sapphire gaze. 'When did you start hearing the voice?'

'I always have. For as long as I can remember.' Frances lowers herself into the chair opposite Shona.

Shona caresses her mug of tea, running her fingertips over its hot surface. 'I suppose I always heard it too…in a way. But I didn't really realise.'

There is silence for a short while.

'Frances waits for her to go on,' mumbles Frances.

'I mean…when I started hearing it properly, distinctly, it was quite different.'

There is another pause, and Frances glances furtively at Shona. She is staring out of the window, her gaze lost in the night.

'When did you start hearing it properly?' Frances asks.

'Becca's birthday.' Shona drags her eyes away from the window to look at the scrawny creature seated opposite. 'Six weeks and four days ago,' she says. 'I don't know if you remember, but we went to Justine's. It was kind of a normal evening. There were about…nine or ten of us. All of us girls were there, and Callum of course, and Steve. Some friend of Steve's came along, and Caroline's boyfriend at that time…I can't remember his name.' She lapses into silence, her soft lips hovering slightly apart.

'Did something happen?'

'Not really,' says Shona, forlornly. 'Only there was this really pretty girl sitting at another table, and the guys wouldn't stop going on about how much they fancied her. It was nothing unusual really, but…I don't know. For some reason it really upset me.' She curls her hair around her fingers, the fine metallic threads gleaming. 'I was just *shocked*, I suppose, by the way Callum went on and on about her. It didn't seem to occur to him that he was supposed to be my boyfriend, so I might not enjoy hearing him say this other woman had a fantastic figure and wasn't she hot and didn't they ought to go and sit at the bar so they'd have a better view up her skirt.' The lock of hair untwists and slips from her grasp. It dangles redly against her collarbone. She turns helpless eyes on Frances. 'It's not that I thought he shouldn't notice other women...and it's not that I minded him saying she was attractive, because she really was, she was gorgeous. It was just upsetting that he kept on about it for such a long time,' she says, trying to explain. 'Of *course* there are going to be other women prettier than me. But I thought he'd be a bit more...caring...than to spend half the evening rubbing it in.' She passes a hand lightly across her eyes. Her fingers come away slightly purple, but she doesn't seem to notice.

'I tried to explain all that when we were on our way back to Callum's, but he didn't understand at all. He kept saying I was making a fuss about nothing. In the end he got quite annoyed with me,' she says, her voice becoming a little less steady. 'By the time we got back to his room I was desperately trying not to cry, because I knew it would only irritate him more.' She raises frighteningly vulnerable eyes. 'I don't suppose you've ever seen inside his room, have you?'

Frances shakes her head, her green hair waving lankly.

'He has these posters of women in their underwear. He has some of completely naked women as well, but he's stuck those up inside of his wardrobe. It didn't usually bother me too much – I mean, you *expect* it. But that evening it made me feel even worse, having all those perfect women crowding in around me, waving their enormous breasts. They were making me dizzy, and the way Callum was looking at me – completely without understanding – it was really hurting me here.' Shona presses a hand to her lower ribs. 'Do you get that? Emotional pain that you feel physically?'

Frances Freak nods wordlessly.

'So I decided to go home. I wasn't going to get him to

understand what I felt, and I was too upset to stay with him and pretend everything was all right.' Shona comes to an abrupt halt. She looks at Frances, then she looks away. She takes a tentative sip of tea. 'But he tried to stop me leaving. He stood between me and the door, and when I tried to get past,' she says, slowly. 'He hit me.'

'What?' says Frances, sharply. 'Shona…'

'Well, he didn't hit me hard,' Shona adds, hastily. 'He was quite drunk. It kind of glanced off my jaw, and I was more surprised than hurt, really.' She clutches her mug defensively in her white hands. She is avoiding Frances' eyes. 'I just stood there and stared at him, wondering what on earth I was supposed to do.' She gazes into the empty air, her eyes a parched and flimsy blue. 'No one ever tells you what to do when your boyfriend hits you, do they?' she smiles, sadly. 'And then he started crying.'

Frances is gaping at Shona, incredulous.

'I'd never seen him cry before,' Shona murmurs, almost as if she is talking to herself. 'He kept saying, "I'm sorry, I'm sorry, I'm sorry," over and over.'

'What did you do?'

Shona's eyes grow huge in her white face. Her purple eye-shadow blurs into the dark shadows of sadness which haunt her lovely eyes. 'I stayed,' she says, softly. 'I held him for a long time and I stroked his hair; and eventually we fell asleep.'

'But Shona,' says Frances, in strangled tones. 'He hit you.'

'I know. But he seemed so sorry. And it wasn't as if he'd really hurt me.' Shona looks about her, bewildered. She attempts a smile. 'Although for weeks I had to really plaster on the foundation.'

'Why?' Frances sounds furious.

'Oh, I bruise really easily…'

'No, I mean *why?* Why did you cover up for him?'

'I don't know,' says Shona, puzzled. 'I suppose I was…embarrassed. And at the time, he seemed so upset about it.' She pauses, staring into the mug she is tightly holding. 'But afterwards…the next day…it was as if nothing had happened. He expected everything to go right back to normal.' She pushes her hair behind her ear, and finds a shred of party streamer in her hair. She crumples it between her fingers and drops it on the floor. 'What he didn't realise was that there wasn't any "normal" any more. Not for me. All of a sudden the voice was *deafening* me…and so much of what I'd thought was real turned out to be…illusions. Just the voice's stories.'

Except for the murmuring thermostat, there is silence in the kitchen. A faint smell of garlic lingers about the room, mixing sourly with the reek of beer. Frances stares at a purple wine stain on the beech effect tabletop, picking intermittently at the frayed cuffs of her pyjamas. Shona tilts her tea from side to side, watching with strange absorption as the liquid laps at one side of the mug's interior, and then the other. When she looks up, an auburn ringlet is trailing across her face.

'Frances, don't cry,' she says.